CROWN OF DRAGONS

CROWN OF DRAGONS

BLEEDING REALMS - DRAGON BLESSED

BOOK ONE

NINA WALKER

ADDISON & GRAY PRESS
WWW.NINAWALKERBOOKS.COM

Copyright © 2019 by Nina Walker

All rights reserved. No part of this publication may be reproduced, distributed, or transmitted in any form or by any means, including photocopying, recording, or other electronic or mechanical methods, without the prior written permission of the publisher, except in the case of brief quotations embodied in critical reviews and certain other noncommercial uses permitted by copyright law.

Ebook ISBN: 978-1-950093-03-8
Paperback ISBN: 978-1-950093-04-5

Published by Addison & Gray Press, LLC.

This is a work of fiction. Names, characters, businesses, places, events, locales, and incidents are either the products of the author's imagination or used in a fictitious manner. Any resemblance to actual persons, living or dead, or actual events is purely coincidental and not intended by the author or publisher.

Cover design by Daqri Bernardo.
Interior design by We Got You Covered Book Design

This book is dedicated to that girl who has never given up on finding her true and unconditional, forever and ever, love story. Even when life seems to be pointing to the contrary, she continues to believe in love. Keep loving yourself first.

This book is for you.

NOT QUITE EIGHTEEN YEARS AGO

THE CHILD WAS BORN WITH *two colored eyes: muddy earth and summer sky. The dragon clans believed her a gift from the Gods, a blessing bestowed on the new generation and a promise of royal strength. He thought it superstitious nonsense, another way the unholy beasts justified their elemental blasphemy.*

He traveled under the cloak of night, pushing his fatigue to the breaking point—he had to move fast. Once the child and mother were deemed healthy enough to travel, they'd be relocated to the castle, and if that happened before he got to her, he'd miss his chance.

The village smelled of filth, of cattle and moody winter and crops gone sour. He curled his lip, slipping between long shadows and past the sentries without trouble, breaking into the hovel and finding her fast asleep. She was a tiny thing, pink cheeked and bowed lipped, with a wisp of raven hair. Some might say she was innocent. Pure. He knew better.

He scowled at the sleeping parents and the child tucked between them, imagining ways he could execute all three—end them while he still had the chance. But no, another Dragon Blessed daughter would be born with heterochromia to take this one's place. That baby might be born of better circumstances. Unreachable.

This one was right here. It had to be her.

The spell was nothing save for a few quick utterances. But he still had to procure the blood. So he cast the second spell, the one that would leave all three inhabitants lost in slumber until sunrise. Their breathing relaxed into the magic and the night grew impossibly quiet. He raised the bed sheet and found the child's foot. It was as small as a baby bird and blushing velvet to the touch. He felt no remorse as he pricked her heel and drained the blood. He let it run, much of it sopping onto the sheets, until his vial was filled. With a flick of his long finger, he erased the mess and wiped her clean.

Tomorrow, the trio would wake, fully rested and surprised at their good fortune. Tomorrow, he would take the blood to its intended target and cast the final spell. He held the warm vial as he would a precious gem and smiled for the first time in weeks.

One day, this blood would prove to be the killing blow against the dragon clans, ending their reign—ending them. It really was a shame the baby had to be born with two colored eyes.

She never had a chance.

ONE

HAZEL

A WOMAN WITH A BUTCHER knife sticking out of her back is pulling my hair. At least, she's trying to. She hasn't quite figured out that I can't actually feel her, so she's gone from the polite ask, to the shoulder tap, to full-on hair pulling.

It's a new low, even for me.

I shift away, biting back an annoyed growl, and attempt to focus on the classroom whiteboard where Dr. Peters is scrawling something about Aristotle. I blink, hoping to tune out this obnoxious lady who's now flashing images of her medicine cabinet at me like she's going to die if I don't help, and I'm seriously about ready to punch her in her dead, pasty face.

Not that it's even possible. But seriously!

"You okay?" Macy whispers from the seat next to mine.

I sink into the padded chair and refocus on the lecture hall as I nod, hoping she'll forgive whatever horrible nonverbals are morphing my expression at the moment. Macy is kind and cool and pretty, and dang it if I don't want her to be my friend.

Yup. I've turned into *that girl.*

It's only been a week since I started my freshman year of college, and I've already managed to join what's turning out to be our dorm's "in crowd." Don't ask me for tips. Considering that I graduated a year early from high school over what Mom so lovingly calls "The Regina George Situation", I don't have any tips.

I moved into my dorm last Sunday, only one day before classes started, because I didn't want to be noticed. I didn't have visions of grandeur, of being tossed a frisbee my first day by my future husband or something equally moronic. Quite the opposite. I was awkwardly trying to blend in with my oversized hoodie from the sales rack at Target, my dirty blonde hair pulled back into a ponytail, wearing the barest of makeup (no contouring here), and hiding behind my nerdy and totally fake black-rimmed glasses. Which, by the way, I love—I'm proud to call myself a nerd.

I shouldn't have stood out, and I definitely shouldn't have made friends effortlessly. But did that stop the other girls living in my dorm from sticking to me like white on rice? No. No, it did not. And so far the "Mean Girls" group in our dorm is turning out to be the opposite of mean. They're like the glittery unicorn group of girly friends I'd always dreamed of having but only thought existed in cheesy made-for-TV movies. Who even knew pretty and popular *and kind* was possible at our age? But Mom promised college would be different, and so far, she wasn't lying.

The dead lady is still hovering right in my eyeline, distracting me from whatever's going on up front with Doctor Peters. It's pretty clear that she was a drug addict and she's going through some major withdrawals. I don't quite understand how that works considering she no longer has a body, and I feel bad for her––I do. But I'm *also* trying to focus on Peters as he goes over the origins of anthropology, and she's making herself rather difficult to ignore. I catch my other new friend Cora's raised eyebrows from across the room, and she points to her phone before turning back to the lecture. Discreetly, I check mine to find her text.

Wanna study for Friday's quiz together at lunch? My treat ;)

I smirk. The dining hall is included in our dorm fees, so it's not like Cora's going to treat me to anything other than the pleasure of her company. I quickly text her back. **Sure. So generous of you ;)**

I'm lucky this class has my two newest besties in it. Okay,

they are the only true friends I've made so far, but still, it's best friend status at this point with the three of us. We've spent nearly all our time together over the last few days since we met. I wish all my classes had them, but no, that's not how college works. We just caught a break with Anthropology. Yay for General Education, or something like that.

Cora waggles her eyebrows with a cheeky grin when she reads my reply, and I'm hit with this surreal feeling of imposter syndrome. I'm suddenly cool, aren't I? How is that possible? It won't last and I hate that I care. This stint at popularity is a total farce that hasn't done a thing to change how I feel inside. I still feel out of place. I still have anxiety every single second I'm around these "normals" because deep down I know these people won't understand me and will probably mock me once they figure out my secret. Because they *will* figure it out. Given time, everyone does. Try as I might, I can't help my freak flag from flying high and following me wherever I go.

Actually, *they* follow me wherever I go. *They're* my stupid freak flag.

But I can't very well go around telling my new friends the truth about them, can I? I can't just announce, "I see dead people," like some kind of female Haley Joel Osment. The kid was a loner in that movie for a reason. And yeah, I guess these days it's cool to be weird and different, but not *that* weird and different. It would be one thing if I read tarot cards and wore a pretty rose quartz on a dainty chain around my neck; that would be passable. That might work.

Talking to the air? No. Definitely not okay to be babbling into the empty aisle, all like, "Oh, hey crazy lady, get off me! And spoiler alert, you're actually one of the dead people. I'll just send you on your way. Go be with Jesus!"

Can I do that right now? Hell to the no.

So that's why I'm about ready to spontaneously combust right here in this padded seat. I should be paying attention to the anthropology lecture. Peters is a campus favorite for a reason, and I actually really like this class if our first lecture was anything to go by.

But there are a lot of dead people hanging around campus. I purposely chose a small liberal arts college in a backwater West Virginian town so that spirits wouldn't bombard me like they do in big cities. Lucky for me, I don't see ancient ghosts, so I wasn't worried about the Civil War history here. It's the recently dead who appear to me. And as it turns out, Hayden College has its fair share. They seriously won't leave me alone now that they've realized I can see them. Even though I'm not talking to them or acknowledging them whatsoever, they sure aren't scared to bombard me.

It's like this: I can see the spirit realm. The ghosties sense that about me and send images to my mind. Sometimes it's moments from their lives, or people they love, regrets they have, but usually, it's random objects that make no difference to me. It rarely makes sense. But they do it all the time regardless of whether I'm busy—like right now, in the middle of class. And oh goodie, I'm supposed to be answering a question.

"Umm, sorry, Dr. Peters, what was the question?" I ask, voice cracking. My face burns as everyone in the classroom, living and dead, turns on me. It's a smallish lecture hall, but all fifty seats are filled. Lucky me.

Peters raises a bushy eyebrow, notices the phone tucked in my palm, and turns to another student. "Mr. Ashton, perhaps you could enlighten us?" The heavy gazes of my classmates turn from me to someone sitting in the back, and I let out a stilted breath. That could have gone better.

A brief silence is followed by a deep silky voice dripping in exasperation. He has a slight accent that for the life of me I can't place. "Anthropology comes from the Greek words anthropos, meaning human, and logos, meaning logic. That's an easy question, Dr. Peters. If people would listen instead of being glued to their phones, perhaps we could all move on to the more interesting bits."

A few students snicker. Shame washes over me, along with that awful feeling of being the butt of the joke. I can't believe he called me out like that! And it's not like I didn't know the answer. I just didn't hear the question because of this crack-baby ghosty hovering over me—who by the way, is still on my case, sending image after image of prescription medicine bottles. The shame burns up quickly, consumed by anger as I grit my teeth. I continue to tune out the dead lady's hysterics and turn back to glare at the know-it-all in the last row.

I'm stunned at what I find. An icy chill creeps over my body.

Whoever he is, he's glaring right back, his expression venomous, and with eyes so dark, I swear they're black. It's unsettling to the point of making my pulse race. He sees me looking but he doesn't turn away. A jolt of electricity shoots up my spine. His jaw is clenched tight, accentuating the sharp lines of his cheeks and the fullness of his pink lips. I take him in, this man with a face made of daydreams and nightmares. He's the kind of attractive meant for Photoshop and glossy magazine ads, not real life. And from his brazenness, I'd guess the good looks come with a crap load of arrogance. Gross. Also, total eye-roll.

The marker squeaks against the whiteboard as Peters continues the lecture, bringing the class back to focus.

But I don't turn back. Not yet. Instead, I sneer at the guy who's still openly staring at me with complete and utter disdain. Like, I'm sorry, but what does he want? He's probably used to women fawning over him, but I refuse to be so predictable and lame. I also don't want to be the first of us to break eye contact. It's as if we're playing a game of cat and mouse, but guess what? Cats are my favorite animals. I have two back home. Plus, I have claws. So back off!

Okay, I don't really have claws. I bite the crap out of my nails if we're being honest. But what I'm trying to say is I'm the cat in this scenario—I'm the winner.

He tilts his head, curls his lip, and averts his gaze.

Ha! I knew I was awesome!

Satisfied, I whip back around and resume my attempts to pay attention. I'm here to learn, dang it! The back of my neck heats all throughout the lecture, like a laser beam is being directed right at me. It's even more distracting than the ghosts all up in my business. But I don't turn around again. Not because I'm afraid of the jerk in the back, but because I don't want to give him the satisfaction of knowing he's bothering me. For whatever reason, the hatred between us is instant and mutual. I smile. It's a nice distraction for a haunted girl.

And lo and behold, a half hour later I find him waiting for

me after class.

"Mr. Ashton" leans against the wall in the hallway and the moment he sees me, he pushes off it, stalking toward me like a lion about to attack an innocent baby gazelle. Yeah, I am well aware I just went from awesome feline warrior goddess to a baby gazelle.

"What are you doing here?" he demands, the accusatory tone slamming right through me.

I stop, Cora and Macy at my side. All three of us seem to be momentarily blinded by both his attractiveness and that continued brazenness. I blink rapidly, downright baffled by this behavior. It was one thing to challenge me in class, but to wait for me afterward so he can yell at me? Who does that? It only takes a second for that stunned feeling to evaporate into one of indignation.

"Back off," I snap, stepping forward in challenge. I almost can't believe my fearlessness. I've always been so afraid of the bullies, so ashamed of my curse, my self-esteem weakened by something I couldn't change no matter how hard I tried. I let the kids at my old school walk all over me to the point of graduating early and running away. But not today. Not with him. Something about this feels oddly different.

I glare up into his face, voice tight, "I don't even know you."

He scoffs and shakes his head, pointing at me until his index finger pushes against my shoulder. "Don't play dumb. I know what you are."

My whole body lights up with recognition, but not in a good way. I step back, nerves rushing through me like electric currents. He knows *what* I am? He knows I'm a medium? How?

"Don't touch her!" Cora bursts forward, her voice an angry growl. She's the kind of person I wouldn't want to mess with, but he doesn't even give her a second glance.

"This is my territory," he says, leaning in closer, hateful eyes trapping me in.

My inner voice is screaming at me to run far, far away. But something else inside me, something base and primal, wants to destroy him, to tear him limb from limb. Who does he think he is?

Our classmates have begun to form around the two of us, mixed expressions of shock and outrage and curiosity and even delight glued to their prying faces. But nobody intervenes. Go figure.

"Your territory?" I question with a laugh. "What is this, Westside Story? Like I said, I don't even know you. And don't you ever lay a hand on me again."

He pauses for a second, looking me up and down like I'm

half diseased, like I smell bad or something. Do I smell bad? I quickly inhale and catch his scent; it's campfire and spice and oddly intoxicating. He's dressed in the kind of laid-back black t-shirt and jeans that cost a fortune to look like he doesn't care about his wardrobe. Typical. I'm wearing butter-soft black leggings and an oversized Gryffindor hoodie. And proud of it! His nostrils flare and that "could cut glass" jaw tenses again.

The moment stretches out between us, taut as a wire. Nobody moves. Nobody speaks. I suddenly grow hot. A ghostly gurgle of water streams across the floor, pooling at our feet an inch thick. I look down and stare, panic rushing through me. *Not now!* It seeps into my high top sneakers. Nobody else sees it. Nobody feels it. Dread sweeps over me. Where did it come from?

"Pack your things and get the hell out of this town," he hisses under his breath, the venom in his tone meant to sting. I blink up at him, out of my element. Then he pushes past me, his broad shoulders nearly knocking me to the tiled floor, into the ghostly water that only I can see.

I'm speechless.

Macy rushes to steady me, her face pale and her wide eyes twinkling with worry. "Are you okay, Hazel? What was that about?"

"I don't know," I croak, confused as ever. Blood rushes to

my cheeks as my adrenaline begins to fade, and I realize that everyone is staring at me. Why is this crap always happening? Seriously, I cannot handle another bully, especially one that *looks like that.* Good Lord, he's sexy and scary and I don't even know what to do with this situation.

Cora slides her ebony arm through mine, tugging me close. The water sloshes around my ankles and I refuse to look at it for too long, to search for whatever spirit is doing this to me. Cora's a physically affectionate person in general, and something about her vanilla perfume and warm skin relaxes me a fraction. I can get through this. With friends like her, I'll be okay.

"Dang girl," she sighs dramatically. "What on earth did you do to piss off Dean Ashton?"

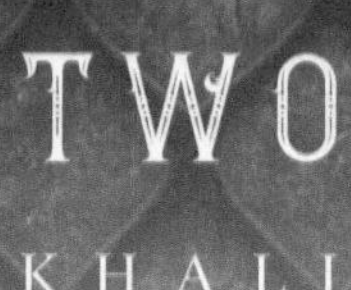

TWO

KHALI

I FLY AHEAD OF OWEN, dipping close enough to crest the water and fling an icy spray into his face. If he were in his human form, he wouldn't cough or cry out, he'd laugh. And then he would send it right back. But in his dragon form, he relishes the water. A loud splash echoes throughout the darkness and the flapping of our wings goes from two sets, to one. He must have gone under, his water elemental magic eager for a ride. I push harder, flying as fast as I can, sticking to the air. While I have an affinity for all four elements, air is my favorite. I'll need the advantage if I'm to beat him to the outer wall.

A torrent of water shoots up, and I crash straight into it. It's quick to twist around my body, dragging me down into the murky lake. Water floods my throat and dulls my senses, and I instantly draw on my water elemental. The magic springs to life, giving my dragon self new life underwater. I thought it was dark above, but below the surface, it's black as ink. Fear clamps down on me, despite my efforts to push it away.

Where are you, Owen Hydros Brightcaster!? I yell at him through our telepathic link. *I am going to murder you! You know I hate going under, especially at night. It's creepy down here.* But it's not only creepy, it's filled with terrible memories that I'd rather not revisit. Ever.

I'm met with a sly laugh. *Don't be such a baby!*

I'm almost a grown woman, you twit, I challenge. I don't even bother to search for him down here. Our jet-black hides camouflage too well in the watery darkness. I tug at my fire elemental, just enough to warm my limbs so I can swim faster to the surface.

Oh, believe me, he replies with that same laughing tone, *everyone has noticed.* His words ring through our link and send my heart skittering.

If I could blush in my dragon form, I would. Not because he and I have anything between us other than a deep friendship, but because there's no hiding the way my body has blossomed. I'm beginning to resemble my mother, who wears her curves like a badge of honor. I could never be like that, walking around court like a prize to be won.

Even though that's *exactly* what I am.

The moment I crest the lake to greet the late summer air, my fear washes away with the water. I hate going down there, night *or* day, and my dragon side doesn't like it much either. Everytime I do, logic vanishes and the animal within demands I get out before the merfolk sense us. Not that Owen and I couldn't fight them off. He's not the least bit afraid of sea monsters, but I'd rather not face those particular demons ever again. As a child, they used me to get what they wanted from the dragon royals, and I'll never be able to let that watery experience go. No matter how hard I try, the trauma follows me.

The familiar shapes of our towering castle home and the surrounding village rise like hands in the distance. The village spreads out over the landscape for miles with a looming stone wall circling the entire thing. The sun has yet to break the horizon, thank the Gods. Owen and I have to be back in our beds before morning, with no one the wiser to our midnight escapade. I stretch my wings to their absolute fullest and push every muscle to maximum effort. I can almost taste my forthcoming victory.

Once a week, for the last year, Prince Owen and I have snuck out at night to race around the territory and practice our magic. The sentries and guards don't mind him, he could walk right on through the gates if he wanted. Princes can do almost whatever they want. *Almost.* It's my presence that requires our secrecy. I've gotten caught out here before and the reprimands cost me dearly. But if he were caught *with* me? There are some things even princes cannot overcome. And yet Owen insists. He's my best friend at court and understands how much I crave to fly. He risks everything to give me the chance.

I love him for it. It's because of his friendship that I'm here, wind rushing off my scales, night shrouding my dragon form, the thrill of the chase nipping at the tip of my wings.

This is the happiest time of my week. Always.

Owen swoops up next to me, and having left his beloved lake behind, he's faster than ever. Sometimes I wish he'd let me win, but I know he won't. He's far too competitive. And I wouldn't be satisfied if he did. I could use one of my other elements to delay him, just as he did with the wall of water, but I don't. I never do. It wouldn't seem fair to use the wind or earth or fire when he cannot. I'm just as competitive as he is and a level playing field is half the fun. So we stick to water and flight.

He's inches from gaining the lead and the outer city wall is closer now, Stoneshearth's Castle rising beyond it. The first one of us to land along the edge and shift back to human form wins. We advance, neck and neck, our wings slapping the wind, until he presses ahead. I quickly veer to the right and knock into him, hoping to jar him off course, but he's bigger than me and it proves futile. Something foreign ripples through me, pulling me down, like weights clinging to my scales. I baulk, confused, tumbling to the rocky ground. Did I just lose my power? No. Not possible. I quickly push the thought away.

Owen circles back, landing next to me with a thud. We shift back, our clothes half drenched. My long hair is a matted mess down my back that will be its own cruel punishment come morning, but still worth it.

"Are you okay?" Owen asks, crouching down next to me. "What happened?"

My breath catches in my throat. I bite back the worry and force a smile onto my face. "One of these days, I'm going to beat you."

"I have no doubt." He winks. His eyes are the brightest blue, even at night. It's impossible not to stare. But there's still something unsettled in his gaze. He's also worried about me, but he lets it go for now.

We sneak back into the castle through one of the many underground passageways. It's musty and cramped. The floor is worn dirt and the damp stone walls are so low we have to crawl in some spots. There are a few places where we travel close to public spaces. We take extra care to go slow here, and even still, every sound sets us on edge. But we're also used to it and, as far as we know, we're the only ones who've found this particular passageway.

We take this risk week after week, knowing that if we get caught together, he'll bear the brunt of our punishment. I'm selfish for it. I know that. For a prince to be caught sneaking around with me is prohibited, and if caught, he—or any one of his brothers—would be given a very public and very painful lashing. But its effect wouldn't be lasting, wouldn't be life or death, and perhaps that's why we tempt fate.

No. It's my kiss that is deadly. Should *anyone* be caught kissing me, they're to be sent into immediate exile. And should they foolishly try to return? Executed. Owen has never kissed me, and I pray he doesn't. Because two years ago, his older brother did, and we haven't seen him since.

"LADY KHALI. PLEASE, HOLD STILL," my ladies maid, Faros, says with a great deal of exasperation as she tugs my corset's strings. I catch her eye in the gilded mirror and shoot her a chagrined smile, but I do what she asks, wincing as she finishes tightening, dressing, and primping me for the day. Faros has been with me for as long as I can remember. I consider her my second mother, though she's much kinder than my real mother who took to court life like a knife to venison, cutting her way to the top.

"Does it have to be Friday already?" I complain. "Let's just skip right to Saturday so I can rest."

The missed sleep from last night weighs heavily on my limbs. That and the pressing worry about what happened. I've never once struggled with my dragon form like that. It was as if one second she and I were together, and the next, we were separated into two different beings. The thought of it leaves me hollow.

Faros clicks her tongue. "You have to give all the princes equal time. You know the law."

I frown. "Yes, I do."

Some of us choose our fate. Most do not. But in my seventeen years, I've come to realize that we all have control over what we believe. Our lives may not be ours to mold, but our thoughts are ours to own. Do the Gods have their hands in our lives at every moment, continually directing us on a course of their choosing? Or is fortune left to chance, left to ambitious men and women, willing to take what they want?

Or perhaps it's both.

I was placed here by the Gods. My past, present, and

future are clay between their fingers. There was a time when I rebelled against my fate, but I've since accepted the truth. And *that* acceptance was my choice. My *one* choice. My path was bestowed on me the day I sparked life in my mother's womb, and, from the moment my eyes fluttered opened as an infant, it was known that I would be the next queen. My status from commoner to royal has never been questioned.

No, the question was, and still is, this: which of the four princes is to be my husband?

I brush my hands along my robin's egg blue bodice, admiring the crushed velvet. Velvet is my favorite fabric, even in summer, and it makes me smile. There's little I get to choose, but this dress is one.

Still, I sigh, returning to the truth of the day ahead. "But why does Bram have to be so boring? He never wants to do anything I want to do. It's all study, study, study with him."

"You would do well to read a book every once in a while."

I fake a gasp of outrage. "I read!"

"Only to satisfy your tutors. I'm talking about taking a real interest in your responsibilities."

I roll my eyes, even though I'm not surprised. This kind of advice is constant. Ask anyone, and they'd tell me to be grateful, to embrace what I've been given. "You sound just like Mother."

"Oh hush," she replies with a twitching smile, breaking her orderly façade.

As if her timing couldn't be any more impeccable, my mother sweeps into my room. Her chestnut hair is neatly done atop her head in a sort of silly bird's nest design and her dress is perfectly pressed silver silk against her tanned skin. She's beautiful and cunning, and I steel myself for whatever she has come to demand of me.

"Tonight is an important night for you," she says coolly, her eyes landing on me like I've already begun to argue.

I roll my eyes. "Aren't they all? You know, I'm tiring of all this fanfare at my expense."

She looks at me like I've gone insane, gathering her thoughts. "Then I'll make this quick. I've come to encourage your courtship with Silas," Mother says. She glides across the room to stand in front of me, placing cool hands on my shoulders and peering into my eyes. "Silas will take good care of you *and* this kingdom when the time comes. You should be nicer to him and stop paying so much attention to the childish twin."

I shrug her off me. "Owen is my best friend, and why does it matter who I pay attention to? The king will choose my mate anyway."

"It matters because people talk. So you'll give Silas extra

attention tonight. Do it for your family."

I fake a smile, but inside I'm boiling. "As you wish, Mother." I want to argue with her, but it's so much easier to give in to her demands.

Not for the first time, I wish my father wasn't gone so often. She never does this kind of thing in his presence. He's too protective of me, and she's too enamoured of him. He's the kind of person who brings out the best qualities in all of us. I miss him terribly, like an emptiness is in my heart and only he can fill it up.

She raises a perfect eyebrow and then leaves me to Faros without another word. The second she's gone, I groan and Faros shrugs, a look of regret passing over her eyes. There's no point in talking about it. These are the kinds of conversations I've been having with my mother for years. She only has a place in this castle because of me and she's desperate to make sure that everything I do stays in her control so that *she* can keep things the way she likes them.

Faros ushers me to the hallway as if the previous scene never happened. I wish she'd stand up for me, but I forgive her for not quite understanding me, because I love her, and at least she doesn't try to control me. It's like that with the people I call my family. With Father and Mother and Faros— even when they try to put me into the tightest of places, even when it hurts me to contort to their ideas for my future, my forgiveness is automatic. Perhaps that's foolish, or perhaps that's normal when it comes to family.

Faros stays close as we walk down to Bram's chambers on the other end of Stoneshearth's Castle. The staff step out of our way as we pass. Courtesans smile and offer cheerful greetings. Around us, the stone floors and walls are polished to gleaming gray. Giant arched windows line the long hallways, letting in rivers of golden light, brightening the glittering dust particles suspended in midair. Beyond the windows, countless dragons swoop and swirl in the distance. Some of our dragon army is practicing, their training drills sending a pang of pure want through my body. I long to be out there instead of cooped up in here, but I know that will never happen.

It doesn't take long until I find myself standing outside of Bram's door. I release a breath and knock against the oak. I hope he doesn't answer. I know he will.

Every day it's a different prince, except for Saturdays, which belong to me, and Sundays which belong to the Gods. Prince Owen is my best friend, and we always have loads of fun together, joking and lounging around with our pals. Prince Silas is witty and intense. He likes to play chess and talk about war strategy. Sometimes we'll go for strolls in the hedge maze, which I quite enjoy. He's fairly easy to talk to, but he doesn't have many friends; he's too critical, too barbed. Nobody stays close for long, nobody wants to get cut. And there's something about him that scares me, something about the way he sees the world, like it's another one of his chess boards. Everything can be won or lost.

But it's Bram whom I struggle to connect with the most. He's as dull as a butter knife. All he cares for are his books and tutors. Whenever I spend the day with him, we barely speak, let alone leave the musky library attached to his chambers. I suppose that's to be expected of someone who isn't Dragon Blessed. It's not his fault, really.

In a matter of seconds, he opens the door, nods once, and goes back to his desk.

"Your majesty." I bow and Faros and I stride into his chambers. All the princes have their own studies and sitting rooms for our meetings, and when we're together, we're never to be alone. At least not until one is crowned King and I'm married off.

Bram's sitting room is dark, with thick curtains drawn over the window, dripping candles burning in the candelabras, and stacks of books piled on every available surface. True to form, he doesn't even bother to look up from whatever he's studying today. I eye the tome in his lap, catching sight of the name of our greatest enemy: The Sovereign Occultists.

I shudder and swallow down the instant burst of fear. The warlocks are terrible in every possible way and, worst of all, they want to eradicate elemental magic. The dragon race is top of their list.

I drop into the closest chair. It smells like dust. Faros shoots me a pointed look and I sit up straight, resting my hands on my knees and smiling meekly. "Do you have any novels in here?" I pick up a book about the Jeweled Forest and toss it aside. Geography is no fun for someone who's never allowed to go anywhere. Not that I'd go *there*, not from the way people talk about it like it's sure to lead to a gruesome death.

"Like what kind of novels?" He doesn't look up.

"Action and adventure," I respond. "Romance, too, of course."

That gets Bram's attention. He peers up at me with mossy eyes like I'm one of the puzzling science experiments dissected in his books. "No," he clips.

I roll my eyes and reach for the nearest history text, absentmindedly thumbing through the worn pages. Neither of us wants me here. There's no way Bram will be named King and we both know it. A Non-Blessed prince has never been king. But the law requires us to spend this time together and so we suffer through it.

A photograph in the text catches my eyes and I gasp.

Bram jumps forward, ripping the book from my hands. "You can't have that," he snaps. But my heart is racing so fast I hardly care what he has to say about it.

"That's not our history," I challenge, "that's from the other realm." My mind reaches back to what I saw. A city of glass buildings towering into the sky like giants, glinting in the sun. I've never seen anything like that here, but I've heard stories of the non-magical realm where people aren't dragons or wizards or seers, but are instead slaves to technology. I don't quite understand what that word "technology" means, but I've had good enough sense not to ask. Whatever it is, it's not for our realm. "Are you allowed to have that?"

Bram's eyes level on mine. "Yes," he says plainly. I don't believe him. But I don't press him on it either. He sighs with exasperation and stands, rummaging through books for a while, until he drops a novel into my lap.

The title says, *A Midsummer Night's Dream*.

"What's this?" I ask, running my fingers along the spine. It's smoother than any book I've ever seen before and glossy in the sunlight. It doesn't seem to belong with the rest of the books in his library.

His eyes dart to Faros, but she says nothing. She sits in the back of the room, busying herself with her needlepoint work, feigning that she's giving us privacy. She's not. But even then, she can be trusted.

He swallows hard and levels his gaze back on me. Something foreign shoots up my spine and I sit up taller. "It's a play. Just read it," he finally says. "You'll like it." Then he settles back into his own text.

I've nothing better to do so I begin reading. The words are lyrical and somewhat difficult to understand, but I soon find myself drawn in, laughing through the tale of mischievous fairies and unrequited love. It's the first time today I'm able to stop thinking about what happened last night with my wayward magic. Finally, after a few hours of nothing but comedy playing out in my mind and my occasional laugh to break the silence, Bram speaks. It catches me so off guard that I jump in my seat.

"Pardon me, what was that you asked?" I close the book but hold a finger between the pages. I don't want to lose my place!

His gaze pins me down. "I said, I'd like to talk to you about what happened with my brother."

My heart jumps and my eyes dart to where Faros sits in her chair along the edge of the room. But she's just as startled and can't help me. "Which brother?"

He raises a dark eyebrow, calling my bluff. His voice is dry as sand, "Who else but the one you got exiled?"

Tears warm my eyes. My lips press together. I knew this day would come eventually, but now that it's here, I can't remember all the lies I'd so carefully prepared.

THREE

HAZEL

THE COMFORTING AROMA OF COFFEE wafts from
The Roasted Bean and wraps me up like a warm blanket.
I sigh and breathe it in, my eyes darting to the shiny glass
door. When I notice the "help wanted" sign, I smile at my
good fortune. I worked at a coffee and bubble tea shop back
home in Ohio, so this place is a perfect fit. Fighting down
the sudden flutter of nerves, I pull open the door and stroll
into the upscale coffee shop. *I am a girl on a mission. I am
a confident goddess. I am the best candidate for the job and
they'd be crazy not to hire me.*

Help wanted? Coming right up!

For a girl like me, receiving a full ride scholarship was
a complete godsend. Growing up with a single mother, we
never had a lot of money. Not that I noticed it too much.

Mom works ridiculously hard as an emergency room nurse and has always made it a point to provide for me in every way that two parents would have. But when it came to paying for college, my options were limited to student loans or scholarships. I earned good grades, and I even graduated a year early from high school, but I wasn't "Miss Valedictorian/Debate Captain" or anything like that. Not to make excuses, but having spirits in my face at all hours was rather distracting, not to mention the bullying that went on in my Ohio hometown kept me from being much of a joiner.

So when all was said and done and it came time to apply to colleges, I assumed scholarships were out of the question. I applied to all the best schools located in small towns that I could find. The day a thick letter from Hayden College landed in my mailbox, I opened it up and my world opened up with it.

The craziest thing about it was that I didn't even think I would get in to this school. It's ranked high and the class sizes are small. And now I'm here with a scholarship? I sometimes wonder if the admissions office made a mistake, but it's not like I'm going to ask. Anyway, if I keep a full schedule and my grades above a 3.5 average, my room and board will continue to be paid through four years of undergrad. All I need is a part-time job to pay for extra expenses and save up for vet school. Easy enough.

There's not a line at the counter this late in the afternoon which makes me a tad nervous. I guess it's now or never. I quickly catch the eye of the barista, a young guy with white-blonde hair pulled back into a man-bun and bright cobalt eyes, and wave a friendly hello.

"Don't I know you?" He grins, and my stomach does a weird flip-flop. He has dimples. Honest to God, all American boy, swoon-worthy dimples. Those might make up for the man-bun situation—not my favorite look.

"Umm, I think so?" I bite my lip, smoothing my hands along my frayed jeans, trying to place him because yeah, he actually does look familiar.

"You're in my organic chemistry lab." He leans over the edge of the counter, hooking me in with his gaze. Okay, yup, I remember him now. He looks even better in his black barista apron than his chem lab jacket, by which I mean, he's freaking hot.

College has turned me into a total boy-crazy lunatic—that much has become alarmingly clear over the last week. I swear, everywhere I go I'm checking out all the new hotties. It can't be helped.

"Landon, right?" I ask, then immediately redden. I remembered his name and now he's going to think I'm a stalker chick or something.

His grin grows even larger. "That's me. And you are?"

"Here to apply for the job."

He gives me a quick once-over with those startling blue eyes of his and I'm not even going to pretend that I'm breathing properly. Oh sweet baby Jesus, if working here means I get to flirt with this cute guy, then please Lord, give me the job. Don't I deserve this?

"Right, let me grab an application. You can fill it out now. I'll give it to the owners myself and put in a good word for you." Landon winks and holds a hand over the corner of his delicious mouth as if to let me in on a secret. "I'm a local. I've been working here for years. This is my family's business."

I smile, the bundle of nerves unraveling inside me like a tangled ball of yarn. He slides the application across the counter, and I snatch it up. If he has any say in who his parents hire, then today just might be my lucky day.

"Thanks," I squeak out.

"So you're a freshman, right? I'm sure I would've seen you before, otherwise."

I nod sheepishly.

"But you're in an upper level chem lab with me, that's pretty impressive."

"Thanks." Is that all I can manage to say to him? Thanks?

"You're welcome. You must be pretty smart, what with

those cute glasses and all. What's your major?"

I automatically reach up to touch the black frames of my fake glasses. Would he think I was smart if I told them they're fake? "Umm—biology. I want to go to vet school." That's better, at least that was a complete sentence.

He smiles and little wrinkles spring up around his eyes and I nearly melt right then and there. I don't even care that he used the most obvious question ever of "what's your major" to flirt with me.

"That's awesome. Good for you. Well." He nods to the application and raises an eyebrow. "I'll look forward to working with you, Freshman."

Oh my gosh! He gave me a nickname. Never mind that he didn't ask for my real name. Never mind that he probably uses that name on all the new girls. I smile back and say something awkward about looking forward to it too, the whole time my face growing scarlet by the second. If only all the guys on campus were as sweet as Landon, this place would be heaven.

The altercation with Dean Ashton has been following me around since yesterday like an ugly cloud hanging over this whole "college experience," and I don't know how to shake the feeling that Dean's not going to let this thing go between us, whatever *it* is. Cora seems to be in the know about everything on this campus and she claims he's the mysterious, bad boy that all the girls want and all the guys want to be. Talk about a total cliché. This isn't some bad 90's movie that's so bad it's also so good. If Dean's really that cool of a dude, then why he is so bent out of shape about me?

Pushing the thought away, I settle into a sleek leather booth and get to work, my mind still spinning at the possibilities of Landon. Back in high school, I never dated. Not that I didn't want to, but I wasn't part of the crowd—any crowd—and nobody ever asked me. People thought I was weird. They stared. And laughed. And besides, I took extra classes so I could finish up early, choosing to spend my time on that goal rather than finding some pimply teenager to date.

The application itself is pretty standard: normal questions about previous employment, available hours, references and whatnot. But I find myself getting distracted. Not by Landon who's looking pretty good behind the counter if I do say so myself—and I do, not by the bell that chimes every time someone enters the coffee shop, and not even by the group of rowdy college kids in the next booth.

No, it's the dead girl sitting in the booth across from me that's the source of interruption.

Seriously, why is this always happening? I can feel her sitting there, staring at me. But I don't look up. My pen scrawls across the application, filling in the information, all the while, a prinkling sense of foreboding creeps up my spine like a needle pulling thread. I can't help it anymore. I look up. My pen drops to the table and rolls to the ground with a clatter.

I know her.

Terror grips me tight and I press myself back into the bench seat. I just met this girl at our dorm welcome activity four days ago while she was alive and well. And now here she is, sitting across from me, dead. A ring of blue blooms around her mouth in a way that usually means death by drowning. Her black hair hangs around her face, dripping wet, exponentially adding to her creepiness factor. And her eyes are so bloodred that I can't tell what color they were in life except for the fact that when I met her, I thought she had the most gorgeous green eyes I'd ever seen. I'd been momentarily jealous, annoyed that mine were a boring hazel to match my name.

Drowned Girl opens her mouth to speak, which I know is impossible. Water rushes out in a gagging torrent. It looks just like the water from the hallway earlier. She's been following me.

I jump up, about ready to scream.

"Oh, heck no," I mutter, adrenaline racing through every vein. I do not want to deal with this, not today, not right now. She stares after me through watery eyes as I gather up my application and shove it haphazardly into my trendy jean backpack. I zip it up so quickly that I take off a bit of the paper on the corner. Dang it all!

"Is everything okay?" Landon calls after me as I scurry toward the exit.

Oh, crap, I'm not acting normal, am I? I slow and turn around, giving him a 1000-watt smile. I probably look like a lunatic. Of course, since I'm the only one who can see dead people, this kind of thing happens a lot.

"Everything is great," I sputter. "Thanks, Landon. I actually have to go, but I'll bring the application back tomorrow." Even as I speak, I can hear the places where my voice sounds high-pitched and dare I say it? Spooked. Landon's expression is questioning but luckily a new customer walks in and pulls his attention off of me. The dead girl is still gargling from the booth, still trying to speak, still spitting water all over the place.

I can't do this.

I don't spook easily. I've seen enough ghosts to make my life a living horror show, so what's one more. But this girl, *this girl* is a different story. She was alive four days ago! I met her, her name starts with a K or C or something. She lives on my floor and has already declared a major in Elementary Education and wants to be a freaking Kindergarten teacher. And now? Now she's one of the ever-present ghosts haunting me.

Tears prick at my eyes and I push my way out the door and onto the street. I try to breathe. I try to calm down. I can't.

What happened to her? She clearly drowned, but how? This West Virginian town of Westinbrook is small, a college town centered in the Smoky Mountains. With only fifteen thousand residents, a third of them being college kids, there isn't much to do here to get yourself *killed* unless it involves drinking oneself to death.

My mind races to any known water sources in the area. There are neighboring forests dotted with lakes, but students have been in school all week. We haven't even made it to the first weekend when the parties are known to kick off. What was she doing out at a lake? Swimming to cool off or something? Or maybe it happened in a pool on campus somewhere. Maybe something crazy went down in the dormroom shower? Visions of the shower scene from the old movie *Psycho* pop up in my head and I shudder. I am officially freaking out!

I turn back to make sure she's not following me.

And she totally is. Awesome.

Water pours off her, an unholy sight reserved only for my cursed eyes. Every time she opens her mouth, I'm met with more of the water. It's not real. It belongs to another dimension: the spirit world. But it's terrifying and horrible and I can't take it. A pang of guilt shoots through me. I should try to help her. She's probably so much more afraid than I am; she might not even know what's happened to her yet. Even though I'm standing in daylight in the center of Main Street, what choice do I have but to try to help?

"What happened?" I croak, looking the ghost-girl up and down. Maybe she can send me images and I can piece this together.

I'm met with no response besides an open mouth and more gurgling water.

"Okay, I know you're scared or whatever but you're literally going to give me a heart attack. You have no idea how freaky this is," I reply in a rush. I haven't engaged with a ghost since arriving on campus and I had vowed not to. That lasted less than a week. Big surprise.

The problem was the few times I've tried to help one of them, I've tended to create more harm than good. Their family and friends never wanted to hear what I had to say. They didn't believe me, called me crazy, a crook, blasphemous, and even once, the devil's child. Not to mention, helping one ghost always means more would show up to pester me.

Turns out, everybody wants something, even dead people.

Mom knows all about my problem—or curse, as I call it. She calls it a gift, which would be downright laughable if it were funny. No joke, we've spent years and years trying to make the ghosts go away, but nothing ever works. Not therapy. Not pharmaceuticals. Not support groups. Not random blog articles with advice about how to cleanse under the full moon.

Nothing.

We've also tried to embrace it. Maybe if I learned how to control the ability, I could pick and choose what I had to deal with. Yeah, all that did was attract more ghosts than before. Scary ones. Nowadays, they are everywhere. All the time. I largely ignore them and try to live a normal life. It's not easy…

But this poor girl! I can't seem to help myself from speaking to her again. She and I could have been friends. We're not that different. If she's dead, isn't it possible I could be in her place right now? We live on the same floor and have things in common. She wanted to help innocent baby humans. I want to help innocent baby animals. Practically the same thing, right?

"What do you need?" I press, stepping closer.

Her face slackens, and she points a thin index finger off into the nebulous distance.

"I'm not sure what that means," I continue, staring back down the street. The area is lined with cute restaurants, shops, businesses, and a few clothing boutiques for tourists.

With the swell of Smoky Mountains as a backdrop and the trees lining the sidewalks, it could be a postcard.

Someone giggles from behind, and I turn to find the same group of college kids who'd been in the coffee shop. They're not laughing with each other anymore. They're looking at me like I'm a crazy person. Maybe I am. Either way, I've become the joke. Embarrassment prickles over my entire body and I grin sheepishly, my eyes probably bugging out of my head. One by one, the group averts their gazes and rush past me.

"I'm sorry," I say, speaking low to the drowned ghosty girl once I'm sure we're alone again. "I don't know what you want and I don't know how to help you, but you're dead. If you see a light or a tunnel or something, my advice is to go to it."

She gapes at me, mouth open like a fish, bloodshot eyes wide and terrified.

Did she not know she was dead? Bile rises in my throat. There's nothing I can do, so with a stab of guilt, I turn from her and hurry away, back in the direction of campus. Of one thing I'm certain—I really need to get a grip on my ghost problem if this college thing is going to work out. I sure hope I don't end up in the loony-bin one day. I say it as a joke to myself and to Mom all the time, but I actually mean it. It's my worst fear. Some days it feels inevitable that my future will involve padded rooms and straitjackets.

"I can help you," a woman steps out from a shadowy storefront. I squeak and stumble, nearly jumping out of my own skin.

I hold up a hand. "Holy Hannah, you scared the bejesus out of me!"

Her smile is playful, her pale blue eyes framed by deep wrinkles and twinkling in their intensity. Her white hair is dreadlocked and even though she's clearly pushing old age, the look works well for her. A knobby finger points up to the name scrolled across the building: The Flowering Chakra.

"Oh, no thanks." I stop her right there, my heart sinking.

"I think you and I could help each other, actually."

Her tone is genuine, but I quickly shake my head and continue on my way. I want to look back, want to give this lady a shot, whatever she's offering, but I know better. Believe me when I say, I've been there and done that. Nothing and nobody can help me, especially not the metaphysical crackpots of the world. Most of them claim to see spirits too, and while that may be true for some, it's never close to what I experience on the daily when it comes to the spirit realm.

These people always think they know, always think they can help me.

They can't.

"Come back," she calls out, her voice as thick as slow-churned butter, and I want to believe her so badly it hurts. It's the familiar ache of old disappointments all lined up in a row, and I hate it. "Come back, soon, my dear. I really do know how to help someone like you."

I shake my head. If only it were that easy.

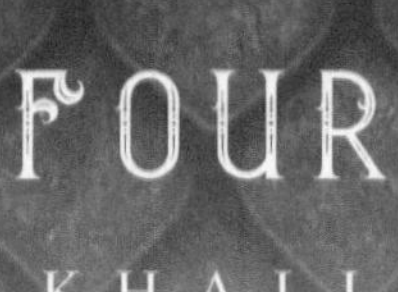

THE ENTIRE DRAGON KINGDOM IS waiting for my eighteenth birthday. Sometimes it feels as if the whole world is waiting for me to come of age so I can be married off. The pressure of every passing day adds another drop of anxiety to an already boisterous ocean. I only have four months left, and Bram isn't making this easier. Sometimes, I think I'll drown underneath the weight.

I narrow my eyes at him. Inside, I'm that ocean storm, but outside, I'm a calm surface. Practiced. Perfect.

"You've had two years to question me about your brother's exile and yet you never said a single word," I quip. "Why the sudden interest?"

"It isn't sudden," he replies casually. "I never believed he would have engaged in an inappropriate relationship with you."

Guilt racks my body and I sit up straighter. "Well, he did and it's over."

"So I've heard."

He eyes Faros for a long second, as if measuring how much she can be trusted. As my chaperone and ladies maid, she's with me nearly all of the time and has been for years. She knows almost everything about me. But even *she* doesn't know the specifics of how and why I got the oldest prince exiled.

"There's nothing you can say in front of me that you can't say in front of Faros," I retort. "She is family. I trust her with my life."

"How lucky for you to trust family so implicitly," he says dryly. "But I wonder if she values the princes' lives above yours. We still don't know who told my father about your alleged tryst with my brother two years ago."

Faros raises her hand to her mouth. "I would never do such a thing." Her tone is shocked, and I believe her.

"Get to the point, Bram," I snap. "Whatever you want to say, say it. This conversation is growing tiresome."

His eyes lock me down. He's never held my gaze for so long and it's unnerving. I haven't had the opportunity to measure how green his eyes are until now. They remind me of a rainy spring that won't seem to end. He runs a hand along his jaw, considering. "What would you do to get my brother back?"

Dark mistrust and bright hope battle through my veins. "Don't speak of the impossible," I reply. "He's gone. And if he returns, he'll be killed."

"Maybe…"

"No, not maybe. It's a fact."

"Before he left, he said he had initiated the kiss. But I find that odd. What I'm trying to figure out is if he *actually* liked you back, because it was painfully obvious how much you wanted him. I believe you kissed him, and I want to know why he didn't just say that."

"You don't know what you're talking about!" I lean back into the padding of my chair, wishing it could swallow me whole. Blood rushes to my cheeks, but I refuse to break eye contact, even if I'm powerless to hide my shame.

"I think I do." He leans back as well, studying me. "I know you had harbored a secret crush on my brother for years, but he never returned your advances as far as I could tell. And yet, he never denied kissing you, something forbidden, something he knew would get him sent into exile. Why would he cover for your blunder? Did he *want* to leave the kingdom?"

My throat turns to ice, freezing the words within.

"He was the most powerful of the princes," Bram continues. "He loved it here, excelled at court politics and would have been a formidable leader and war hero. Besides that, everyone knew he was my father's favorite. He was destined to be crowned our next King."

"Perhaps." My voice is steady but my nerves are a riot.

"And *you* would have been his queen. You would have gotten the prince you desired since your girlhood."

That part is true, but I swallow my response.

"But the two of you ruined it. I want to know what happened and why."

"I am not speaking to you on this matter. It's none of your business." I gather my dress while still holding onto *A Midsummer Night's Dream* and stand, rushing toward the door. Guilt nips at my heels, but I promised more than just myself that I wouldn't tell anyone and I won't break that promise, especially not for someone as frustrating and sure of himself as Bram.

"Now you only have three brothers left to vie for your bed, but of course you and I both know I'm about as likely to be crowned king as a horse," Bram calls after me. "So why keep secrets from me, Khali Elliot?"

Faros stands at my side but I don't dare to look at her. My shaking hands press against the cool wood of the door. Outside, children's laughter echoes down the corridor. Careless and free.

"I'm suddenly not feeling well," I say over my shoulder.

"I apologize, but our meeting must be cut short. I hope to see you at the ball tomorrow night, Your Highness." I end the conversation and burst into the hallway, my heart hammering against my ribcage.

"Do save me a dance!" Bram's mocking words reverberate through the open door. Faros slams it shut.

I growl and grind my foot into the stone floor. My dragon raises her head within me, eager to take out the frustration in our favorite way, but I can't shift without permission. And I *never* have permission. My dragon may be the reason I'm here, but she's just as caged as I am.

Faros and I hurry back to my chambers and all the while, Bram's words ravage my thoughts. He was right about too many things. I did have a crush on his older brother and I do have a secret about what happened that night. Just thinking about how it unfolded sends my heart twisting and my jaw clenching so tight that pain shoots through the bone and into my teeth. I take a steadying breath and count to ten. Just because Bram's a keen observer and the smartest of the princes doesn't mean I'll ever confess the truth. Not to him. Not to anyone.

THE CLAWING FINGERS OF THE corset dig into my skin. I straighten my spine like a puppet on a string, but it doesn't help the pain. I take a breath, double check that my gown is in immaculate condition, and slip into the ballroom. Tumultuous thoughts of what could have been slip in with me. Drat! I haven't been able to stop thinking about Bram's accusations since he laid them out yesterday. This party had better be a good one.

My gaze travels over the members of the Court, and I click my tongue. The disparity of wealth among Blessed and Non-Blessed families is becoming more and more noticeable, from the degree of fine clothing, to the level of desperation behind masked expressions. Had I not been born with my peculiar set of eyes, I wouldn't even be here. I'd most likely be starving in the backwater village on the edge of nowhere. We may have all descended from dragons, but not everyone in the Kingdom of Drakenon is actually Dragon Blessed and can shift. Furthermore, it's only my two colored eyes that clued others into my elemental powers, that marked me as something *more*.

"Princess, there you are." Silas appears, dipping in close. His voice is as smooth as the black silk tie around his neck. "I've been looking for you. I wanted to get the first dance."

I smile calmly and he takes me into his sturdy arms, twirling me around the ballroom in a familiar waltz. I'm reminded of growing up with the brothers and learning this exact dance during our hours upon hours of painstaking lessons. Silas didn't enjoy dancing then, but he certainly seems to be enjoying himself now. Everyone watches us. He watches me. Is it because my birthday is approaching that his indigo eyes glow with pride? And with something else—something hard to place. Confidence, perhaps? No, not confidence. Determination.

King Titus and Queen Brysta preside over the party in their raised thrones but seem to care little for the guests below. The monarchs draw in the most ambitious among us. Several Dukes and Duchesses flit around the pair like moths to the flame, keeping the royal pair busy with flattery and politics. My mother is among the group, of course. She hasn't looked my way yet but I know she will soon. Her dark tresses are piled on her head in complete perfection. It's only a matter of time before she glides over to remind me of our earlier conversation about Silas. At that thought, he tugs me in closer.

"You look radiant tonight," he says, his gaze running over my face and then landing playfully on my own. "I'll never get over how beautiful and unique your eyes are, Khali. Truly extraordinary."

Wow. I'm used to his flattery but he's really going for it tonight.

I scoff and raise a brow. "Your mother has the same eyes. It's not *that* unique."

He shakes his head. "But they are. I love my mother, but you, you are vastly different from her." His eyes flick to my lips and I glare and stiffen.

"You know the rules," I say sharply. "You know them better than anyone."

He only smiles. It's all a game. Silas is far too ambitious to be tempted to kiss me now. I can only assume it's the other way around. He wants to be the one to tempt me, wants me to want him. Ultimately, the King will decide which one of the brothers I'm to wed after I turn eighteen, but it will be easier to convince his father if the court is talking of how much I longed for his lips during the Autumn Equinox ball. I stiffen, because while I consider Silas a friend, I'm not charmed by his ambition. And while I do find him attractive, it's the kind of attractiveness that comes with a bite.

"May I cut in?" Owen's cheerful voice is that of pure salvation. He swoops in before Silas can argue otherwise and steers the two of us in the opposite direction. I give Silas an apologetic look as I go, but inside, I feel nothing but pure relief. Silas keeps his mouth in a thin line, his eyes zeroed in, his jaw tight. He never looks away.

"Thank you," I whisper to Owen.

Owen just laughs, his glorious blue eyes brightening. He never takes any of this seriously. It's all a big game to him, too. But he's not playing to win; he's playing to enjoy himself. Between him and his two brothers, I'd rather marry Owen in a heartbeat. He is my best friend, afterall. Though deep down, I know it will be Silas. The Court loves Silas. His father dotes on him. Silas's ambition is unmatched, and because of that, he's best suited for the job of future king. My stomach clenches into a ball of nails knowing what that will mean for me.

"How many here do you think can shift?" I ask, trying to take my mind off of Owen's twin. We turn to take in the guests. The ballroom is packed fuller than normal for one of these parties. They flutter around like desperate moths to a flame, each one seeking to be part of the light. But it's the ones who are Dragon Blessed who were born to burn brightest. I wonder if some of them are part of the dragon army I saw training earlier. What would I give to be one of them?

Owen shrugs, running a confident hand along his suit jacket. "Maybe half."

I bite my lip and nod. That's what I thought, too. To be a dragon and not permitted to shift openly, like myself, is a cruel way to live. Does Queen Brysta hate it as much as I do? Does she long to break free and fly, to be her true self? If she does, she's never shown it in my presence. Maybe it would have been better to have been born without the ability to shift, like Bram.

"Do you ever find it strange that we're called the Blessed because we're simply the ones who can shift into dragon form?"

Owen shoots me an odd look. "Well, it's a blessing to the kingdom, isn't it? Dragons can do incredible damage to any invading armies. It's why we've stood strong for as long as we have."

"I guess so," I say. What I don't say, is that I don't feel so blessed. The closer I get to my birthday, the closer I get to having a husband thrust upon me and the less fortunate I feel. My job here is to become queen and produce elemental Dragon Blessed heirs. I'm lucky to have all four elements. Rare. So rare, they can't risk losing me.

I think of how *easy* it would be to fall in love with him when I glance up at Owen's deep blue eyes that fit his ability so well. Prince Owen Hydros Brightcaster. His element is water and his personality is as fluid, even if he is my rock. Like water, he can be gentle and calm, or wild and unpredictable, and underneath the surface, his personality runs deep.

Prince Silas Skylen Brightcaster is Owen's twin, though the two don't match in any way. Silas possesses the elemental magic of sky and is a formidable warrior. Not only can he cause the winds to blow so hard that they lift entire buildings, he can conjure storms and wield lightning to strike his opponents dead where they stand. I haven't seen it with my own eyes, but I've heard the stories brought back from the battlefield over the years. And I've seen what his father can do, how his moods direct the weather around the castle. A chill skitters down my spine.

I peer around the room for Bram but I doubt he's here. He rarely comes to these things, and nobody cares. He probably wasn't serious about dancing with me, thank the Gods. Bram doesn't dance. In fact, he doesn't do much of anything besides study and scowl and study some more. But Prince Bram Oaken Brightcaster never shifted, so nobody bothers him about dancing at these things, or even attending. Had the magic not skipped him, he would've been able to manipulate earth. He could have caused the ground to shake and rise, could have caused entire crops to flourish or crumble and die. And he would be here at this ball with his brothers, asking for his turn to dance with the future queen. I find it strange that Bram's eyes are still bright emerald to match his element, like his brothers' eyes match their own gifts. Sometimes that's what happens, though. Sometimes, entire families can be dragon shifters, their bloodlines thick as chainmail, save for one lone outcast, one weak link.

Life isn't always kind.

But I don't feel too bad for Bram. He's still a Brightcaster Prince and still enjoys the luxuries that come with the title. All that freedom with none of the responsibility. No, I don't feel bad for him at all.

"What is going on in that pretty little head of yours?" Owen asks. We've stopped dancing and have found ourselves outside on the terrace. The cool night washes over me, softening my dark mood. We lean side by side against the balcony, inches apart. Music and party guests float in and out. The night is a blanket of darkness and stars, our lands reaching far, far beyond what I can see. My future kingdom.

An endless prison.

I turn to Owen and search his concerned expression, looking for a sign of some sort of go-ahead. Should I tell him about Bram's questioning? As my closest friend, surely he'd understand. But then again, what if it made him question me further? Question our friendship? In the end, I make up nonsense about a tiff with my mother and we fall into companionable silence. He accepts my story without question. Lady Alivia Elliot and I are always at odds and my father is rarely around to buffer our spats.

Pesky thoughts creep back into my mind—the consuming ones about the eldest royal brother, the man we never speak of. His eyes were so different from any of his younger brothers. They were black as coal, which makes sense considering he was the strongest fire elemental dragon in generations and more dangerous than all of his brothers combined. He would have been the king we all needed, the one who would've ensured Drakenon's safety and prosperity for generations.

I peer over the glittering city into the dark horizon and wonder where he is, knowing he's utterly unreachable. Maybe even dead. It's my fault. Because of me, Dean Ashton Brightcaster will never be the king of anything.

FIVE

HAZEL

CORA AND MACY'S HIGH-HEELS clack on the sidewalk as we head across campus toward the first party of our college careers. Their bare arms are laced through mine, which is actually quite appropriate considering how badly I'm struggling to walk in this dress and the accompanying high heels. Is it luck that Cora and I are both a size seven shoe and I could borrow a pair from her, or that Macy and I are both a size six dress? They would say yes. I would not.

In fact, I'm convinced the weird wobble my legs are doing is making it look like I have to pee. In my defense, I'm not used to high heels or the suffocating fit of the dress, even if the bright white fabric looks great against my leftover summer tan. I keep telling myself to suck it up––it's just for one night. It's my own fault. I was super nervous about the party so I went against my better judgment and gave into peer-pressure.

"You look hot." Cora slaps my hand away from where I'm tugging at the short hemline. "Seriously, stop worrying about it, Hazel."

"You two are bad influences," I shoot back.

"Oh, you know you love it," Macy interjects. "Doesn't it feel a little good? Whenever I'm sad I go shopping and curl my hair and go out on the town. It makes such a difference!"

I raise an eyebrow. "No. I can't say I've ever done that." My voice is deadpan and something about that makes my friends bust up laughing.

Truth be told, I don't have *anything* like this outfit in my closet, and now that I know how impractical it is, I don't plan to go shopping anytime soon. Doesn't matter how sad I might get. I just hope Cora is wrong and this isn't the standard attire at these things, because if that's the case, then I'm screwed for all future parties.

"Should we establish a code word?" Macy grins, changing the subject. Her curtain of perfect strawberry hair flashes under the street lights. If she wasn't so freaking nice, I'd hate her. "You know, if one of us needs to get away from a creeper or something."

Cora laughs, pointing a sharp finger at Macy, her silvery bracelets jingling together. "Just tell the guy to back the hell off, and if he doesn't then he can deal with me." She flexes her bicep and waggles her eyebrows in that endearing way she does.

Macy rolls her eyes. "The point of a code word is to get out of a sticky situation without causing a scene."

"That's so sad, though, right?" Cora protests. "We shouldn't have to have a code word. Men should be respectful. And actually, if something does happen, if someone does make a woman uncomfortable, she *should* cause a scene instead of always trying to be polite."

I study Cora for a second, taking in her smooth chocolatey eyes and the way she's narrowing them at Macy. She's way more passionate about this than I first thought, but why shouldn't she be? Everything she's saying makes a lot of sense. "You're right, Cora." I nod. "I am going to do a better job at that."

My thoughts flash to the drowned ghost girl from yesterday. Maybe what happened to her wasn't an accident. Maybe if she'd made a scene, she'd still be alive. Either way, I haven't seen her since The Roasted Bean and I hope I don't have to again, especially now that I've been refreshed on her name.

Katherine.

Not Katie. Not Kat. Katherine. I remember her saying it.

Her school I.D. picture appeared all over campus this morning on "missing persons" leaflets. I know better. She may be missing, but she's more than that. And I've been debating all day about going to the police with a tip to go look for her body near open water sources. But I can't. It would make me a person of interest. They'd never believe the truth. Who would? Even I can't believe it sometimes.

As if sensing my thoughts about Katherine, Macy speaks up, "I wonder what happened to that girl. I hope she's okay."

"She's probably dead," Cora says, her voice going dark.

"Don't say that!" Macy gasps.

"Well, if they don't find her within seventy-two hours then her chances drop down to like 1% of survival or something crazy like that. It's already been three days. I'm sorry but that girl is as good as gone. Don't you watch any cop shows?"

"You're seriously freaking me out." Macy squeezes in closer. "None of us go outside at night alone, okay?"

"Deal," I say. But that's all I say. I keep my mouth shut about Katherine even though the backs of my arms are stinging with all the little raised hairs, even though my conscious is begging me to do something more, even though I might be able to help her family recover the body.

"This is it." Cora stops, guiding us toward the white-pillared house looming up ahead. Lanterns light the porch and the front of the house where huge Greek letters are hung. It's a surreal sight. Even from here, the stench of booze and bad decisions wafts through the night. Going to frat parties is what normal people my age do in the movies. This isn't what I do.

Well, I guess it is now.

When we walk into the Alpha Sigma fraternity house, the first thing I notice is the awful smell. The second is the noise.

The place reeks of old beer and too many sweaty bodies, and the offensive rap music blasting through the place is worse than nails on a chalkboard. *Not my thing.* I scrunch up my nose, already eager to leave this party and never look back. I'm sure it'll be overrated. But from the looks on Macy and Cora's faces, leaving already is not going to happen. Macy's blue eyes are wide and glittering with excitement, and Cora's got a knowing smirk on her face, her gaze fixed on some lucky schmuck across the room.

"I'll see you two later. It looks like I've got myself a date," she says, her silky voice dripping with confidence.

She pushes her way through the crowd of college kids, taller than most of them, even the guys. Her bare ebony shoulders and head of thin black braids bob above the sea of students. She's cool in a way that I could only dream of, and I'm suddenly filled with gratitude, and confusion, that of all the people she picked to be her first friend at college, she picked me.

I raise my eyebrows at Macy, curious if she knows where

Cora is off to, but Macy only shrugs.

"Let's get a drink," she suggests warmly, grabbing my hand and tugging me toward the kitchen.

I've never drunk any alcohol before and still haven't decided *for sure* if I want to when the red cup lands in my hand. It's not legal. I'm only seventeen so I have years to go. Logically, I should say no. But this is college and it's not like most of the people here are twenty-one. And this is part of the whole coming-of-age experience, is it not? I eye the foamy substance wearily but the weight of my insecurities hits me hard and before I can make a choice one way or the other, I'm drinking.

The taste is not good. Not even close to good. It warms me right up and before I know it, I'm reaching for the keg and helping myself to more. Macy does the same and then we head toward the dance floor, a tad wobbly, but ten times more courageous than when we first walked in here.

My defenses are down, and the music pulses louder but it's not so annoying anymore. My body moves with the throng of people, and I'm not the totally awkward dancer I thought I was—I might even be good at this. I find myself laughing and enjoying myself as one song fades into the next and sweat glistens my skin and maybe this dress isn't such a bad thing after all and where did Macy go? She was just right here. Oh hey, is that Landon? I should go dance with *him.*

But just as quickly as I see him, Landon disappears into the crowd. I blink, dread prickling through me, as the crowd itself shifts, the college kids overcome by transparent shapes, gray and colorless, ghosts appearing out of thin air, approaching me, surrounding me. I stand frozen in my heels, my knees turning into elastic.

That's when the spirits attack.

Maybe attack isn't the right word, but it sure feels that way. They bombard me with images flashing one after the next after the next. People laughing and fighting and tucking their children into bed. A car screeching. Someone lying on a beach, watching the surf as it crashes against the sand. Another running, headphones tucked into his ears, his breath heavy. Someone dropping a dish, the white porcelain splintering and scattering across a wood floor. A woman screams.

They're all kinds: all ethnicities, all ages, with all manner of death bleeding out on their ethereal forms. I don't know where to look or how to block them out, even a little bit. They press down on me, their thoughts louder, my heart pounding harder. Somehow, I've opened myself to a flood of these images and they just keep pouring in. They're from a contemporary time; I've never seen a ghost older than a few decades, at least. It's the one shred of silver lining here. But even then, they won't stop their attack on my senses. They're relentless.

The thing about spirits is they don't care as much about the living world as you'd think. They have no issues walking right through us, squatting in our homes, or scaring the bejesus out of us. And as it seems, they have no problem crashing a college party to get to me. They don't care that I'm trying to have a good time, trying to be normal, *to blend in*. In fact, something about the alcohol in my system has made me defenseless.

But they know it. Oh boy, do they know it.

And I can't seem to get control back. My head is spinning, and their lives are flashing before my eyes in one giant lurch of movement. I push my palms over my ears and squeeze my eyes closed, not that it helps. I need to get out of here. I stumble forward but there are too many people on the dance floor. They're caging me in, bodies pressing me back. I gasp, tears springing to my eyes. There's something seriously wrong with me, the alcohol has hit me way harder than I anticipated. Am I drunk? This is not fun. My balance is crap. I'm sinking to my knees, hot tears ruining my mascara, when two male hands steady me.

Landon? I smile weakly, despite the terrible situation I've put myself in.

My eyes flutter open, expecting to find my favorite cobalt blue gaze, but what I get are two dark as coal eyes, angry, with a tiny flickering line of orange-red around the pupils. So, not Landon then.

"You! What are you doing here?" I sputter at *the* Dean Ashton. The words are thick on my tongue, like I'm trying to swallow peanut butter. Something about that image of peanut butter stuck in my mouth is the funniest thing ever and I can't suppress the giggles. What the heck is wrong with me? How is anything funny right now? I'm a mix of terror and laughter and I don't even know what to do with myself.

"I should be asking you the same thing," he growls back, lifting me to my feet. The high heels suddenly feel three times higher than they were earlier tonight and I fall, my ankle twisting, but he catches me in time. "I'm taking you back to the dorm," he sneers.

I want to snap back, to tell him to leave me alone, but instead I mutter, "They're everywhere, please make them stop," and I turn away from the barrage of spirits still throwing their problems at me with such ferocity I can't tune them out. My head is ringing. The noise of their stories is growing, and I can't make out what Dean says next over all the racket. My face presses flush against his rock-like chest, and I close my eyes again, trying to ward off a spirit-induced migraine.

He expertly maneuvers me through the crowd and before I know it we're outside in the cool air, the noise fading away, and he's plopping me into a shiny black car like I'm a bag of bricks. "If you puke on my leather seats, I swear I'll make you clean it up yourself. I don't care how drunk you are."

Okay, rude much? The door slams and I squeeze my eyes shut.

A few minutes and a gloriously quiet car ride later, I'm blinking them open and we're parked in front of the freshman dorm. My headache has cleared a little, and the alcohol has worn off enough for me to know I'm in a car with someone who's not only much bigger than me, but who hates my guts. The feeling is mutual. I almost can't believe I got myself into this situation but then again, knowing me, nothing is out of the realm of possibility.

"Why did you help me?" I ask, braving a glance at the man who challenged me in class, accosted me in the hallway, and has now saved me from a terrible situation.

His grip on the steering wheel is so tight that his knuckles are stark white. His face is forward, the same profile, same chiseled features and clenched jaw. His anger is a pulse, a heart beating so wildly that it circulates the emotion through the car, and I swear I can feel his body heat. But no, that must be the beer playing tricks on me. Never again!

"I'm not helping you," he says. "I'm helping myself. First of all, I've already told you that this is my territory, and whoever you are, you need to leave before I force you to leave. Second of all, what were you thinking, drinking that disgusting human alcohol? Are you trying to get yourself killed? Are you trying to expose yourself? To expose me?"

I have no idea what he's talking about.

"I have no idea what you're talking about." I want to laugh at the way it comes out as an echo to my thought, and I would, except I think he'll probably kill me if I do. I laugh anyway.

He whips around, his glare deepening into two black coals. The car grows even hotter, prickling against my skin. My mouth slams shut. So, maybe not in my imagination? What is going on? I peel away from his gaze to fumble with the controls on the dash, looking for the AC and the heat button. Both are off.

He slaps my hand away. "I don't believe you," he snaps. "Did someone send you to spy on me? Which clan are you?"

My head spins again. A prickling of exhaustion hits me and all I want to do is crawl into my bed and sleep this horrible feeling off. Good heavens. If this is what alcohol does to people, why does anyone drink it?

"Thanks for the ride," I grumble, wishing I had the energy to deal with whatever this guy is going on about. My words are a bit slurred as I continue, "Seriously, I don't know what you're talking about and you're being a total jerk and I'm just trying to get an education here. I can drink whatever I want. I'm a big girl."

This time, *he* laughs. "How old are you? Aren't you a freshman?"

Yeah right, like I'm about to tell him I'm still seventeen. I point, my index finger jabbing at him with each word, "I'm done with this conversation, Mr. Ashton."

I wrench open the door, peel myself off the leather seat, and wobble to the entrance of the freshman dorm building. When his fancy-pants car peels out of the parking lot, I don't look back, and I'm a teeny-bit proud of myself for that. It's a small consolation. I'm developing a headache, my stomach churns, and worst of all, the spirits are back! They don't travel with me inside cars, but they aren't bound by a body the way we are, so it's easy for them to pop up just about anywhere. The creepers follow me inside, still demanding things of me with all their life stories. I've never had so many of them come at once. Ever. There's got to be at least fifty of them.

I can't take it—not for another second!

By some miracle, I make it to the second floor and stumble into my small room with enough time to text Cora and Macy that I'm home safe, put on my noise-cancelling headphones *with* music on, rip off the awful high-heels, and crash into my pile of blankets.

Free at last! Free at last! God Almighty, I'm free at last!

As I'm drifting off to sleep, the annoyingly handsome image of Dean Ashton's face floats across my mind, taking center stage above all the others. And those startling black eyes, they pin me down--those black, knowing irises with a ring of orangey-red around the pupils. Now that my head is clearing, I have a chance to think about what his eyes remind me of…

Fire.

But no, I must have imagined the fire in his eyes. But I didn't imagine the heat in the car and he did say something totally weird about drinking "human alcohol". Like, what other kind could there be? And what's with all this talk of territories or the accusations about spying and exposing him? Even as I'm drifting into the reprieve of sleep, even as the numbness in my limbs starts to melt into the warmth of blankets, one thought roots itself into my mind.

Dean Ashton has a secret and it has something to do with me.

SIX

I EYE THE BLOODRED DRAKENON wine in my chalice but don't drink. Nobody pays me any mind. They've already filled themselves with several rounds of wine, not to mention the delicious meal of roasted pheasant with its mountain of trimmings. I sigh and try to listen to the inane conversation going on around me, but I'm itching for this evening to end.

Midnight can't come fast enough.

All week, as I tended to my responsibilities, my skin crawled with the need to escape the castle, to fly into the void and let my dragon breathe free. I rarely get the opportunity to be my best self unless it's during my weekly secret rendezvous with Owen. Afterall, I wasn't brought here to fly. That's a fact King Titus has made clear to me many times over the years.

So it's every Thursday night after the prominent families of court dine together, gorging on fine food and drinking themselves into oblivion, that Owen and I risk our futures and sneak away using the underground network of tunnels hidden beneath the castle. Tonight should be no different.

The court grows boisterous and sloppy as the hours-long meal nears its completion. Queen Brysta looks as if she's about ready to fall asleep at the table, but my mother, The Lady Alivia, is sitting next to her and chatting cheerily as if she doesn't notice the Queen's boredom. I look just like my mother except for our eyes. Nearly every time we're together, someone points that out, much to my annoyance.

All the ladies are dressed in elegant gowns of silk and velvet, jewels dripping from their necks, and I'm no exception. Everyone dresses their best for these gatherings, the royal family especially. The Queen's emerald tiara glitters in the candlelight, weighing her down even further. I see myself in that image and have to look away.

"No," King Titus grunts, his fist pounding on the table and clattering the dishes. "We have to focus on our borders first, let the other kingdoms fend for themselves. We especially don't owe the *Fae* anything." He says Fae like it's a dirty word.

"Quite right, Father," Silas agrees with whoever happens to be the most powerful in the room, as usual.

Next to him, Bram rolls his eyes and I still, a little shocked. I almost want to laugh but I don't dare!

Silas and the King have been engaged in hearty conversation all night, going on about our greatest enemies, an army of warlocks who call themselves The Sovereign Occultists. The more those two drink, the less sense they make as they try to piece together war strategy. The King's round cheeks grow rosier as he slurps more wine, a stream of it running down his chin without notice. He is the older, and fatter, version of Silas.

"We can't come to anyone's rescue right now," Silas continues. "Nor is that our duty. We must keep our borders strong and our armies numerous, as we've been doing. Should they dare attempt to brave the wards and cross into our territory, we'll be ready for them."

It's the same old story we've been hearing for *years*.

Owen catches my pained expression from across the table and waggles his eyebrows until I *do* giggle. This kind of behavior is exactly why he and I picked Thursday nights as our weekly midnight flight. It's easy to slip away unnoticed once the meal is complete and when those who would care about our whereabouts are either busy sleeping off their hangovers or sleeping with each other. Plus, by the end of these nights, I'd do just about anything to get away from the castle.

A servant dressed in black pads over, presenting a silver plate of steaming blueberry pie. The aroma is tart and sweet and perfect but my mouth doesn't water. I feign enjoyment as I pick at it, but inside, I'm a bundle of nerves, waiting to be excused—waiting for a few hours of peace. I set down my fork and tuck my arms in close to my bodice. The vast room has grown chilly and outside the rain smatters against the stone walls and glass window panes. It won't stop Owen and I tonight. He lives for water and I can navigate any element with ease.

"Owen," the King's voice breaks through the chatter. "What are your thoughts on all of this?"

I expect Owen to shrug or offer up a joke. I suspect his family does too, because we all look surprised at his answer.

"The Occultists have taken over our entire realm save for our kingdom." Owen's face changes, turning serious. His blue eyes deepening, his gaze hardening. A blonde curl drops across his forehead as he leans in. "It's only a matter of time before they make another move on us."

"Well, I could have told you that," Silas scoffs. "They want our lands. They want to destroy us."

"But it's not just our lands that they want," Owen replies. "Nor do I truly believe they wish to destroy all the Dragon Blessed, not when they need us."

"What else could they want?" The King asks, growing just

as serious as his sons. The room quiets and curiosities are piqued. Rain pitters against the windows.

"The human realm," Owen offers.

His answer is met with a spattering of laughter.

"What could they possibly want with a useless realm where the magic is so stifled?" Silas challenges. And it's true. In the human realm, nobody's magic is strong. Many lose it entirely. It's considered a terrible punishment to be sent there. But...

"It makes sense," I cut in, my voice rising as I realize what Owen means by all this. All eyes turn on me, a mix of puzzlement and irritation. Women aren't supposed to talk politics around here. "As far as we know, only the Dragon Blessed can move between the realms, *but* is it possible we could take an Occultist with us? They are born of magic. Sure, they lack our same elemental magic, but that doesn't mean it would be impossible. Maybe they could use us to somehow boost their spells."

Throughout our realm there are hidden ley lines where portals meet. Those with elemental blood can use these portals to travel between this magical realm and the human one. But it's rare anyone does—nobody has good reason to leave. But maybe the Occultists feel divinely called to travel to the non-magic realm for some reason or another. Those wizards are known to be crazy, afterall. Owen could be right.

"They're thirsty to extend their rule and enforce their religion on others," Bram adds nonchalantly, speaking for the first time all night. He's so quiet and easily overlooked, that people often forget he's there.

His interjection quiets the room even further. Bram might not get a lot of respect when it comes to magic, but everyone knows that when it comes to logic, he's the smartest person in the room. He leans forward, his elbows resting on the table. "I've been considering this for a while, and I have to say I agree. Why wouldn't the Occultists want to take over the human realm? It's the next logical step, assuming they can get to us first. They'll need the Dragon Blessed to get them through the portals, but I do think it's possible that ruling the human realm as well as this one could be their end goal."

Because Bram isn't Dragon Blessed, he isn't always taken seriously. Dragons don't shift until reaching the age of puberty, around twelve or thirteen years old. And even then we don't exhibit any elementals right away. Those take time to develop, if they're going to develop at all, which they don't for most shifters. I was no exception to waiting. It wasn't easy to be patient, to wait for my first shift, for the powers that followed. But in time, everything happened. It happened for Dean, for Silas and Owen, too.

But it never happened for Bram.

Because of that, not everyone took him seriously. But the King has always been smarter than to underestimate his son. The King looks at each of us now, from one to the next, to the next, until his eyes finally land on me. They match Owen's, the son with his legacy element. And he smiles broadly, a light seeming to go off in his mind. "Princess Khali, I didn't realize what a good team you and Owen make together. Perhaps I'll need to rethink my plans for your birthday?"

My heart leaps, and I nearly choke on my breath. Do I dare to hope it could be true? It's not that I dislike Silas--who is turning so scarlet, his eyes are bulging from his head--it's that Owen is my best friend. I truly believe our relationship could one day shift to love, but if not, life wouldn't be bad with him as my husband. Once king, he would let me fly whenever I wanted, would do anything to give me a life of happiness.

"Owen might be the perfect king to your queen," Queen Brysta speaks up, fully awake now and with a happy twinkle in her eye. She rarely offers an opinion, rarely speaks at all. She's my opposite in that way and my jaw drops at her admission.

My mother kicks at me under the table and I close my mouth and smile meekly. Mother has always said love is not in the cards for me, that I was dealt a much better hand. Silas is her choice to play that hand best. But is it so wrong to want both love and respect? I clear my throat and gather my courage, laying those cards out on the table for everyone to see.

"I think so, too."

EVERYTHING HAS CHANGED.

That night, after Owen and I spend a glorious hour racing around the countryside, we shift back into our human forms and face each other. We stand next to the lake's edge, and I try to ignore the bubbling fear I always have around water. I step away from it's black surface and look at my best friend.

We can't wait a moment longer—we have to figure this out. The rain has stopped but the air isn't clear; nothing is clear. Things between us are murkier than ever. Water drips down his face in long rivulets. His clothes are soaked, his blonde shaggy hair matted to his cheeks. I'm also soaked to the bone, but I don't feel an ounce of cold. All I feel is the change—the change between us.

He feels it, too.

Even in the darkness, I can see it in his crystalline gaze. The way he looks at me now is entirely different, like he's seeing me for the first time. But is it for the better? I can't read him well enough right now to say. And that is the part that kills me. I've always been able to read Owen before. What if this is the moment where he rejects me?

His eyes flick to my lips.

I take a step back. No. We can't risk it. Especially now that there's a chance for us.

I clear my throat. "I hope that was okay," I say awkwardly. "What I said tonight. About us."

He exhales and turns away, peering into the night, running a hand through his wet hair. I want so badly to ask him what he's thinking, but I don't say a word. We stand side by side, a few feet from the lake's edge. The landscape is smooth, a line of gray on black, save for the crest of the castle wall two miles behind us. The clouds obscure the stars and moon, darkening everything more than normal. The air is thick with humidity, the ground beneath our boots sticky with clopping mud.

"I never wanted to be king," he admits quietly. "My whole life, I wanted it to be Dean, and then when he left, Silas." He tilts his head toward me and smiles. "You know me. I've always wanted to be free, to travel, to be my own man. Being king comes with so much responsibility."

So he's rejecting me after all. I'm met with mixed emotions. Sadness for myself, but love for my friend. I can understand his need for freedom. I want that for him, too.

"If you don't want it," I say, swallowing the lump in my

throat. "I would never force it on you. Only one of us has to bear that responsibility. And Silas will make a fine king."

"I'm not finished," Owen says, smiling again. "I never wanted to be king. But I've *always* wanted you."

I blink, my heart skipping.

"I can't have one without the other," he continues, inching closer, "but I never thought I would get either, so I didn't even try to get you, and I certainly didn't try to get the throne."

"Oh." It's all I can manage. But I smile, too. Ultimately, I want my friend to be happy. I want what's best for him, even if sadness sweeps through me at the thought.

"I want to kiss you right now, but I won't. I won't risk it even though it's killing me. I won't risk it, because even though we're alone now, once I start, I know there will be no possible way I could stop and we *will* get caught." He reaches out and takes a lock of my hair between his fingers, twisting it. "So I'll wait… and I'll start trying."

This time, my smile is real.

Thunder cracks across the landscape. Lightning flashes through the darkness, brightening everything for the briefest of moments. Owen and I jump apart and search the sky. My nerves tangle into knotted fear, recognizing the storm for what it is: magic. A massive black dragon appears between the clouds and swoops down, landing feet away from us with practiced grace. The air around him crackles with electricity as Silas shifts into his human form. He's dressed head to toe in black, blending with the night, but there's hatred on his face and *that* stands out.

"There you two are," he sneers. "I thought I might find you out here."

Neither of us speak.

He steps closer, the hem of his long black cape brushing the mud. "Oh, you didn't think I knew about your little Thursday night illegal activities, did you?"

Owen raises his hands. "It's not what it looks like, it's just for fun."

"I thought it was just for fun." He turns on Owen, pointing a long finger. "I overlooked it because I care about both of you and I trusted you to be an honorable man. But I can't overlook it anymore, now can I?"

"What do you mean?" I challenge, widening my stance. "You're not going to turn us in, are you?"

Silas ignores me, stalking toward his twin. "You just couldn't let me have it, could you? You saw that I was going to be given the throne and you had to get in the way, even though everyone knows I'm the best man for the job."

"It's not like that," Owen replies, his voice growing dark,

but Silas doesn't care, he moves in close anyway, rage rolling off him in waves.

I expect that at any minute, they'll fight. Brother on brother. It will be a wild mess of crunching bones and flying limbs and hurled insults, and it could take a turn for the worse, with Silas drawing on his air elemental and Owen his water. But I've seen the brothers fight before. First as boyish children, then as sparring young adults, and it's nothing I can't break apart with my magic if it comes to that.

What I don't expect is the knife.

Silas draws it from his pocket so quickly I nearly miss it. He rushes forward, slicing the blade straight across his brother's throat in one quick motion. Zero hesitation. I gasp, disbelieving. This isn't real. But it is. *It is.* Silas cut Owen wide open, the blood pouring from the wound too fast to comprehend.

Owen's eyes are wide as saucers as he crumples to the mud.

I scream, shock slamming through my body, and charge forward. I have to save Owen. Somehow. I have to help. Have to stop Silas. Have to do something!

Silas jumps out of my way and I fall into the mud, grasping Owen's lifeless body in my arms. He's still warm, but he's not there anymore. His eyes are vacant. There's too much blood. His soul has been sliced from his body and I can't believe this. This can't be happening. This can't be real.

"What did you do?" I cry up at Silas. The rain has started again, heavier than before. This time, I feel the chill, feel it right past my bones and down into my very soul. "You killed him!"

Silas takes a step back, his eyes round and still. At first I think he's realized what he's done, regretful. But then his eyes thin and he glares at me through thick lashes. "Did I?" he spits back. "No elemental powers were used here. Anyone could have slit his throat had they caught him by surprise."

"What?" I sputter through hot tears mixing with the rain.

"My brother shouldn't have been so stupid as to sneak out here at night. And what with our enemies out to get us? Terribly careless. Senseless tragedy. This could start a war."

He's going to deny what he did? I swallow back bile as the realization sinks in. He's not only going to deny that he murdered his brother, but use it to feed his political aspirations. He pretends that all he wants is to protect our borders to keep his father happy. But it's Silas. Of course, he wants more.

"How could you? You're a monster!" I choke out.

"How could *I*?" He shakes his head, his eyes filled with certainty. "No. How could *he*? How could my own brother betray me? How could he suck you into his clutches like that when he *knew* I was going to be crowned? I did what I had to do for the betterment of this kingdom and for *your* own safety, Khali. In time, you'll see I had no choice. He made me do it."

I pull Owen's limp body into my lap. My tears run cold and loathing consumes my every word. "You'll never be king. I'll tell everyone what you've done here tonight, Silas. You have murdered a royal—your own brother. You will be executed for this."

"Nobody will believe you," he sneers. "I have an airtight alibi already in place at this very moment. And actually, I'm certain everyone will blame you for Owen's unfortunate death if you present lies about me. Once they discover he was out here with you, so you could fly around like a couple of lovesick idiots, ignoring the danger, ignoring the *law*, they'll know it was your fault my brother was killed."

"Murdered," I spit back. I don't want to believe one foul word, don't want to listen to his murderous mouth utter another lie. But a small part of me wonders if he could be right. Will they blame me? Should I blame myself?

We never should have come out here. Never.

I glare up at Silas, the weight of my bad choices a million pounds on my heart. "No matter what happens, mark my words, you will *never* be my husband."

He smirks. "I'm all you have left, sweetheart. Four more months, and you're mine."

I shake my head.

"And one more thing," he adds. "If you tell anyone about this, mark *my* words, everyone you love will end up like Owen."

I'm going to be sick. I always knew he was intense, but never did I imagine he was capable of something like *this*.

He smiles mockingly, blows me a kiss, then shifts back into his dragon form.

I don't watch him go.

I can barely see through the tears. Violent sobs take over my body as I hold my friend for the last time. Owen's face is so pale now, it's almost white. His dead eyes are open, lifeless, peering into the afterlife beyond. Water drips down his cheeks. Not tears. Rain. Rain that will never wash away this moment or the terrible way his brother stole everything from us.

SEVEN

HAZEL

I HOLD THE FINISHED APPLICATION for The Roasted Bean in my hand as I walk down Main Street—a girl on a mission. I'll turn it in, get the job, and that will be that. I should smile, but I can't. All I can feel is sadness. Behind me, Kathrine's ghost follows in my footsteps. She's been tailing me all day and my heart is broken for her. There's nothing I can do. She keeps sending me images from her life, but they're just random, and none seem to have anything to do with what happened to her. I don't know what I can do to help her or erase the guilt I feel.

At least for now, Cora, Macy, and I have made a pact not to go anywhere alone, unless it's out in public. I haven't told them about my curse, they don't know what I know, but at this point, they're not the only ones who believe Kathrine is dead.

The smell of coffee leads me to my destination, but just before I get there, something stops me cold in my tracks, like cement has been poured around my boots. I stare across the street at The Flowering Chakra shop. The store sign's script is purple and flowy with the "o" in "flower" shaped like a daisy. It's actually pretty cute. The place has a welcoming energy about it that's undeniable.

It kind of pisses me off.

It pisses me off because it pulls me in like a magnet and before I know it, I'm crossing the quaint little street. I stand right in front of the cute red brick shop, my nose pressed to the front window. Hoping to see what? I don't know. An answer to everything, maybe. As if that'll happen. Katherine stands with me.

Inside are several rows of glass cases filled with jewelry and crystals of all shapes, sizes, and colors. Geometric art pieces made from a variety of metals hang from the ceiling, twirling gently. Two large distressed wooden tables stand centered in the airy space with a variety of trinkets expertly laid across the top. A row of matching bookshelves lines the back of the shop. I expected clutter. But this is organized. Loved.

The door swings open. "Well, are you coming inside or what?"

I scrunch my nose and take in the older lady from last

week, the same one I swore I would avoid because I can only assume she's out to scam me. Her eyes glitter like sapphires as she smiles knowingly. I don't want her metaphysical mumbo-jumbo or whatever it is she's offering, but then again, why am I standing here?

"Come." She reaches out to embrace my hand. Her skin is soft and thin, cold and wrinkled with age, but her touch is oddly relaxing. "We have so much to discuss."

She leads me inside, flipping the open sign on the glass door to CLOSED and locking it behind us. My natural guardedness is screaming to get the heck out of dodge, but curiosity keeps me from that.

"Is that really necessary?" I ask, folding my arms over my chest. "I don't plan to stay long."

She shrugs the question off and leads me to the back of the shop to a dark purple door. "Reading In Session" is written across it in bold letters. She pulls it open and inside is a pale lavender box of a room with a couch, two puffy chairs, a little black card table, and one window covered with a bamboo shade.

I'm struck with a feeling that's not quite déjà vu but close enough. I've been in rooms similar to this one before and the experiences never ended well. I can't go through more pain of false hope, and I'm struck with cold-feet and take a step back. What was I thinking, coming here?

"Sit down, dear," the woman continues in a calming but firm tone. "I promise I don't bite." She winks and then spins around, sitting down and watching me with that same knowing smile from before. "My name is Helen Marnie but I've gone by Harmony for sixty-seven years and don't plan to stop. I'm a woman hellbent on making this earth a better place to live in and when I said I could help you, I meant it. In order for that to happen, *you* have to be willing to at least sit your butt down in that chair there and hear me out."

I bite my lip. Something brought me here, didn't it? I don't know if it was fate or if I even believe in fate, but all I can think is I ought to at least give this woman a shot. What's the worst that can happen? I can't imagine anything could be worse than the incident on Friday night, what with those spirits hounding me until freaking *Dean Ashton* had to save me. Even if she makes things harder for me in some way, nothing could be worse than that.

I release a deep breath and settle into the center of the cushy brown chair across from her. "All right, Harmony." I say her name awkwardly, part of me wanting to laugh at the "Helen Marnie" of it all. "How is it exactly that you can help me? Do you even know what's wrong with me?"

"Of course I know what's wrong, but it doesn't have to be

considered wrong. It's all a matter of perspective."

"Okay…"

"You have eyes for the spirit realm and you don't know how to manage it. Not that I blame you. It can be a particularly challenging gift."

I gape at her. I didn't expect her to hit the nail on the head on her first try. How did she know?

She raises an eyebrow. "How did I know?" Her question mirrors my thought, leaving a trail of goosebumps over my body. "If I told you, I'm not sure you'd believe me. What's your name, by the way? Are you ready to tell me?"

I sit up a little taller and clear my throat. "I'm Hazel and I'm a haunted girl. But I think you already knew that. So whether or not I'm going to believe you… how about you try me."

"Well then," she quips back. "I like a girl with some sass. Okay, what do you want to know?"

"How did you figure out my problem so quickly? Do you see them too?"

The silence spreads between us as she studies me with a knowing gleam in her watery eyes. The mood shifts like afternoon shadows, growing more serious.

"All right then, Hazel, I'll tell you about me. No, I don't see the spirit world. What I can see are the paths."

I blink. "Ehh, the what now?"

She leans forward. "When I meet people, I see many paths laid out in front of them, those future possibilities that could play out in their lives. When I saw you, many possibilities spiraled out in front of you, all involving the future of your spiritual gift. In one of those futures, I was helping you manage it and you were thriving."

I blink at her. I have no words.

"And that's how I know you're going to agree to work here and not at The Roasted Bean."

I suck in a breath, catching the musty scent of sage mixed with sweet lavender. Part of me wants to latch on to this woman, to make her spill everything that might or might not happen to me. The other part of me wants to run far, far away. She's probably a crook. She's probably bad news. But then why the interest in me? How did she know my secret with only one chance look? I try to picture myself working here. But I can't. It feels too... confrontational. Too real.

"Even if you are the real deal, I'm sorry, but I can't work here," I say, my walls growing thick. "No offense, but this isn't really my kind of place."

She laughs. It's a joyful sound and it catches me off guard. "Hazel, my dear, no offense to you but this is exactly your kind of place. And as for what you'd do, I thought that was obvious. You'll do readings for the shop."

I raise an eyebrow. "And by readings, you mean?"

"I'll keep to psychic readings, and you'll do the mediumship readings."

Now it's my turn to laugh. "You're crazy! I can't do that."

"And why not?"

"Because if I open myself up to the spirits, they won't leave me alone." Even as I say it, that long-held hope flares to life. Maybe this lady is the answer to controlling my problem. *But what if she's not*, my mind reels, *and she makes everything worse?*

She nods and a white dreadlock falls over her bony shoulder. Understanding shines in her eyes. Empathy, too. "And are there any spirits in here right now?" she asks kindly. "Go ahead, look around."

I blink, realization practically slapping me across the face. Kathrine didn't follow me inside the shop. In fact, none of the spirits did. Something a lot like hope spreads over my entire body. "Wait, how did you do that? Where did they go?"

"I can teach you how to create dedicated safe spaces where only invited spirits can enter. And I can help you protect your person when you're out and about so that they don't bother you as much. And in return, you can work for me. How much does that coffee place pay, anyway?"

"The application said $10 an hour plus tips, which are

probably pretty decent. They needed someone for ten to fifteen hours a week."

"You can work *here* ten to fifteen hours a week instead. I'll pay you the $10 an hour when you're on the sales floor but give you half commission for any readings you book. That's $50 an hour right into your pocket for those. Plus, I'll teach you anything I can to help you manage your gift, because, Hazel"—her eyes grow soft, shifting from business woman back to compassionate matriarch—"it *is* a gift. You're going to do great things with it."

"I just want to do normal things, to *be* a normal girl." I'm overcome by the words and everything they hold.

"Oh posh! No you don't! Normal is for the birds. You have a big, big life ahead. It's coming for you whether you're ready or not, so you might as well get ready."

I close my eyes for a lingering minute, breathing in the quietness of the room, the solitude of this space. No spirits. No ghosts. It's downright glorious. I can't believe what I'm about to agree to, but then again, how could I not? My eyes pop open and I extend my right hand. "Harmony, I can't believe I'm saying this, but you have a deal."

THE NEXT FEW WEEKS FLY by in a blur of classes, work, friends, and studying. Needless to say, I don't touch another alcoholic beverage, nor do I plan to. But thanks to Harmony, this college thing is going better than I ever hoped for. I've made my dorm room a ghost-free zone with large black obsidian stones strategically placed in the four corners. Now they can't come in unless I invite them. Hahaha, suckers! That's never going to happen!

My classes are going splendidly well because I finally have a quiet place to study. I've started recording every lecture just in case I get too distracted while in class, but my new obsidian necklace has lessened a lot of the spirit realm's noise and images. Life is flipping fantastic. Who knew the black stones could be so powerful at blocking the spirits?

Landon and I have been flirting during organic chemistry labs on Tuesdays and Thursdays, and I always stop by his work on the way into mine. I'm certain he's going to ask me out on a real date soon—he asked for my number this afternoon. And even the perpetually grumpy Dean Ashton has inexplicably decided to leave me alone. Guess he gave up on the territorial stuff? The man doesn't even *look* at me anymore. In fact, I'm pretty sure he's avoiding me. Not that I care. Sure, I still want to uncover his big bad secret, but every time I allow my mind to go there, I end up shutting that nonsense down. The possible explanations are too... weird. Which says a lot coming from me.

I finish ringing up a chatty customer, when my phone vibrates in my back pocket. Once the customer has left the store and the place is again empty, I slip my phone out and find a waiting text from Landon.

Hi, Gorgeous. How's work going? Caffeine wearing off yet?

I smile and bite my lip. Ya, I know it's a stupid pick-up line, but him calling me gorgeous sends a flutter of butterflies scurrying through my chest anyway. Sometimes I am *such* a girly girl.

I type back.

Starting to, but working here is interesting enough to keep me awake. :) How are you?

His reply comes in almost immediately.

Still wish you would've applied here instead. And I'm doing good. It's dead here right now. So bored.

...

The three dots on the phone blink for a second before another one of his texts pops up.

I'm lonely. Wish you could keep me company.

The butterflies are having an all-out war in my chest now,

and I'm considering asking Harmony if I can take my break when she comes bounding in from her back office with the kind of cheeky grin that makes her look twenty years younger. Oh, no. This can't be good.

"Guess what I just did?" She rushes to put her arm around my shoulders. She smells of her usual sage--not my favorite scent in the world. I hold back a cough, my eyes instantly watering. The stuff sells here by the boatload, so it comes with the territory, but I swear I'm allergic or something.

"What?" I grit my teeth and smile.

"I just booked your first reading! Your customer will be here in five minutes."

I blink at her, my heart stopping and then furiously catching up to the fear. I knew this was coming. She's been preparing me on what to do and putting feelers out with her regulars. But I'm not ready.

"You *are* ready, Hazel." She lets me go and glides through the store, arms outstretched like this is some kind of "world is your oyster" moment. "Remember what we talked about?" Her watery blue eyes travel up and down me. "You let the customer sit and you invite any spirits of the light to join them and then take it from there. Let them ask questions. Tell them what you see and hear. Simple. The hour will go by in a flash. And if anything weird or uncomfortable happens in there, you're allowed to end the session early."

I gulp and nod, forcing my expression to relax. "I'm going to be cool as a cucumber, even if more than five minutes notice would have been nice."

Harmony only laughs and busies herself with one of the displays. I guess the $50 commission will have to make up for this sudden attack on my nervous system. Harmony's been saying that it's only a matter of time before I'm completely booked for these "psychic medium readings" and not able to work on the sales floor anymore. If that happens, I'll be earning several hundred dollars a week. Maybe even $750 a week if I can work up to the full fifteen sessions. That number is staggering for a girl who grew up in a single parent household and needed a scholarship to be able to attend college without going into serious debt. It's the kind of money that could go a long way in getting me through veterinary school one day. It's true what they say, vet school is just as costly as medical school without the fancy BMW waiting ten years down the line. Sigh…

Okay, I can do this. It's a great opportunity.

The door opens and the little bell chimes. My whole body lights up with nervous energy.

Nevermind, I can't do this!

I take a steadying breath, once again clearing my face of

fear, and look up to find my first customer, a fake smile frozen on my lips. He strides into the shop like he owns the place, like he knows exactly how this day is going to go for him and it's going to go *super well*. His scruffy dark hair is curled around his ears and somehow, my own hands twitch, my treacherous fingers wanting to frolic through those silky waves.

What is wrong with me?

My eyes travel down the curve of his arms to where his hands are pushed into the pockets of his jeans. The man is sporting a leather jacket that oozes so much sexiness, it's completely unfair. I can only pull off the nerdy girl look. Not the "hot librarian fantasy nerd" version. Just the regular one. But it's his dark eyes, those two black depths, no longer lit by fire, that send an icy shiver over my entire body. The shiver battles with the nerves already there!

He's no longer the man who knows exactly how this day is going to go, in fact, his expression is saying quite the opposite. But that doesn't make sense! Dean Ashton is scowling at me, eyes blazen, lip curled, jaw tight, and all I can think is that now would be a good time to quit my new job.

EIGHT

KHALI

WITH EACH PASSING HOUR, I shift from chilling numbness to staggering grief. Every small action seems like a mountain of overwhelm that I don't care to climb. I can't eat. I can't sleep. Mourning has left every muscle aching and even that isn't enough to push away the turmoil. And the worst part is that my thoughts of Owen are tainted with guilt for having put him in that vulnerable position in the first place. We shouldn't have gone out alone unprotected. And we never should have trusted his brother. I always knew Silas wanted to be king, but how could we have underestimated him?

Because after two weeks of hell, I'm beginning to think Silas is going to get away with what he did. He's the only Dragon Blessed heir left. He'll get the crown by default.

I stare up at my stone ceiling and force myself to replay

what happened; all the tears dried up days ago. Parts of it are hazy. I still don't know how long it took the guards to find me with Owen's body. After Silas threatened me and left, I stayed. I stayed and I held my best friend's body in my arms, sobbing until the rain stopped, the sunrise bled over the horizon and they found us.

I was a babbling mess and they were quick to take me into custody, locking me in my chambers. And I've been here ever since. Every time Faros comes in with a meal or to help me bathe or dress, I plead with her to send King Titus and Queen Brysta to come speak with me. They need to know what happened. Why don't they come? But Faros says they've refused to see me and forbidden anyone but her to come in here. I haven't even received a visit from my mother.

At this point, I'm waiting for my death.

Because why else would Owen's parents refuse to talk to me if they didn't believe I was responsible for their son's murder? If I could just explain what happened, warn them about Silas, then they could punish Silas and protect Bram. He might not have magic, but that doesn't mean Silas won't find a reason to end his life too. Besides, perhaps the King and Queen could find it in their hearts to bring Dean back from exile. Surely they could override the law? What good is being a monarch if you can't do that? If they knew the truth, they'd have to agree that anything would be better than Silas getting away with murdering his twin.

I drift into sleep, exhaustion taking over like a spring mud, thick, heavy, and bitter cold. I sink into it, letting it take me. Anything is better than to be left alone with my thoughts.

Sometime later, I wake to find my mother sitting at the end of the small bed. Her hair and makeup are done perfectly. She wears a black mourning dress. Her eyes are red but she doesn't look sad. She looks angry.

"What did you do?" she spits out.

I don't have the energy to entertain her right now. I roll over, pressing my face against the cool stone wall. It smells of winter.

"Khali Elliot, you *will* talk to me." She grabs hold of my leg. "What happened? What did you do to Owen?"

I shift to glare up at her, yanking my leg away. "Maybe you should ask your buddy, Silas, about what he did to his twin?" I hiss.

Her eyes widen. Her body stills. I can see her mind is racing as she puts it all together. I don't know what I expect from her. Shock? Sadness? Anger?

I get none of these. Instead, I find fear on her face.

"Silas must have been provoked," she says calmly.

"No!" I snap. "Silas killed Owen in cold blood."

"Shh--" she jumps forward and slams her hand over my mouth. "Don't you ever speak those words again. That's treason."

I want to laugh. To cry. To bite out every angry word I have for her. I do none of those things. She stands, brushing out her skirt, and leaves without a backwards glance.

She doesn't come to visit me again.

And all I can think about is how much I miss my father. I miss him with every fiber of my being, but he never comes through that locked door, despite how many times I plead with the Gods. He's still gone from Court, I'm sure. If he were back in our suite at the castle, he would have noticed my absence and upon discovering what had happened to me, demanded an audience. But his missions for the king are so secretive that his travel locations and lengths are left to my imagination. I never have any idea when he'll return and this latest absence is no different.

What use is thinking about it? It only adds to the pain I already have to live with.

The days spread into nights and back again, until finally someone comes through that door who isn't Faros. He enters alone, dressed in his own version of the black mourning clothes. His eyes are rimmed in red with long shadows under each and the stubble on his cheeks is days old. For a moment, he looks so much like Owen that it kills me all over again.

"King Titus." I scramble from my bed and curtsey. "I'm so glad you finally came to hear what I have to say." Genuine gratitude blooms within. "Thank you."

He closes the door with a thud and strides forward, holding up a hand. "I didn't come here to hear what you have to say."

That gratitude is plucked away in a second. "But Silas—"

"Stop," he commands. "I do not wish to hear it from your mouth and I forbid you from ever speaking of what Silas did, do you understand?"

My throat goes dry as sand and I blink in surprise. "You already know?" I wonder if my mother told him but I can scarcely believe it possible she'd be so bold.

"Yes," he says evenly. "Brysta and I know what Silas did to Owen."

"Then you have arrested him? Where is he?"

He shakes his head and narrows his eyes, stalking in close. The man towers over me, and a prickle of intimidation claws across my flesh. The laugh lines around his eyes and mouth no longer look welcoming. Something tells me this meeting isn't going to go how it should.

"Owen is gone," he says calmly. "There is nothing anyone

can do about that fact. Silas is the only heir left that could possibly take the throne. You will never speak of what he did to Owen, do you understand me? Owen was murdered by an unknown assassin. That's it."

His words push at my wound, twisting the knife Silas put there to begin with. "What about Bram? What about Dean?" My voice rises in disgust and anger.

"You are forbidden to speak that name," he roars, meeting my volume with his own demands. "He is in exile and to bring him back would be to void the treaty of the dragon clans. It will *not* be done."

"Well, Bram is still alive," I challenge. "Why can't he be king? At least he isn't a cold-blooded murderer!"

"Bram is useless!" King Titus scoffs. "He can never be king!"

I stumble backward until the back of my knees hit the edge of the unmade bed and I stare up at the King, seeing his true self for the first time. He has always been intense, powerful, with an air of superiority that leaves other men cowering, but the boiling anger in his tone is so startling, this demand so terrible, that the breath is ripped from my lungs. Tears prick at my eyes, and I clench my hands into fists. I'm not upset for being yelled at, though it tilted me off my axis. I'm horrified by the unjust way Silas's treason is being treated. He really is going to get away with this, and his parents, the ones who should want to avenge Owen, are going to make sure of it.

"How can you do this to Owen? He was your son, too!" I'm crying now. I can't help the burning tears that splash down my cheeks but I can't be bothered to wipe them away or feel weak in front of this man. I'm a roiling mess of emotions and the elemental powers within are demanding to break free. I hold them down because I know there's nothing I can do with them, not in here, not with *him*. This isn't right. This isn't fair. This is sick.

"Silas will be the next king." He glares, speaking softly now. "There is nothing anyone can do about that. Not you. Not me. Not my wife. Not anyone. If what Silas did comes out and he is punished for his crime, the clans will rebel and we will lose our royal line to another dragon family."

I nod, giving in, because what else am I to do? But I'm already running through all possible options in my mind, trying to stay strong. All I can think is while the Brightcaster family will lose everything, I won't. I'll be forced into a loveless marriage with some other son of some other noble family, but at least I won't have to take Silas as my husband. The Gods offered me as Drakenon's queen but I'm not bound to *this* family. I'm bound to whoever takes the throne.

If I marry another, at least I won't have to lie about what happened to Owen, to live my life at Silas's side, to go to bed with him and give him elemental dragon children. The thought of a marriage to Silas leaves my stomach twisting with disgust. I can't do it. I won't.

"Fine," I lie, meeting King Titus's eyes. "I won't say anything. I'll keep your secret and go along with Silas as the next king, but you have to do something for me."

He smiles ruefully, his eyes narrowing into stormy slits. "Oh, darling, this isn't a negotiation. In fact, I came here to tell you that should you betray my trust, your parents will pay for your folly."

My hands shake. I hold them against my chest, feeling the breath leave my body. "What are you talking about?" But I already know. Like father, like son.

He tilts his head. "It's a pity. I never wanted it to be like this. I like your parents. They've been friends of mine ever since you were an infant and we brought the three of you to live here."

"Just tell me what you've done," I snap.

"Your father is fortunate enough to have the privilege of traveling the kingdom on my behalf. Should you betray me, Princess Khali, I can promise you that you won't ever see your father alive again."

Can he do that? Neither of my parents are Dragon Blessed. How would they defend themselves against this wicked man?

"And not only will your father die, but your mother will be ruined. I know all her secrets. Lest you forget, Lady Alivia is quite the court politician. She's made errors over the years in her climb to the top, and I know of each and every one of those errors. If you break my trust, Khali, I will make certain your mother is the joke of the entire kingdom. It won't matter who takes the throne, she'll be the outcast." His air elemental crackles behind his stormy eyes, a promise of what's possible.

My mother probably does have terrible secrets. She and I don't even get along, surely he knows that? But then again, I'm not cruel. I don't want her to be unhappy, and as much as she and I butt heads, she's usually the only family I have around. I would never want to see her ruined, but is that enough to stop me from avenging my best friend and keeping his murderer off the throne? My father's possible death is King Titus's best play and I don't know how to use it to my advantage.

"And if that isn't enough," he continues, catching on to my thought process, "well, I can always have your mother killed as well. Gods know she has enough enemies. And what about that maid you love so dearly? She's a cousin to your mother, is she not? She could easily be taken down with the rest of them."

"You're sick." I shake my head, the extent of the betrayal sinking in deep. "You would do that to your own friends? To innocent people? My family has been completely loyal to your family since day one. They moved me here, didn't they? I've heard stories of other future queens being hidden away, but not my parents. They came forward the moment I opened my eyes. And since that day they've encouraged me to embrace the role I am to play, even during those moments when I didn't want it."

He leans in close, his eyes shining, and I catch the faintest scent of Drakenon wine on his breath. "You may possess all the elements, Khali. You may be used to the incredible power flowing in your veins, but you have no idea the kind of *royal* power you're dealing with. The Brightcaster family has held this throne for over a century and you will *not* cross us."

My mind races through my options but I don't see that I have anything tangible. He's right. Even if I do stage a coup, he will still extend his power long enough to hurt or kill the ones I love. Silas going to prison won't mean he'll automatically lose his throne, but it will mean he will have years to torture me until it's time for him to step down and give up the line to the next strongest clan.

"Owen is gone," he says, his voice catching. Deep-rooted pain crosses his features. "It never should have happened. But it did."

I won't let it change me. "How dare you grieve Owen," I sneer. "He deserved better!"

The slap comes fast, charged with electricity. The pain blossoms on my cheek and I fall to the bed.

The King continues as if nothing happened. "After we started questioning the events, Silas came to Brysta and me to confess his sins. He is remorseful over what happened. He lost his temper and things got out of hand. *He's sorry.* We all are. But he can't take it back and we can't lose our royal line over this one mistake. So we won't."

I rub my cheek and sit up, contemplating my lack of options moving forward.

"Do we have a deal?" he asks. It doesn't sound like a question.

"I don't see how you are giving me a choice," I finally relent bitterly. "But King Titus." I meet his gaze square in the eye. "You raised a murderer. I was there that night and I can promise you, it wasn't an accident. It was a planned murder and Silas had zero hesitation or remorse before or after the event."

His face pales but he says nothing.

"You had better watch your back, because Silas wants your

throne and the only one left standing in his way is *you*."

"He wouldn't—"

"He murdered his twin brother," I say between gritted teeth. "He would. You're a fool to protect him."

NINE

HAZEL

"SHE'S THE MEDIUM?" DEAN ASKS, gaping at Harmony like she's gone and lost her mind.

"Best there is," Harmony replies, shuffling forward to wrap Dean in a loving, familiar hug—as if he were her favorite son. But I know for a fact Harmony never got married or had children. It's too bad, she would have been great at family life. But then again, what she's doing is pretty great, too.

I'm standing behind the register, my hands balled at my sides, my breath caught in my chest. I'm a mixed bag of shock, defensiveness, and a heck of a lot of confusion. I thought Dean knew what I was. He certainly acted like he knew exactly what I was when we first met and that my presence was this massive affront to him and his "territory." I assumed he had a problem with mediums or perhaps he was something similar. I don't know.

None of this is making any sense.

Then another thought comes to my mind so quickly and I can't help myself from blurting it out. "*You're* a regular *here*?" I let out a laugh, then try to cover it up with a fake cough as they both turn on me.

Harmony's lips purse, and I know I should feel utterly terrible that she's hurt by the comment but *come on*. I hold up my hands in defense. "I'm sorry. He just doesn't seem like the type of guy to frequent The Flowering Chakra, that's all."

Dean glares, folding his arms over his chest. He towers over Harmony, all muscle and petulance. "You don't know anything about me."

I almost want to laugh again but I hold it in for Harmony's sake. I mean, he's not wrong, except I know that he's a cocky prick. Even when he drove me home that Friday night a few weeks ago, he could have redeemed himself and been a gentlemen about it but he chose not to be. And in Anthropology, he totally has a superiority complex, acting like he's the smartest guy in the class.

I meet his challenging stare with my own. This is my work and my town now, too. So the way I see it, he's in *my* territory. I tilt my head, realization dawning on me. Are his cheeks turning pink? Because I think they are and it is totally making my day. Who knew the big man on campus would turn out to be a patron of the metaphysical arts? This is too good. Cora and Macy are going to love this. Would it be mean to make fun of him behind his back? I'm not normally that kind of person but something about Dean Ashton makes it too easy.

"So if you two are ready," Harmony says, clearing her throat and attempting to clear the air, "we can start the reading."

I step back, shaking my head vehemently. "No way," I blurt at the same time Dean says, "I've changed my mind."

Harmony's head bobs between us, her gray eyebrows knit together. "Why on earth not?"

"Are you kidding me?" I laugh, sounding crazed. "This guy's been a total jerk-face to me from the moment I met him."

"Jerk-face?" He questions my choice of words like I'm a child. "How old are you?"

I ignore the question even though I'm burning up with the implication. I shrug at Harmony. "I'm sorry, Boss, but there is no way I'm going into a room with him to do… *that.*"

Okay, did that sound bad? Because I'm pretty sure I made it sound like my readings come with "extras". His eyes flicker to mine, and he snarls like he just smelled raw sewage. My cheeks burn even hotter with utter embarrassment.

Harmony is unfazed. "I'm *so* sorry, Dean. I didn't know you two knew each other. I'm wondering why I didn't see that?" Her voice trails off and she looks at us for a minute, humming to herself. I clear my throat and it snaps her out of it.

"Anyway, Dean," she continues. "If you'd like me to give you a reading instead, I'd be happy to help. I don't have the same gift as Hazel but perhaps I can still help."

His lips are a thin line, and he shakes his head. "No, I don't need a reading from anyone today. I'll grab a few things and be out of *Hazel's* way." He says my name like it's the same raw sewage he smelled earlier. But how is that fair when he's the one who's been awful to me? Besides, I have a right to turn any client away that makes me uncomfortable. That was the agreement.

The shop is filled with crystals, books, herbs, and all sorts of metaphysical paraphernalia. I can't pretend that my curiosity isn't piqued. What "few things" would *he* need?

Dean turns his back on me and meticulously picks out three of the sage smudge sticks from a nearby wicker basket, and then he approaches the register, tossing them onto the wooden tabletop for me to ring up. My eyes travel from the sage on the counter to his eyes, my lips slightly parting in a smirk. He glares again.

I'm sorry, but I can't help it. Dean Ashton smudges? Okay,

this is getting weird. What kind of college guy uses a smudge stick, let alone knows what it is? The bundles of dried sage leaves are tied together with twine and even have a few sprigs of dried lavender mixed in. People light them up and then use the smoke to get rid of bad energy in their homes and funky stuff like that. But they smell pretty gross so even I don't use them *and I work here*!

Harmony clears her throat again. "Hazel, can you please ring up our customer?"

"Of course." I plaster a smile on my lips and get busy.

As I scan his items, Dean casually slips a piece of folded up paper from his back pocket and hands it to Harmony.

She unfolds it and her face pales. "Another one?"

"Second one in as many weeks," he replies grimly. "I don't know what to make of it."

I lean over the counter to get a better look. Is that nosy? Sure. But I don't care. And the second I see the Missing Persons flyer, my breath catches.

Harmony turns to me. "Have you seen this one?" She slides the black and white image of the girl to me. I know what she means. Not, have I seen her in person. But have I seen her dead. Her name is Alexandria Burk, she's 17, one of the students at the high school. Her smile radiates from her round face. She wears a cheerleading outfit, ribbons tied up in a high ponytail.

"I've never seen her," I say. But I wonder, if I took off my obsidian necklace, would she come to me? Is she dead like the other ones?

Harmony puts her hand on mine. "Good," she says, "but watch for her. Let us know if she comes to you."

I swallow hard and nod. Then I finish up the transaction. "That will be twelve dollars and forty cents." He hands me his card then turns back to Harmony.

Through all of this, Dean hasn't acknowledged me in the slightest. He's no longer angry or shocked or questioning. He's indifferent. He treats me like he'd treat any other clerk he didn't have a history with. His attitude is aloof and when we're done, he turns away without saying goodbye or acknowledging me. *Not even a smug retort? No glare? Nothing? Where's the Dean I know and hate?* It bothers me. And the fact that it bothers me, *really* bothers me.

The second he walks out from the store, Harmony spins around and raises an eyebrow.

"Really, Hazel? You hate him? Why? *What was that?*"

"Okay, I can see that you're less than happy."

Her mouth is slack, her eyes two bulging marbles, and her face is nearly the same shade of pink as the watermelon tourmaline crystals in the locked display case behind her.

"I'm sorry," I continue, feeling like the totally ungrateful brat she must think I am. But what was it that Cora said? If a guy is a jerk to a girl, she should be allowed to make a scene instead of always having to be polite. And Harmony did say I didn't have to finish a session if I was uncomfortable. This is kind of the same thing as far as I am concerned.

But I don't want to fight with her or sound ungrateful. I like Harmony. I like this job. I take a deep breath and hope that I can make her understand.

"I promise I can explain. Thing is, Dean accosted me the first moment he met me. We have a class together and basically, we don't get along. I have no idea why he hates me, but he does. He hates my guts. Neither of us would want to spend an hour together in that room."

She nods slowly and runs her hands over her face. "I've never been so embarrassed. Dean is one of my favorite customers. He's such a good boy."

I somehow doubt this is the most embarrassing moment of her entire life, and the idea of Dean as a "good boy" is questionable, but I take a deep breath, knowing I didn't handle myself very well and I need to fix this. Not that I want to, but Harmony has changed my life, and I hate to see her so disappointed in me. My stomach hurts just thinking about it. "I'm truly sorry. I will go and apologize to him right now if that helps." Maybe a bit reluctantly, but I'll do it for her. "I'm still not going to be able to do the reading for him though. Is that okay?"

She mimics my deep breath and her zen-like state returns. Her expression has cleared of the earlier torment, and she's back to the woman I've grown to know and love over the last few weeks. "I guess that will have to be okay."

She points to the door with a flick of her wrist. "Go before he's gone. He drives an unnecessary sports car. It's black. You can't miss it."

"Oh, I know all about that car," I mutter to myself, skipping through the store and out the door. Truth be told, the car is hot. Dean is hotter.

It's all so annoying and I've decided not to be effected like other girls.

The world outside has that shadowy late afternoon filter that hits a few hours before sunset. It's colder than it's been all month, and I wish I'd thought to grab my sweater. I'm only in a thin black t-shirt and blue jeans. I wrap my arms in close to my chest, and glance down both ends of the sidewalk to search for Dean or his "unnecessary" car. Main Street is gorgeous, sprawling before me like a storybook. A few of the leaves are starting to change color, but it's pretty void of people at the moment.

As far as I can tell he's not here, nor is his car parked on the street. I hurry past a few storefronts to the side parking lot at the end of the block. There are more spots there and I'm betting if he's one of Harmony's regulars, he knows all about them, especially if he likes to keep his visits to her establishment discreet. I mean, the man must have some pride, right? He has a reputation to protect. Since I've worked there, The Flowering Chakra hasn't had many college-aged patrons, certainly none that were male—until Dean.

Sure enough, I round the corner just as he's getting into his car.

Part of me wants to turn back and pretend I didn't catch him in time, but I can't disappoint Harmony. Nor would I want to lie to her. I've already embarrassed her and she's been nothing but good to me. Even if I don't want to do a reading for Dean, I still want to do them for her other customers. I want to learn. I need that kind of $50 an hour money and I want to prove to her that she made the right choice in hiring me.

I swallow my pride and stride up to the car, tapping on the driver's side window. It's tinted to complete darkness––like a celebrities car or something. Typical. It rolls down and Dean is there, his expression unreadable. Again, I'm struck by his almost inhuman beauty. I sort of hate him for it, but that's not what I'm here for. I sigh.

"I'm sorry about what happened back there," I say in a rush. "I wouldn't ever want to upset Harmony and even though you and I don't get along, I hope you won't take it out on her."

He blinks at me for a few moments as the quiet stretches between us. His fingers flex around the steering wheel and he leans back in his leather seat. "How hard was that for you to say?"

"Umm—pretty hard."

"I thought so." He laughs bitterly. "But I would never take it out on Harmony. It's you that I hate. Not her."

I scoff at him and step back. Is he serious? "Hate is a pretty strong word there, buddy. What possible reason could you have to hate me?" I can't help but ask the same question that's been driving me crazy. I've never done anything to him. He doesn't know me. How could he say he hates me? It's utterly ridiculous and doesn't make any sense.

He pins me with that smokey gaze, and I'm reminded of what I saw in those eyes that Friday night. This man has secrets. "It's clear to me that you're hellbent on pretending that you don't know the reason for my disdain, so if that's the way you're going to play it, it's better we don't talk and you stay out of my way."

Well, okay then...

He rolls up the window and the car purrs to life. I turn and scurry back to the sidewalk, more than ready to be finished with this conversation and be done with Dean Ashton.

As I'm about to round the corner, something swoops in on me. Something monstrous, black, and of the spirit world. But it's nothing like any spirit I've experienced before now. It swoops again, closer, and I'm knocked to the ground, landing hard on my back. White-hot pain shoots through my hips and elbows. I cry out, more surprised than anything. I scramble back until I'm pressing against the brick building. Blood whooshes through my ears, and I can hardly breathe.

Images flash through my mind so quickly I can't grab onto a single one. Images of castles and courtiers and a girl with two different colored eyes. I blink until the images are gone.

The creature settles to the ground in front of me, huge and terrifying. My heart basically stops—I can't believe what I'm seeing. And yet, it's clear as day, clear as if it were flesh and blood and fire and smoke. It's a … dragon.

A freaking *spirit dragon* has come to visit.

TEN

KHALI

THE FUNERAL PYRE GLOWS AMBER against the yawning gray sky, a solemn dance of flame and smoke. It's been hours since it was first lit and still I've held my tears at bay, watching the pyre burn and burn and burn. What started as an inferno, hungrily consuming Owen's cloth-wrapped body, has since dwindled to a pile of fiery coals. I stand on the crunchy grass, my velvet black dress gripping my torso, the suffocating corset underneath holding me up. The matching black cape hoods my face and hides me from the barrage of unwanted stares.

Once they cool, Owen's ashes will be split in two. Half will be taken to the sea that's nearly one hundred miles away as tribute to his water elemental, and the other half will be laid to rest in the castle cemetery alongside his ancestors.

Perhaps then, his soul will be free.

But I'll still be here, a prisoner to fate. Here, without him.

It's only fourteen weeks until my birthday when I'll be forced into an engagement with Silas, and soon after, forced into his bed. The Gods will bind me to him forever. He will be my jailer, locking me to his side again and again with each child. The cruelty of it leaves my mouth tasting of soot that no amount of water will wash away.

A thick gust of smoke blows in my direction, swatting my cape from my head. The smoke burns my eyes and throat until I finally look away from the pyre. That's when I notice most of the funeral party has left, returning to the warmth of the castle—the warmth of life. I can't bare to join them. I can't will myself to move from this place until there's nothing of the wood left, and even then, I don't know that I can leave. Because I'll have to face them.

"My daughter." Lady Alivia's voice is smooth as pearls as she appears at my side. "It's time to be done here. Come, let's share a pot of your favorite tea together. Lavender?"

I don't answer her, but I take in her perfectly made-up face, expertly covering her few wrinkles, and the long dark curls styled to add to her youthful appearance, but it's the twinge of triumph shining behind her amber eyes that tell me all I need to know of my mother's true beauty. This funeral is not too sorrowful of an affair for her, not when Silas is next in line for king and whatever he's promised her will come to fruition. I look away bitterly, longing for my father. *He* would understand.

"The depth of your heartache will not do you any favors," she tries again, more forcefully this time. "People will question your relationship with the water brother if you continue on in this manner."

"Let them," I challenge through clenched teeth. "Owen was my best friend. I don't care if my grief is too strong for you or anyone else."

"But *Silas* is to be your husband now," she interjects.

"Do not speak to me of Silas again," I snap. "You got your wish. Whatever he has promised you is yours. There is no need to gloat. Now leave me to my heartache and let me grieve in peace."

She folds her arms over her chest, peering at me like I'm nothing but a petulant child, but she relents with a wistful sigh. "Very well. I will see you at the dinner tonight. I trust you to behave."

As she leaves, I don't dignify her with another word or glance. When did she go from being my loving mother, looking out for my needs, to being simply another person looking to use me for personal gain? She has no idea how lucky she is that I care about her life and reputation enough to protect her against the King's threats. Anger towards her and everyone else who has wronged me and Owen grows stronger. The dragon within rages to be let free, to take revenge, starting with Silas himself. But I cannot give in. *Not yet.* All I can do is stand here and watch the coals fade to white.

Hours later, I change into a different mourning dress of head-to-toe black, this one comprised of hideous piles of lace that itch with each movement. I'm sitting next to what is left of the Brightcaster family, trying not to break my "deal" with King Titus. I can't even look at the man without wanting to scream and scratch out his eyes. Nor Silas. And Queen Brysta, her tear-stained cheeks mean little to me. She's an accomplice in all of this too. The one with more elemental power than any of them, but who stood back and let it all happen.

Bram is quiet and withdrawn, watching the members at our table like he would one of his experiments, green eyes alight with questions. That's how he is, always in the background, nose in a book, but somehow, always keenly aware of what's going on around him. Today there is no book, and his eyes keep darting to me and then to his other family members. His earthy brown hair is more messy than usual, like he's been running his hands through it over and over.

Does he know what happened to Owen? Would he go

along with his parents' wishes and cover for Silas? He is smart enough to figure it out on his own but suddenly, I have the urge to tell him. Even so, he may already know. He may be just as terrible as the rest of them. The thought of it stings like ice. I want to believe the best of Bram, need to believe he's the last good one left. But I don't know that I can.

Queen Brysta is seated to my right, the King at the head of the table next to her, the two brothers across from us. Everyone dressed in black seems like a slap to Owen's memory. I glare at the brothers. Save for their height, the two look nothing alike. Silas is fair-skinned and white blonde, polished, confident and oozing with lust for power and glory. If I thought he was open about his wishes to be king before, this is ten times worse. And Bram? Bram couldn't care less about power and glory. His unkempt chestnut hair flops haphazardly in front of his observant eyes, his shoulders hunched over in exhaustion. Down our long table and the ones adjacent, the rest of the party dines. This is not a night of wine and raunchy behavior. The conversations are muffled. The energy is tense. And eyes are shifty.

I do not speak to a single person. I fear I'll proclaim the truth and ignite Titus's threats against my family. I do not care to pretend that I want to be here as I've done every day previous to this one. I've always done my duty, gotten in line and smiled through the pain. I had resolved to go along with my predetermined future years ago, believing that my feelings didn't matter more than the betterment of the kingdom. All that mattered was what the Gods wanted and they wanted me Queen. That was it.

Well, I don't care about my fate anymore.

What have the Gods ever done for me? What did they do for Owen?

Nothing.

I'm done with this. I don't want to be a queen. I don't want to play this part or try to fit in with these people. This role is wicked and it makes me ill to play it. What is power and glory without loyalty and love? These people don't understand anything of either and the whole lot can rot in hell for all I care.

The crowd is a sea of richly embroidered dresses and tunics, many belonging to desperate or scheming faces. People who would do anything to get on the throne, so why must I prevent them? There are hundreds of Lord's daughters and thousands of untitled peasant girls living within Drakenon's borders who would kill to be sitting in my seat, so why didn't the Gods give this burden to one of them?

I catch Bram's gaze across the table and his eyes narrow. He is always curious, but tonight he is filled to the brim with unanswered questions. Those eyes lock me in, intense and demanding. Then he flicks them to Silas so quickly, that I almost miss it. But I don't and the question is there. Bram returns his stare to me, willing me to answer through our eye contact alone. I can't know for certain what he's asking, but I'm no fool. Bram is wondering if Silas had something to do with Owen's death. Indecision rocks me. I shouldn't do it; it risks too much. Let Bram figure it out for himself.

He stares at me. And I stare back. *You know the truth,* I direct my thoughts to him, knowing he can't hear me. Only in dragon form could he and that's impossible for him, but still, I shout the words inside my mind. *You know who your family is! You know what they're capable of! Don't be fooled! Silas killed Owen!*

He's waiting, waiting for me to indicate the truth. I look away.

Nobody else notices me, it seems. King Titus and Queen Brysta are occupied with Silas, the trio of serpents speaking in low tones, and none the wiser to Bram or myself. I let out my own sorrowful breath and return to spreading a heap of mashed potatoes around on my plate, uninterested in eating a single bite. In the presence of all these people, in my regular seat at this table, without Owen here, it forces the weight of his death onto my shoulders. I doubt I'll ever live without this pain. It might lighten with time, but it will never be completely lifted from me, nor would I want it to.

I'm so sorry, Owen. You didn't deserve this.

King Titus fists his silver goblet and stands, a splash of cranberry colored wine dripping onto his meaty hand. The room falls into silence and the guests turn toward their leader. If only they knew. I eye some of the more prominent members of the Drakenon Court, noting their fleeting looks of sadness and sympathy, but also the distrust in their eyes and the unanswered questions held on their tongues. Maybe they don't know the full extent of it, but they have to suspect. Titus was right to assume some would make a play for his throne should it be revealed that Silas committed an unforgivable crime, and there are no other Dragon Blessed heirs. I smile. Maybe I won't have to say a thing; maybe the Brightcasters will dig their own graves.

"I want to thank you all for coming to mourn the death and celebrate the life of my son, Prince Owen Hydros Brightcaster of Drakenon," Titus says. "He was a gifted young man with a promising future." Tears spring to his eyes, and I bite the fleshy inside of my cheek, holding back a torrent of angry words. "Our family is distraught over what happened. We are still in shock that we lost our gifted, humorous, beloved son. He had a vivacious taste for adventure, a cunning mind for battle, a generous heart for leadership, and the kind of water elemental power that outshined his peers. We loved him and he will be greatly missed." He raises his goblet high. "To Owen, may your adventures continue in the next life and may the Gods guide you."

"To Owen," the court echoes. I join in, even though it guts me.

The King doesn't sit. He shifts his stance and continues, "Now, as you may have already heard, my son was murdered in cold blood." A few gasp but most are quiet. Word travels fast around here and surely they all spent the two-week mourning period spreading rumors. "No elemental magic was found, nor any traces of the death being the result of a dragon attack."

His eyes harden as whispers erupt. They were not expecting this, it seems. Something about that makes me gleeful. Bram isn't the only one who suspected foul play here.

"It could have been someone in this court," the King says louder, his booming voice quieting the whispers. "But more likely, it was an enemy assassin or a foreign spy. But no matter what, I can assure you we will not rest until Owen's murderer is caught and his death is avenged."

What he really means is he won't rest until he can pin it on someone believable, and most likely someone who would suit his plans. I can't help but glare.

"Our investigation started the moment he was found with Princess Khali," he continues, as more whispering ensues. "She did not see what happened. She discovered him after he was already gone and I would kindly ask that you do not question her any further. She's been through enough, poor thing." Every eye in the room is trained on me and my face is practically in flames. Titus's patronizing tone makes me want to scream.

"Until we have answers," the King goes on, his face growing softer, kinder, "we must protect the family we have left. Silas and Khali, will you please stand?"

Icy dread pours over my body as I rise on shaky legs. I knew this was going to happen, everyone did. But it seems knowing something is coming and actually experiencing it are two very different things. My stomach rolls over in protest and tears prick at the corners of my eyes. I force myself to smile and the action physically hurts my heart, like a knife is running right through its center.

This isn't fair! I wasn't supposed to get engaged until my eighteenth birthday. That's how it works. That's how it was for Queen Brysta, and Queen Isabel before that. A ring and vow on the eighteenth birthday, followed by six months of engagement. Then the marriage and all that comes with it.

Titus smiles, charm reeling us in. "I am pleased to announce that Silas has proposed to our kingdom's elemental princess and Khali has graciously accepted."

The crowd claps along and a few even go so far as to cheer. My mother winks at me like I'm the luckiest girl in the world. My breath is lodge in my throat, my vision narrowing. Silas stands and saunters around the table to my side, wrapping an arm around my shoulder and softly kissing my cheek. He's laying his claim. I don't breathe. I don't speak. I don't move an inch.

"Normally we would expect a longer engagement," Titus says, "but given everything that has happened, my wife and I feel the Gods wish this union to start the day Khali comes of age. The pair will be married on December the fifthteenth, on Khali's eighteenth birthday."

I want to rip away from Silas and demand justice. Instead, I blink back hot tears and smile through the pain. Maybe I will look like the picture of happiness instead of rage. If the members of court suspect my true feelings, they don't dare show it.

Either that or they don't care. And why would they? Arranged marriages happen all the time in Drakenon. I'm no different. And I'll be queen, the second highest position in the kingdom. Nobody will have an ounce of pity for me. But just because the position is ranked so high, doesn't mean anything to me. I see the way Queen Brysta acts and her complete lack of power. She's caged just as I am—just as I'll always be.

A clang reverberates throughout the dining hall. The massive oak doors burst open. Everyone turns toward the noise, guards and warriors unsheathing their swords. A man stumbles into the room, his dark hair ruffled, his eyes wild and afraid.

"Father?" I gasp, breaking free of Silas and rushing toward him. "Are you all right?"

Dirt stains his rumpled clothing, and it's as if he sees right through me, right through all of us. He can't focus on one person or one thing. *Has he been struck mad?*

I reach him, my hands gripping his. They are ice cold. "What's wrong, Father?" He does not hear me.

My mother pushes her way to us, her dress billowing out behind her. "What happened?" Her voice cracks. There's shrillness there, a fear in her voice I've never heard before.

He shakes his head over and over, as if a demon has possessed him. "There was a spell," he finally speaks, his voice garbled and frantic. "There was a spell. She's not safe. She's not safe. She will die!"

"Who's not safe, Father?" I beg him, pulling him closer. My mother is right there with me, urging him to relax. His wayward gaze finally locks on mine. His pupils are blown, black covering the entire iris. But he must see me because his face crumples and he breaks into gasping sobs. I squeeze his hands tighter. I'm so shocked I don't even move. I have no words. I've never seen my father cry. Not once.

"You," he says. "You're not safe!"

Me? That can't be right. "I'm right here," I say, bringing his hands to my face. "See? I'm fine."

"No! No! No!"

"What are you saying?" my mother pleads. "Calm down and explain yourself."

We're both holding him now, and I'm filled with hardened terror. The spectators surround us, the royals at the front of the pack. But nobody knows how to make this behavior stop or what to do with a man who's lost his mind. He has been a respected member of court for years. He is known for his level head and calm demeanor. This isn't like him.

He coughs and blood spurts from his mouth, black as tar. It sprinkles across my face and down my bodice. "Father!" I scream, my voice sounding far away--not my own.

His eyes begin to shift again, the earlier presence of madness before he could speak sweeping over. Finally, they land on me. Fear takes hold between its clawed talons.

"You're going to die!" He grinds out before his eyes roll back and he collapses to the floor.

ELEVEN

HAZEL

NO. THIS CAN'T BE HAPPENING. I'm losing my mind. I must be, because this kind of thing only exists in storybooks and make-believe. *Dragons aren't real.* They're just not! My body is alive with tingling horror, and my injured elbows are screaming out in protest, and my pounding heart is about to escape through my chest… and I can't do this, I can't do this, I can't do this.

I press my palms tight against my eyes and stand on legs of elastic. Little gasping breaths slip from my lips, one following the next and the next. They're supposed to be slow and steady, supposed to calm me down, to shore me up, but my lungs aren't cooperating.

It's okay. I'll open my eyes, and that dragon, or whatever it was, will be gone. It will all be a figment of an overactive and over-caffeinated imagination. That's all. I remove one hand and start with the left eye, slowly opening it.

Bad idea.

The dragon is still there. It's at least twice my height, towering over me and seething hot air out of its gruesome mouth. Its eyes are like a blue ocean rimmed in blood, its body like tar, its scales like that of a venomous snake. It sits on hind legs, outstretched claws as long and thick as scythes. The creature stands, growing even more massive, and I scream.

I take off, running back down the side of the building toward the street, my feet slamming against the pavement. I'm not fast enough. Part of my brain is reminding me it's a spirit which means it's already dead. It can't hurt me. But the other part of me is stuck on the whole "run for your life" option. Because what if it *can* hurt me? I comb through my recent memory as my breath pumps in and out and legs push forward.

Did the dragon physically knock me over at first or did I fall from shock and fear? I don't know. But I don't want to wait around and find out.

I probably look like a raving lunatic running down this street but I don't care. There are a few living people, several more dead ones, all with startled expressions locked on me as I sprint down the sidewalk. My necklace bounces against my neck. It's there, but it doesn't seem to be doing its job well enough.

Harmony. She'll know what to do. She'll be able to help.

A car screeches to a stop just up ahead—a black shiny one that sends my nerves into an all-out frenzy. Dean tears himself from the driver's side and rushes toward me. His black hair flops in front of one eye, giving him a rare frazzled look. His jaw is tense and his mouth is set in a line.

"What did you see?" he demands.

When I move to get past him, he grabs my elbow. I screech in protest but he hangs on.

"Tell me, Hazel," he presses. "What spooked you? What's there?"

I shake my head. No way I'm telling him anything.

"I have to go!" I try to push past him but his grip is iron tight.

He tugs me toward his car and throws open the passenger side. "Get in. We need to talk."

"No. I need to find Harmony. I need—"

"Absolutely not! You can't tell her and risk exposure! I'm still not sure if she can be trusted."

I've been looking past him, toward the Flowering Chakra and my getaway plan. But his final words shake me from that haze and I whip around. What is he talking about? Harmony already knows all about my gift. He's obviously aware of that.

Of course, she's trustworthy.

"Seriously, get in." His eyes bore into mine, more intense than I've ever seen them before, and the fire dancing around his pupils has returned. A sharp breath catches in my throat. So it *was* real… It's so small, it's almost unnoticeable. But I do notice and it both chills and burns me. It's wild and unnatural and I should run far, far away.

But I get in the car.

TWENTY MINUTES LATER, AFTER A silent car ride and a chance for my nerves to settle, Dean parks us in the middle of nowhere. There are fat pines and about a million trees alive with the colors of autumn, but that's it. We're alone out here. My nervous energy comes racing back. Katherine is dead and now there's another missing girl to think about. I shouldn't be so careless.

"Are you going to murder me out here or something, because I'm pretty sure a bunch of people saw me get into this car so it's not like you'll get way with it," I ramble, my words may sound like a joke, but I'm only half-kidding. I don't really *know* Dean.

"Come on," Dean orders before stepping out of the vehicle

and slamming his door.

I slip my phone from my pocket and check it, planning to send a message to Cora and Macy with my whereabouts, in case Dean really is a crazy murderer. It's a no-go. I don't have any service. Fantastic. But hey, at least the location services are on so if the cops need to search for me they'll have a place to start.

I huff out a breath, trying to keep calm, and open my door.

"What did you see?" Dean asks again. His voice crawls through the clearing, and I glance back to the empty stretch of one-lane highway.

When I don't immediately answer, he stomps around the side of the car to stand toe-to-toe with me. He's so close I can smell the campfire and spicy aroma that is distinctly his and distinctly intoxicating. His eyes bore into mine, coal black and no longer dancing with flames. My prickly nerves relax a fraction, and I remind myself that no, he didn't bring me out here to murder me—he brought me out here because he wants to know what I saw.

And I want to know what he's hiding.

"Why should I tell you?" I ask, genuinely curious. Because what good does it do me to tell him what I saw? "Are you going to help me or something?"

And do I even need help? *Hazel, you saw a dragon. You*

clearly need help.

He rocks back on his heels instead of answering my question. "You're a medium, right? So you see the spirit realm?"

I nod once. I thought we'd already established this. I thought he knew that about me all along. This situation is getting weirder by the second.

"Who's your father?" he asks sharply.

The question is so unexpected, it's like a slap to the face. Not that I care about the "sperm donor" but because I don't like to think about the missing part of my life too much. I look away into the distant trees and frown. "I don't see how that has anything to do with you."

"It has everything to do with me," he barks out.

I whip around on him, both intrigued and annoyed. "Why? Why is the identity of my father any of your business? What could it possibly have to do with you?"

More importantly, what isn't he telling me?

His jaw is tight but once again, he doesn't answer my question or react to my anger with anything other than his own calculated hatred. I can see it in his eyes, see how much he despises me. And now it might have something to do with the "sperm donor"? Dean's not the only one who can ask questions here. He's left me confused and it's a tangled feeling I need to unravel.

I fold my arms over my chest, widening my stance. The earthy smell of the autumn forest brushes past us on the wind, whipping my hair behind me. "I don't know who my father is, okay? He was a one-night stand and my mom never got his name." I narrow my eyes on Dean. "Why do you want to know about him?"

His gaze is hooded and he thinks for a minute. "Who's your mother?"

I scoff. "You're going to dodge my questions but keep asking more of your own? No, I don't think so."

Apparently, he doesn't care what I have to say. "Where does she live?" he continues, his expression intense. "What does she do for a living? Is she… normal?"

I roll my eyes. This is getting ridiculous. "She's an ER nurse in Ohio and she's a wonderful person and perfectly normal except for her terrible taste in men. Okay? The end." I lean against the car before shifting closer to him. "The way I see it, if you want answers from me, I should be able to get answers from you."

He raises an eyebrow. "When you see the spirit realm, what does it look like?"

Okay, maybe not.

I exhale and rub the goosebumps on my arms. It's colder

now than it was earlier, and it was chilly before. More shivers run over my skin and I rub at my arms even harder. I really don't want to answer, to play victim to his interrogation or whatever this is but I find myself spilling the truth anyway, "I see spirits. Usually the people who have recently died. They don't talk but they show me images from their lives. It usually doesn't make a lot of sense."

"That's it? Just people?"

I pause. That was it. Until today.

"Did you see something that wasn't human today?" he presses, guessing—or maybe it's not a guess. Maybe he knows. Maybe it's part of *his* secret. Nervous energy spreads through me at the thought.

Somehow he's even closer now, and he slowly reaches out and grips me above my wrists. He runs his hands delicately up my arms, warming me up. I hold my breath, the nerves now firing like crazy. His hands are so hot and wonderfully smooth and they remind me of warm summer days and of a time before things got complicated.

I nod once.

"Was it an animal?" He's inches from me now. So close that I can see flecks of gold in his eyes, can smell the spearmint on his breath.

Should I tell him? I don't want to tell him and I do want

to tell him at the same time. Before I can catch myself, I'm speaking, "I guess you could say that," I whisper.

His eyebrows furrow together. "Did it show you anything? Any images?" I notice that he doesn't acknowledge *what* it was, only speaks as if he already knows. But surely, if I said, Dragon, he'd laugh at me.

"Hazel." He shifts closer. "Did it show you images?"

I blink and nod.

"It's okay to tell me."

"It was black… the creature," I say, my voice low. "It showed me a castle and several people but it focused on one girl in particular. I think she might be in trouble. I think it wanted me to help her."

"What did she look like?"

"She had two colored eyes. One blue. One brown."

He cusses and rears back, ripping the moment in two. "Khali."

I'm stunned. "Who's Khali?"

He shakes his head. "I have to go. Do you have a driver's license?"

I look around, confused. What just happened? "Yes… go where?"

He reaches into his pocket and pulls out his keys. Frantic, he removes the black key fob and presses it firmly into my palm. "Drive yourself back to the shop," he demands, his words quick and decisive. "I'll pick up the key from Harmony later."

I gape at him. "What? Where could you possibly go all the way out here?"

But he doesn't answer me, doesn't even seem to care that he brought me out here in the first place. He takes off running into the forest of all places. There's nothing out here but trees. Where could he possibly be going? Any traces of the man are gone within seconds and I'm still standing here, still bracing myself against the cold and the sudden loss of his heat.

TWELVE

KHALI

THE COURT PHYSICIAN LEANS OVER my father one last time; the wrinkles around his eyes deepen in examination. He stands to offer his conclusion. "Lord Paul Elliot has been hexed."

Mother gasps, and dread spreads through me like boiling liquid. I was worried it might be something like this. I don't know too much about magic, but I know if he's been hexed, it probably was done by a dangerous hand. He's lucky to be alive, to have made it back to us, but I don't know how much time he has left. Tears spring to my eyes and I grasp his feverish hand.

I can't lose you too, Dad. I plead to his sleeping body and to the Gods, wherever they may be. *Please, don't die.*

"Are you certain?" King Titus stands back from us, keeping

his distance. A crease forms between his bushy eyebrows, but something else flickers in his gaze too: something suspiciously like acceptance. He must have been worrying about the same thing. Did he know this was going to happen?

"There is no other explanation for the way his symptoms are presenting," the physician says. "This isn't an illness. This is dark magic."

I place my hand on my father's sleeping back, rubbing small circles as I hold back tears. He's warm again. Sweat beads his ashen skin and wets his white linen shirt. He rolls over, mumbling incoherently, and the black stubble on his chin brushes against my hand. Since his arrival in the banquet hall and subsequent collapse, he hasn't woken. Not once. It's been four days, and Mother and I have stayed by his side, alternating shifts when one of us grows too tired. His temperature has spiked and plummeted a dozen times. He is going to waste away in front of our eyes.

"Who would hex him?" My mind races through the possibilities but I don't know where to start. Witchcraft is a forbidden art in Drakenon and punishable by death. As far as I know, the craft has been eradicated from our kingdom. We have dragon shifters and elemental magic but nothing like witchcraft. That is an entirely different beast that was slain long ago when the Brightcasters took the throne, saving us all from those who'd want us dead.

Oftentimes, our dragon ancestors were slain as ritual sacrifices for magical purposes. The idea of it sends a terrified shiver down my spine. The Brightcasters may have their own levels of evil, but at least they're nothing like the Occultists, who worship demons.

"Could he have left the Drakenon border?" the physician asks, his eyes bouncing from each of us in the room.

"He travels around the kingdom," Mom says defensively. She's even more of a mess than I am. "He is exposed to all sorts of people, but he isn't foolish enough to leave the borders."

The physician nods sympathetically but I catch a twinge of guilt from King Titus. His eyes are shifty, like he can't look at any one of us for long. It's his biggest tell. I've known these people for as long as I can remember and I know when they're hiding something. And he's *definitely* hiding something important.

"Did you send him beyond the borders?" The accusation leaves my lips before I can think it through.

"Khali!" Mother chastises, but her eyes tell a different story. She wants answers as much as I do.

"Of course not," King Titus says automatically.

I don't believe him but I hold my tongue.

Nobody leaves the borders unless in exile or to spy. We obviously aren't privy to who the King's spies are, lest they be compromised. Drakenon sits on the eastern edge of a larger, very contentious continent called Eridas. The other kingdoms consist of witches, fae, elves, mages and all manner of wiley beasts. They constantly vie for power over each other; bloodshed and broken treaties and entire family lines murdered are the norm. But not the dragon clans. Our borders have been warded by elemental magic for three centuries and only those with dragon lineage can enter. We keep to ourselves, protected from outside invaders. It's inside the border that we have to worry about threats, but the clans have been at peace for one hundred years under the Brightcaster's reign.

So why would my father leave the kingdom?

Several things click into place at once. "Is my father a spy?" I turn back to the King, my heart hammering. When he doesn't immediately reply, I have my answer. "He is, isn't he? He hasn't just been traveling around the kingdom for you, he's been crossing the border into enemy territory at your request."

"No," Mother says. "Paul wouldn't take that risk. He promised me."

"Tell us," I beg the King in a raspy whisper. Tears break free and run down my cheeks, two hot trails of pain and sadness. "Please, you know what I've done for your family, what I am doing for you now. I deserve the truth."

Titus stills, his shoulders softening, and turns to the physician. "Would you please leave us for a few minutes?"

The man, pale as a ghost, takes no time scurrying out of the room. It's just the four of us now. If I wanted, I could shift into my dragon form and assassinate the king where he stands. It's the only thought I've had in days that gives me a moment of relief.

"It's complicated." The King lets out a slow breath, finally stepping further into the room and approaching my father. "But yes, Paul has been crossing the border for me."

Anger burns deep, ripping its way out to the surface. "How could you ask him to do that?" I seethe. "You know the risks! My father considers you one of his closest friends."

He ignores me, and I'm over it. I'm over the lies, over the choices others have made that have hurt me. The Brightcaster clan may be beloved and powerful, but they have cost me too much.

"Is he going to make it?" Mother asks, tears shining in her eyes. For as much as she and I oppose one another, we've always had the same soft spot for Father. He's the only thing that keeps us together.

"We've seen this a few times before with our spies," Titus

says. "I'm afraid he won't die but he won't wake, either. He'll be stuck in this torment."

The room is silent as we all stare at my father.

"For how long?" Mother asks.

"Until we end his misery."

Mom and I both shoot him deadly glares, outrage burning us up. As if that is an appropriate answer. How dare he even consider it?

"No," she snaps.

My voice is shrill, "How do we cure him?" My elements are rising underneath my skin, especially the fire. I will not let *anyone* hurt my father. I will kill them first!

Once again, his silence tells me all I need to know and the anger only doubles. Titus doesn't have a way to help my father. Would it be more cruel to leave him like this? Should we end his suffering? Those are the unspoken words that die on my lips because I do not have the strength to consider it.

"You have to do something," I challenge. "You have to at least try to help him."

"Of course I will do everything I can to help your father," the King states matter-of-factly. "But for now I must take my leave. I assure you both"—he levels his gaze on my mother and I—"we will keep searching for a way to break this hex."

Again, I don't believe a word that falls from his mouth.

"Wait," I call out as his hand rests on the doorknob. He didn't bring any guards with him today, stupid man. He should know better than to underestimate me. Again, I'm tempted by the idea of assassination. "You never told us why you were sending him over the border. Don't we deserve to know what was so important to risk his life?"

He turns back and clenches his jaw, his kingly stature returning to his broad shoulders. "It's classified," he snaps, leaving us with more questions than answers.

I hate him.

THERE'S A STORM OF EMOTIONS raging inside, destroying my heart, but hopelessness is perhaps the worst of them. All I want is for things to return to what they once were. For Owen to be alive and for us to be on our way to starting a life together. For my mother to carry on with her courtly intrigues instead of hovering over my father like a ghost. And for my father to be safe, whole, and healthy once more. But magic doesn't work like that, at least not mine. I have no means to change my past, and my future has spun so far out of my control, I can scarcely recognize it.

It's all hopeless.

I walk down the corridor alone, a rarity for me, but I couldn't stand to be in that room for a second longer. The night fell hours ago, and the castle has since grown quiet. I need to change and bathe, to gather my thoughts, sleep for a while, and then I'll return to my parents, and Mother and I can brainstorm ideas for Father's healing.

I'm hardly ever alone. The sensation is a little nerve-wracking, but also freeing. I usually have Lady Faros to attend me or one of my semi-friends from court to chirp in my ear as I go from one duty to the next. I call them semi-friends because they don't really care about me, they only care about what I can do for them. They're nowhere to be found these days.

Since Owen's death and Father's subsequent illness, I haven't been available for socializing, and they haven't been available for consoling. And I saw no need for Faros to stand around aimlessly while Mother and I tend to Father during this time, so I dismissed her until further notice. She didn't want to leave me. I didn't really want her to leave me either. But I did it anyway. Nothing is how it was. King Titus never sent any of his guards to watch me, foolish as he is; he must have decided I wasn't a threat or in any danger. Why would I be in danger when the murderers around here all need me alive?

I'm almost to my chambers when a faint giggle drifts

through the corridor. That's a sound that isn't so strange around this massive castle, considering so many live here. I ignore it, as I always do. What do I care for affairs and romantic secrets? It's always been beneath me.

A man's voice whispers darkly and cackles. I stop. Apprehension crawls over my skin. I know that voice. I should leave. Whatever this is—and I'm sure I already know—is none of my business, but I tiptoe toward the hushed voices anyway. Around this corner lies a darkened alcove, one of the many that rarely get decent light during the day, and at night, are used for their shadows. I'm certain that's where this couple is, and if it were anyone else, I would ignore them and move on.

But that damned voice…

The woman giggles again and then she lets out a deep sigh. The man mumbles and groans hungrily. I hold my breath, not quite believing I'm going to follow their promiscuous noises. But it's not like anyone else is forbidden from the act of kissing before marriage as I am. I peer around the alcove, straining against the wall of darkness, wondering if perhaps I should announce myself. My eyes adjust, and I see them for myself.

Against the far end of the alcove, two figures press together. The man towers over his partner as his hands greedily rove up and down her body. So not *just* kissing. I gasp, stepping back as the pair breaks apart. It's exactly who I thought. Silas. Silas and… not a woman… but a girl by the innocent looks of her.

The girl smirks at me, her wide eyes twinkling as she runs her hand possessively along his arm. I try to place her. Her clothing is disheveled, the bodice of her mauve dress far too loose and her pink rouge smeared across her cheek. She doesn't seem to care, but rather wears her appearance as a badge.

"Come to watch or did you want to join in?" Silas grins, turning toward me.

"Do you have no shame?" I snap, disgusted.

He shrugs and the girl laughs. I recognize her as a Duke's daughter but I can't remember which nor can I recall her name. She's at least two years younger than my seventeen, maybe three, and certainly not of age to be behaving this way with a man of nineteen. This kind of behavior may be normal around here, but not for a girl so young.

"Oh, Khali," Silas says. "If you could see your face right now. You really thought I was saving myself for you, didn't you?"

I bite my tongue, holding back the hate I'm dying to speak. Of course I knew there was a double standard when it came to me and the princes, but it's never been thrown in my face before tonight. I've heard whispers, seen flirtations now and then, but I assumed it was all harmless. This is so callous, I don't even know what to think.

He sighs, tucking the girl closer to him but making no attempt to leave. "My father is an anomaly, did you know that? He's chosen to stay monogamous with my mother, the darling man. But most kings before him kept courtesans and I intend to do the same. Gods know you're not going to come to my bed without force." He runs his tongue along his lips. "We'll both learn to appreciate my playthings to keep me company."

The girl smacks him but then runs her hand through his hair and roughly pulls herself closer to him. He laughs and returns to kissing her hungrily. "Let's go to my room," he says, loud enough for me to hear. "I need to get you back into my bed before I take you right here."

She giggles. "Would here be so bad? We might enjoy it."

"If you insist," he replies excitedly, lifting her skirt like he's done it countless times.

Bile rises in my stomach.

My entire body is alive with shock and disgust, and I stumble away, hurrying back to my chambers. I slam the door behind me and lean against it for strength, struggling to catch my breath. I can't. I run to the bathing chamber to empty what little contents I have in my stomach. It takes several minutes to calm the ache before I can return to my bed and rest.

Silas is my *fiancé* and yet he's carrying on like it means nothing. And that foolish girl is far too young to have already turned herself into his mistress. He's taking advantage of her and she's a willing participant. How long has he been carrying on like this? Do her parents know? Are they encouraging it?

I'm a fool to have thought I knew anything about the Brightcaster family and their moral character. A guilty thought comes to my mind, a thought that says I'm just like that girl. I'm also a willing participant in all of this, even if I tell myself I'm not happy about it. I'm here, aren't I? I'm engaged to that vile creature, am I not?

My mind runs and runs into the early morning hours, sleep too far away to grasp.

Is Silas carrying on with other women besides this one? I don't know the answer but I do know that Silas choosing to be in that alcove by my chambers wasn't an accident. He wanted me to catch them. He wanted me to see that while I may become his queen, he will still carry on however he wishes. That *he* is the one with the power and always will be.

I'm nothing but a prize to be won, unwrapped, used, and then cast aside.

My chest heaves up and down, and I clench my fists so tightly that I draw blood. I'm not hurt—I'm livid. And no matter how much power Silas thinks he has over me, I won't stand by and let him continue to flaunt his power. One way or another, I'm going to end Silas Brightcaster. But first, I have to save myself.

THIRTEEN

HAZEL

THREE DAYS AFTER THE INCIDENT with Dean, Katherine Donahue's body is pulled from a nearby lake.

The police called a press conference and announced their suspicions comfirmed of foul play, opening it up as a murder investigation. That was yesterday and now her death is all anyone can talk about. That, and the fact that two other college girls have gone missing over the last two years: Tessa Smith and Charlene Connelly. Both brand new college freshmen when they disappeared, just like Katherine. But their bodies were never found. It's not lost on anybody that there's a connection. The pattern is unmistakable.

And now that there's a high school senior missing as well, everyone is on edge.

"I didn't know any of this when I picked Hayden College,"

Macy complains as the three of us walk to our Anthropology class Wednesday morning. "Had I known, I would've gone somewhere else. I mean, I was waitlisted at Vanderbilt. I should have pursued that more."

"I didn't know either," I complain, looking around the beautifully landscaped campus. It's everything pictured from the brochures, with its sprawling manicured lawns and red-bricked buildings. "It's not like these missing girls showed up in a Google search for Hayden College." Once again I'm struck by the fact that I not only got into this place, but I received a full scholarship. It was the only scholarship I got and I applied to a lot of schools that weren't as highly ranked as this one.

What if it wasn't an accident? What if someone wanted me here for a specific reason that has nothing to do with academics? An icy shiver runs down my spine. *No way. Don't be ridiculous.*

"Well, the world is going to know all about this creepy school now!" Macy says, smoothing out her glossy strawberry hair. As if it could get any smoother, it's always perfect.

Cora rolls her eyes bitterly. "Girls our age go missing all the time. Especially women of color and especially women on tribal lands. The amount who just up and disappear is disgusting. And do most of these women get any sort of news coverage or fanfare?"

I shake my head, hating the answer as I say it, "They don't."

"That's right," Cora continues. "They don't. But this is different. This is a possible serial killer targeting beautiful *caucasian* girls. It's bound to get national attention if it hasn't already."

We continue discussing the unfairness of news coverage giving preferential treatment, all the while goosebumps spread over my body. This is so creepy. No, it's more than that. This whole situation is downright terrifying. But at least I haven't seen any more of these girls' ghosts. Just Katherine. But since meeting Harmony, even Katherine has disappeared. I make a mental note to thank Harmony again. The woman may be an oddball but she certainly knows her stuff. I don't feel haunted anymore. I still see ghosts now and again, but thanks to the little black beads of obsidian around my neck, they can't send me images unless I allow it.

Well, except if they're spirits of the dragon variety.

Then, apparently, they can send me all sorts of images without my permission. I shiver to think of that monstrous creature lurking around here, and the striking girl with the mismatched eyes also returns to my memory, followed by the castle and the way they were all dressed like it was medieval times. The things I saw that didn't make any sense... and the frantic, fearful energy surrounding it all. Dean seemed to understand it, even if I didn't. It's all been running through my mind on a loop for days.

I still haven't seen Dean since he ran off like a crazy person. I was tempted to keep the car and force him to come find me so he could explain his behavior, but I chickened out and returned his car to the parking lot near The Flowering Chakra like he'd ordered. I gave Harmony his keys and that was that. His car got picked up between my shifts and come Monday morning, he didn't show up to class.

Just as we're about to go inside our building, someone taps me on the shoulder. I turn to find Landon and dare I say it? I become giddy with excitement.

"Hey there," Landon says, smiling his big goofy smile at me. Perhaps he's excited to see me too. "I haven't seen you in The Roasted Bean in a while. Are you getting your caffeine fix somewhere else?"

I laugh and give him a hug. He's warm and smells of coffee and cologne. "Hey, yourself. I haven't seen you in The Flowering Chakra in a while. Getting your crystal fix somewhere else?" I tease.

"You know it!"

Cora and Macy exchange a knowing look and raise their eyebrows at me.

"No, truthfully, I've been trying to lay off caffeine for a while. I haven't been sleeping well, what with everything going on."

He nods. "Ya, it's pretty crazy."

The silence between us grows awkward as we think about the missing girls.

"Well, I better let you go," he says, running a hand through his blonde hair. It's not in its usual manbun and he kinda reminds me of a guy on the cover of a romance novel. "Just wanted to say hello. I'll see you in lab later, ya?"

"Absolutely." I grin as he leaves and Cora and Macy pull me into our building, both gushing about how cute he is and asking when I'm going to make a move on him. I don't know what to say to that, I've never made a move on anyone, but I can feel the smile pressing against my cheeks and the blood warming my face.

If he doesn't make a move, then I guess I'll have to learn how.

We stroll into the lecture hall with its theater style seating and my eyes dart to the last row where Dean's usually camped out. I ignore the quick pang of disappointment when I don't find him. Why do I care? I'm being ridiculous. I shake off the weirdness of my fascination with Dean and I turn toward the front of the room where I like to sit.

There he is.

He's lounging in one of the chairs like he owns the place. He raises a dark eyebrow at me before looking away, shifting his weight toward the pretty girl sitting next to him. She says something, and he laughs that wicked laugh and he's flirting and I hate it.

Wait, what? Ugh! Stop it, Hazel!

But he's in the front row. He's right next to the seat I've been in all semester and *that* can't be a coincidence. He must want to talk to me again.

Being the grown up I am, I slide into the empty chair next to him, Cora and Macy filling in the rest of the row. This is my spot after all. I don't need to avoid Dean. My girls both shoot me odd looks but all I do is shrug at them. I mean, let's be honest, it's not like I have a clue what I'm doing sitting next to Dean Ashton either. They *know* I hate the man. I'm just not sure if I know it anymore.

He finishes up with "Pretty Girl" and turns towards me. The way he looks at me, it's like I'm the only one in the lecture hall. Like he doesn't hear or see the other chatting students. It's unnerving. I'm caught in his black eyes and his intensity and his campfire woodsy scent, realizing with clarity what it is he smells like.

When I was growing up, I'd spend one glorious week

at Y-Camp each summer. I loved every minute of it, from the camp songs, to the horse rides, the canoes, the hikes, the swimming, the temporary friends and heart-stopping crushes. All of it. And without fail, every single summer, there would be a night that the campfire would get rained out. We'd be sitting around it, doing our skits, or singing songs, maybe building the perfect s'more, when the thunder would roll in and the rain would spill from above. Nature would come together, blanketing everything in this wondrous scent of burning wood and thick raindrops and fresh air and perfect, perfect summer night. And everything inside of me would buzz from being alive.

That's exactly what Dean Ashton smells like… and oh my Lord, I've totally got a crush on him. *Shoot! How did that happen?*

A wistful feeling comes over me. I miss that time at camp more than I realized. Those are some of my only memories of being myself and having fun with other kids who didn't make fun of me. It was easy to fit in at camp because everyone was a little bit different. Maybe that's what college is like, too? And maybe that's why I like it here so much.

"Can we talk after class?" Dean asks, his focus still steady and solely on me. One ebony lock of hair curls around his cheek and his eyes narrow into a hooded gaze. "Alone."

Oh, boy…

I bite my lip, considering if "talking alone" with him is a good idea. But who am I kidding? Of course I'm going to say yes. Hot or not, I have a lot of questions for the man. I need to know if what I saw was real. I need to know what he has to do with it. I need to know who that girl with the heterochromic eyes is and why she matters to him. And I also need to put this ridiculous crush aside because he is *so not right for me.*

"Please?" His voice drops an octave, and his thick black lashes flutter closed for the briefest of seconds and I can't seem to pull my gaze away from him and sweet baby Jesus, *I'm in trouble…*

"Sure." I swallow hard. He looks at me for a long second, as if sensing the effect he's having on me, then turns away to talk to "Pretty Girl" again. My heart drops into my butt. Gosh, dang it, why am I so bad at this?!

Doctor Peters clears his throat, starting the lecture and ending the embarrassing moment. Bless him. I do my best to take notes and stay attentive over the next ninety minutes but Dean is too close. I can't stop thinking about this newfound discovery of my crush, or feeling the heat of his body against my side.

I thought I hated him. I really did. Actually, I'm pretty sure I still do.

But I'm obviously *attracted* and I can't help but want to spend time alone with him, to unravel whatever it is between us. Because despite the sheer anger he seems to bring out in me, he also draws me in with the mystery, intensity, and challenge.

How messed up is that? Maybe I should get my head checked.

I DON'T KNOW WHAT I expected but this wasn't it. Naive little ol' me figured we'd go chat in the hallway or at least *somewhere* on campus, probably to yell at each other— like usual. But instead of any of that, Dean is leading me across the street to the posh neighborhood adjacent to this part of campus. He doesn't utter a word as fallen leaves crunch beneath our shoes and the earlier chill is thawed beneath the mid-morning sun.

My limbs grow hot under my cherry-red peacoat, especially with the long sleeved t-shirt I've got on underneath. Dean could be one of those aerobics speed-walking ladies at this pace. He's three steps ahead and being a socially awkward weirdo.

"Could you slow down?" I ask in a huff.

He doesn't slow down. And this, this kind of thing right here, is indicative of why I should abandon any crush on

Dean Ashton. His black suede boots continue forward. I peer down at my white Converse, wondering if the little blue constellations I drew on them are childish.

We turn onto a tree-lined street with houses that are at least a century old, all beautifully refurbished with immaculate curb appeal. There are plenty of rental houses around campus where many of the upperclassmen live, but this area is most definitely not home to college-aged renters. Of course it would be home to Dean.

"I'm right here," he mutters, turning up the drive of a darling red brick cottage.

Ivy sweeps across one side where it meets with the sloping roof. The house fits right in with its neighbors. It even has a turret. A turret! Once again, Dean has surprised me. This time, I know better than to laugh and piss him off. The guy buys sage and is a frequent visitor to The Flowering Chakra, after all. It's a sensitive subject.

He leads me to the massive four-car garage and quickly keys in a code before I can catch sight of a number sequence. Not that I was snooping. Okay, I totally was. The garage door opens, revealing his fancy black car in one spot next to a shiny bullet bike. The rest of the garage is a home gym, complete with giant tires and those huge ropes guys like to throw around.

I just learned three things about Dean. Number one, he

likes to workout alone. In fact, I rarely see him with anyone, so he must like to do most things alone. Number two, he apparently has a deathwish, because he has a bullet bike and those things are terrifying. And three, he's much wealthier than I'd originally guessed.

"This is your house?" I ask the stupid question, but seriously, what kind of college kid lives like this? I mean, isn't living off ramen noodles and five dollar pizzas some kind of right-of-passage? Maybe he lives with his parents. He must.

He doesn't bother to answer as we walk into his house. I have to consciously keep my jaw from dropping once we get inside. If the outside belongs in *Town & Country Magazine*, the inside belongs in *Modern Home Magazine*. It's all clean lines and chrome, concrete and wood finishes, stark white against caramel brown and slate black. It's gorgeous in a way that makes me feel separated from it, like I don't belong. I'm too cozy and relaxed for a place like this.

"So, your parents are loaded, huh?" My mouth gets away with me *again* and heat spreads across my cheeks. "I'm sorry, that was a rude thing to say."

He shoots me an unreadable glance, still not saying a word, and goes to the kitchen, pouring us both tall glasses of ice water. I follow his lead and take off my backpack and coat, setting them on the nearest chair.

"I live alone," he finally says. "I bought it when I moved here for school."

He bought it? Again, I'm left with more questions than answers when it comes to Dean.

He downs his glass of water in one go and then fills it up again, drinking more. And then he does it again. The guy must be the poster-boy for water or something, either that or the gallon challenge. Mom would love that. She's always harping on at me to drink more water and ditch the soda, as if that will ever happen. Dr. Pepper for life! I miss her. We talk on the phone almost daily but only for a few minutes each time. There's not much to say now that our lives are in two separate states.

"So what did you want to talk to me about?" I ask. I'm supposed to meet Cora and Macy for lunch in an hour and I have an English Literature class this afternoon that I still haven't finished the reading for, but I don't say any of those things. I just wait. Because I'm pretty sure I know exactly what he wants to talk about and it's exactly what I want to talk about.

The spirit dragon!

He puts both of our empty glasses in the sink and comes to stand across the kitchen island from me. His fingertips press down against the sleek countertop and he gazes at me with a questioning glint. I'm not sure what happened to the air in here but my lungs aren't cooperating fully. "About Friday… I wanted to apologize for my appalling behavior and running off as I did. I shouldn't have left you so vulnerable."

Ummm, what just happened? I never thought I'd see the day. "Why do you suddenly care? I thought you hated me." I tilt my head at him, looking for a crack in his exterior. I don't find one.

His jaw tenses as he considers. "I don't hate you, Hazel. I hate that you're *here*. You're not supposed to be here if I'm here but I don't want to leave, either."

Again, what just happened? He doesn't want to leave either? "We've been through this before, Dean. This whole, 'you're not making sense' and this thing is getting old."

He holds up a hand. "But I've come to realize that you aren't lying and you truly don't know what you are."

I know what I am. He knows what I am. I narrow my eyes, trying to figure this out. "Yeah, about that, what on God's green earth are you even talking about?"

He continues as if I didn't interrupt with a really important question, "I've also accepted that you're not going to drop out of school on my account. And I'm not going to leave because you're here. Especially not when you have certain talents that could be useful to me. So I want to call a truce."

I can't help it. I laugh. "I have certain talents, do I? You're talking about the whole psychic medium thing, am I correct? So, suddenly, I'm of interest to you and you're going to be nice to me when you were a total asshat to me before? I don't think so."

He lets out a slow breath and walks around the counter, moving toward me with the same kind of intensity as always, like a predator hungry for his next meal. This time, I won't let him scare me. And he should, I know that. I feel it deep in my bones. He's the predator. I'm the prey. But maybe I like it. And maybe he does, too. His eyes flicker over my body, over my folded arms and the jut of my hips, before lingering on my lips and then finally resting at my eye level. A shudder runs through me. It's annoying, what one look can unravel inside.

"You've always been of interest to me," he says. "Since the first moment I saw you and you didn't see me. Do you know it took you three days to notice me? That doesn't happen often."

"Wow, Dean. How fascinating," I deadpan. "Are you always this arrogant?"

His smile is wicked. "Comes with the territory."

It sure does.

"So I was wondering if you would help me?" He steps closer. "I need to know more about what you saw the other night. Anything at all."

I consider it. I actually do. He runs a fingertip along the

edge of the counter, coming to a stop when it hits my elbow, but he doesn't move his hand. "And if possible," he continues, "I'd like you to do a reading for me. Tell me what spirits you see surrounding me. Try to communicate with them. I'd be happy to pay for your services."

"A reading here or at the shop?" My breath stalls and my eyes search his, looking for the catch. Because there has to be a catch.

"Here. Not to cut Harmony out or anything, but now that I know what you are capable of, we have to be incredibly discreet."

"You don't trust Harmony?"

He tilts his head. "I don't trust anyone."

I look around the kitchen some more, taking in how barren it is. It's perfectly clean, perfectly normal looking, but something tells me he doesn't have people here often, if ever. So why me? He must trust me to some degree to let me into his home, and yet he's a closed book.

Part of me wants to give in, to say yes. But the other part can't ignore the red flags. This guy has been a jerk from day one. He threatened me the first day I met him and has constantly argued with me ever since. And then, after a terrifying ordeal, he convinced me to get in his car, took me out to the middle of nowhere, and left me.

Besides, women have gone missing and a girl was found dead. There is a serial killer still on the loose and here I am, the smart one who decided it was a good idea to come into this house alone with him, without telling anyone where I was even going. What if Dean is the murderer? I don't want it to be him and I don't *feel* like it is, but who really knows. Fact is, I *don't* know.

There are too many mysteries when it comes to this man.

"I don't feel good about it," I say at last. I press my fingers against the white countertop. It's ice cold to the touch and just as smooth. "It's not about the money. I mean, good for you and all, congrats on being rich or whatever, but I don't want your money." I'm rambling but I can't seem to stop. "Truth is, you scare me and this whole situation scares me."

"And why is that?" he whispers, coming to stand mere inches from me.

I give in. "I know what I saw. I saw you with fire in your eyes, twice. I felt the intense heat when you got angry that night after the party and it wasn't the alcohol and it wasn't normal. And what I saw on Friday, the spirit that came to me. I can't even say it out loud, it's too crazy."

"Not crazy," he mutters, licking his lips.

For a second, I can't breathe. "If it's not crazy, then *you* say it."

He says nothing.

Silence stretches between us until I speak up again, "Dean, if you want my help, you'd better be willing to shed some light on all of this and answer my questions."

"I can't do that." He steps back, adding to the secrets already between us.

"Are you kidding me?" I scoff, walking around the kitchen island. I need to put some distance between us so I can think clearly. "You want me to help you but you won't do anything for me in return?"

"I said I would pay you."

I fold my arms over my chest. "And I said I don't want your money."

He glares, his jaw clicking. "But I thought you needed money. Why else would you be working at The Flowering Chakra? You're a scholarship kid. You don't have a dad in your life. You must need financial help."

Outrage grips me, tearing me up from inside out. There is something about his pitying look that makes me want to burn this pretentious house with all it's glossy, unloved surfaces, to the ground. "Who even says something like that?"

I grab my stuff off the chair and push past him, heading for the front door.

"Wait," he follows. "That came out wrong. I'm sorry."

"No, you're not. Just leave me alone." I make it to the front door and open it, all in two seconds flat, storming outside. A pattering of booted footsteps follows behind. Dean actually has the audacity to follow me? I shake my head. Unbelievable!

"You don't understand. I need you to help me. You have to."

"No," I shoot back, keeping my eyes straight ahead. "I don't!"

"You can't say no to me," he growls, reaching out and grabbing my arm. Burning heat presses against my long-sleeved shirt and I yelp, jumping back. My eyes don't want to believe what I'm seeing but there's no denying it. There's a hole in my shirt sleeve, singed around the corners. The pungent smell of burned fabric wafts through the air between us.

I whip around. This time it's my turn to make demands.

"Explain this!" I point to the black mark against the white cotton. He looks, but he doesn't say anything. "Explain why your eyes have fire in them right now," I continue. "Explain why your body heat raises when you're angry, or why you just burned a hole through my shirt. Explain why I saw the spirit of a dragon when I was with you on Friday and why you act like I have something to do with all of this. Tell me everything, Dean, or don't ask for my help."

He shakes his head, pained. "I can't."

"It's always been just me and my mom," I say, my voice cracking. "For me, letting other people in is super hard. And I get that, I get that you don't want to let me in."

His eyes search mine, but he doesn't say anything.

"I get it, because I'm the exact same way." I pull my arms into my jacket, covering the singed material. "I can't let you in on my secrets without you returning the favor. I'm sorry, but this is how this works for me."

He grimaces. "It's too risky for me to answer your questions."

Does he think he's the only one who has risks involved here? The disappointment is heavy, but I know what I have to do. I step back onto the sidewalk, my voice calm and my resolve strong. Maybe I'll regret this, but right now, I'm fresh out of options.

"I'm sorry, but I can't help you."

FOURTEEN

KHALI

I HOLD MY FATHER'S LIMP hand in mine. He's no longer feverish. He's cold. I don't know which is worse. Mother lays next to him, pressed against this back. She's asleep and her face is swollen with grief. Her dark hair is a tangle around her head. I've never seen her look so unkempt. It's unnerving. She won't say it, but I can tell she's starting to give up hope. How much longer can we go on like this? Someone has to do something.

And yet, nobody seems to be doing much of anything.

After my run in with Silas the other night, I've noticed more and more guards following me around. He must be keeping a closer eye on me. That, or King Titus decided to consider my father's words before as a real threat.

It all races back to me, the horror of it, the confusion, the terrible moment my father said I was going to die before succumbing to the hex. At first I didn't want to think on those words, but now that several days have passed, I can think of little else. If my father is right, and I'm in trouble, I need to know why. I want to know what I can do to stop it. But the Brightcaster cage is tightening around me each day, and if I don't get out soon, I fear I'll never find the answer.

"Alivia," I say. She doesn't stir. I say it again, just to double check that my mother is truly sleeping. There's no response, not even a flicker. Satisfied, I pull the pack I stashed out from underneath the bed along with the thick velvet cape, slipping them on. I go to the infirmary window and crawl out onto the ledge. If I fall, I'll shift and fly, so I know not to be afraid. But logic does little to calm my racing heart.

I only need to climb one floor down to get where I'm heading. My fingers grip the stone but it's harder to hold onto than I'd anticipated. In some places, I'm holding on with the tips of my fingers and the edge of my boots, nothing else. I keep my breath steady and force myself to move, climbing down inch by inch until I find the glass window pane.

I breathe out a sigh of relief. It's still unlocked, just as I'd left it.

I slowly push it open with my foot and stand on the window's edge, then slip silently inside. This part of the library is as empty at night as it usually is during the day. Tucked back in the corner with nothing but musty old books, people rarely venture back here. I'm quick to find the passageway hidden behind one of the shelves. I'm betting my life that nobody else knows this is here.

Once inside, I'm careful to keep my breath steady as blood thunders through my ears. My shaky fingers trail along the cold wall, urging me down a narrow set of stone steps. My vision strains in the pitch-black darkness. I've memorized every nook and cranny of this castle so this should be easy. At least, that's what I keep telling myself. But it doesn't mean I'm not terrified. I count out ten paces until I reach my target, and thankfully, the torch is right where Owen and I last left it. I draw on my fire elemental and light the flame. It will be enough to get me out of here.

There are mazes of secret passageways between Stoneshearth's walls, and Owen and I had spent most of our adolescence searching them out. Some are meant for the servants, some for the royals, but when we found this one, it was so filled with dust from disuse, we considered it ours. Now it's just mine. I swallow the lump in my throat and hurry along the path, careful to keep my footsteps quiet. What if others know about this passageway? It's unlikely, but possible. They could look for me here. They could be looking for me right now.

Around the castle are two thick walls I'll be able to go right under. One wraps around the castle itself and the other protects the village. I could fly over the walls, but that was how I got caught sneaking out a few years ago. It's not an option. I'll sneak through this passageway to where it exits near a pile of rocks next to the lake. Once I'm far enough away, I'll shift and my black dragon scales will camouflage me against the inky night. I'll fly far away from this place and begin my search. I won't return until I've found a cure for my father.

I pray that right now, the King assumes I'm still tending to Father's bedside as I've done all week. My mother is sleeping, but even when she wakes up, she'll still be a mess. She won't think to look for me right away.

I hear a scraping sounds behind me, like a boot catching against the edge of the wall. I stop mid-step. Gooseflesh prickles over my body. It could be an echo, or something from the other side of the wall, but I can't risk it.

I run.

I'm careful to keep my footsteps light and quiet. The fire of the torch lights the way, and I can only hope that if someone is following, they don't have the same advantage. After a few heart-pounding minutes, I approach the break in the path.

The left passage leads to back into the castle and the right path will take me to freedom. I go right.

I make it to the first wall in record time. One floor above, the castle guards patrol. As far as I know, there is no exit down here. They know the tunnels, as that's their job. But they don't know this one, because if they did, Owen and I would have seen them down here at least once.

The stone of the outerwall is different than the stone of the castle. It's thicker, blacker, and burrowed deep into the earth. I press my hand to its slightly damp surface, imagining it to be as old as the Gods themselves. Then I crouch low, to where the passageway will allow me to crawl out. From there I'll be able to follow an underground tunnel beneath the city.

My hand doesn't hit dirt, it hits rock. I pull it back, stunned. *There is no more tunnel.* It's caved in. I curse, tears instantly welling up. Desperation claws its way in, decimating my hope, as I try to think of a plan. I could use my earth elemental to get through the rocks, but it will be felt by those above, or it might cave in the rest of the tunnel. How did this happen? The King or Silas must have known this was the passage Owen and I had been using and closed it in. What am I going to do now? I have no other way out. I kick the wall and grit my teeth in frustration, wiping at my eyes.

Footsteps tap down the passageway behind me and I

freeze, quickly snuffing out the fire. I pray it's not Silas. I don't want to be alone with him. He scares me, sure, but at this point I'm more afraid of what I'll do to him. If I have the chance, I'll kill him. I know I can—at least, my dragon can. But I don't want to be a murderer, even if he deserves to die. I don't want him to take away another shred of my innocence.

"Khali?" a deep honeyed voice whispers. "It's okay. I'm not here to hurt you or turn you in."

"Bram?" I cry out, a little shocked, and scoot back out to stand. Magic travels through my hand, and I light the torch again, and sure enough, it's Prince Bram before me. His green eyes shine gold against the fire's glow, and they're filled with so much emotion, I have to step back. He's dressed head to toe in black, blending him into the darkness behind.

"You're running away, aren't you?" he asks. It's not an accusation but an observation. I see no point in lying so I nod.

"Why?" he questions further. "To get out of marrying my brother?"

"Silas is a monster," I reply, my voice sharp. "He murdered Owen. You need to watch your back around him. He'll kill you too if he feels threatened."

Bram twists his lips, thinking hard. He doesn't seem surprised. Sorrow flits across his features but so does acceptance. "You saw him kill Owen? You're sure it was him?"

He deserves to know the truth. "Not only am I sure, but your parents know it, too. They're blackmailing me to keep it all a secret."

Brams sighs. "I was afraid of that."

"You suspected?" I whisper, accusation rising. "Are you part of it, too?"

"My parents are very protective of the Brightcaster legacy," he says, his voice thick with disdain. "But I would never do something like that. Don't you know me better than that?"

I scoff. "I hardly know you at all."

"We've grown up together."

"Yes," I say. "But you've barely said more than two words to me at once."

He's quiet. It's not like he can argue with me. All those times we were forced to spend time together, he largely ignored me. And I him. The accusations he shot at me about Dean a few weeks ago were the only real conversation we'd ever had.

"If you run away," he says, "you won't be able to help your father."

I don't know if I can trust him. I want to.

"That's exactly why I'm running away," I say. What else can I do but admit the truth? I'm at a dead-end and I'm not going to hurt Bram. "I'll come back when I have figured out the cure to break the hex. I left a note hidden in my chambers indicating as much. Faros will find it. Only once I cure my father will I willingly become queen."

What I don't tell him is that I have no intention of letting my king be Silas. I no longer care about King Titus's threats against my parents. Somehow, I'll find a way to protect them in all of this. I expect Bram to argue with me, to try to convince me to return, but he smiles like I've impressed him.

"Fair enough."

I turn back to my ruined exit. "But I might have to resort to going back up to my chambers and flying away. My exit was destroyed."

He kneels down and eyes the area with a frown. "So it is. But flying out of here will never work. You'll be seen instantly. You won't get far."

I sigh, because I know he's right. "Do you have any other ideas?"

His eyes shine in the darkness, the cunning intelligence I've seen there a million times sparking within. "I know another way out," he says, "and I'll show you if you do something for me."

Of course his good news would come paired with a price. He is a Brightcaster, afterall. "What do you want?" My voice is guarded. The tunnel grows quiet. The scent of rock and dirt and smoke fill in the space between us.

"I want you to take me with you."

I shift back, shaking my head. "Are you serious? Why would you want to leave?"

"I have reason to suspect your father was crossing the border."

I shrug. "I already know that."

"But do you know where he was going? Do you know why? Do you have any leads at all? Because I do."

He's got me there and he knows it.

"Go on."

"I believe he's been visiting my brother Dean to make sure he's okay in his new life."

My eyes widen. "Do you know where Dean is?"

He's quiet for a moment, eyeing me as if calculating how much he can trust me. "I think he's in the human realm," he says matter-of-factly. "And I believe your father has been using the ley lines in the neighboring elfin kingdom to travel to Dean."

This is news to me. I can't even utter a coherent response. I would have never guessed this. Dean wasn't supposed to go to the human realm. He was supposed to be exiled into the larger continent to fend for himself and never to return to Drakenon again. But the human realm would be the safest place for him, even if slowly losing his magic would be torture.

"I wouldn't have put it past my father to have somehow helped Dean sneak into the human realm, not only as a favor to your parents, but because he loved Dean as much as we all did," I say quietly.

Bram nods, but doesn't say a word.

"I have no way to know if any of this is true," I grumble, wishing this were easier. The memory of that night when I kissed him trickles to my mind and I can't lie to myself anymore, Dean took the fall for me and willingly left. He almost seemed *resolved* to leave, like some kind of martyr. Why would he have done that if there wasn't something else going on beyond my comprehension?

"We can't know for sure if that's what happened given our limited information," Bram says, "but you're running out of options. And it gives you a tangible lead. We can go there together and find out if Dean knows what happened to your father."

I swallow, wanting to argue, but knowing I will not.

"Fine," I say. "Lead the way."

He nods once and turns. I notice the pack slung over his shoulders. So he assumed I would say yes? Or he just planned for the best? I have something similar on my back, it's not like I can blame him for preparing. A sudden suspicion leaves me cold. Could Bram have been the one to block this passageway, essentially forcing me to go along with his plan? He's smart enough to have thought out all of this. And if there's anyone who spends a lot of time in our musty library, it's him.

I don't have time to question him and nor do I want him to know my suspicions. So I keep my mouth shut and follow as he hurries back the way we came. He takes the left fork in the passageway, the one that leads back around to the castle's center, and navigates us through the labyrinth of passageways with more expertise than Owen or I ever had. How much about Bram have I underestimated?

Soon we make it past the first wall, under the city, and out past the outer wall. I step into the cool air and let it fill my lungs like a healing balm. I could leave Bram here. I could break my word and forget him. But I can't help but think he might be onto something with his hypothesis. He knows more about the world outside Drakenon than anyone I know, what with his nose constantly in a book. If anyone can help me solve this mystery, it's him.

We begin our journey by foot, careful to avoid detection. The castle is surrounded by vast fields and the miles-wide lake which I would do anything to avoid. Further away to the east is the sea. In the other direction are the mountains and plains. The kingdom stretches for thousands of miles, filled with our villages and people. Those families who are Dragon Blessed are the ones most likely to live in the capital city or close to it. The further out someone lives, means the less magic they'll have. Of course, I was the exception to that.

But my family and I were moved from our home and brought here. Stoneshearth's castle, the surrounding city, and the fields beyond are all I've ever known. With each step I take away from it, I'm met with both apprehension and relief. The Brightcaster family may have dominion over all I can see, but soon I will leave this behind where my life is no longer theirs to claim. Once I return, I'll save my father, and then I'll tell everyone the truth about Owen. Silas will pay for his crime, the Brightcasters won't have a Dragon Blessed heir, and I'll be free of their family for good.

FIFTEEN

HAZEL

I'M WALKING THROUGH CAMPUS THE following afternoon after leaving Dean standing there on that sidewalk, preoccupied with my busy mind, when I spot Landon and stop short. *The boy looks good.* He's lounging in one of the grassy areas with his friends, the sun lighting up his white blonde hair like a halo. I wish my hair did that. Mine is what we call "dirty," which is such a terrible but accurate description for the shade caught between two colors. At least I bothered to style it in loose curls today. His looks so good that I don't even mind how it's tied up in a manbun.

It's an unseasonably warm day for October and probably one of the last we're going to get for the year, so everyone is soaking it up. The women are in shorts and skirts, nobody has a coat, and apparently, some of the men have decided shirts are optional.

Landon and all his friends have their shirts off, and even from here, I can spot the dewy sweat on his tanned and muscled torso. I can also spot the myriad of girls making eyes at the half-naked dudes all lined up in a row. It seems none of us ladies are exempt from staring, not that I'm complaining. A bright yellow frisbee lays a few feet from their crew.

Feeling brave, I smile and walk over, picking up the plastic disc. "Are you guys practicing for your competitive frisbee league, or what's going on here?"

The four guys laugh up at me but my eyes are locked on Landon's. I can't help it. His dimples are showing and those baby blues are sparkling like crazy in this light, which is good because I don't want to get distracted by those abs. But my eyes flick down to ogle them anyway. He catches me looking and my stomach flips. Whoops!

"Freshman." He practically purrs my nickname. "Have a seat. Come meet my boys. Boys, meet *the* Hazel Forrester."

I hand him the frisbee and plop myself down on the grass next to Landon. He reaches in for a side hug. He's so attractive that I don't even mind the sweat, which is kind of gross. He introduces me to his friends, Tim, Garret, and some guy they've nicknamed Howdy.

"They're in my fraternity," Landon explains happily. "Tim's

the president. Garret is a ladies man. And Howdy's the fun drunk."

I nod and smile and try not to look judgy even though I totally might be judging them right now—Landon made it so easy introducing them that way. The three guys shake my hand and turn back to their conversation.

"And what does that make you?" I ask flirtatiously.

"I'm the serious one," he says. And then we both burst out laughing. If there's one thing I know about Landon, it's that he likes to keep things light.

We lay back on our elbows, gazing up at the expanse of clear blue sky.

"When is your next class?" he asks, scooting closer.

I close my eyes, letting the moment settle over me like a warm hug. "Actually, I'm done with classes for the day." I open my eyes and grin at Landon.

"Very interesting. So am I," he replies, his eyes lingering on my lips. My heart jumps to the point of heart attack status because I'm pretty sure we're going to make out soon!

"But I have to work in an hour," I add, a little disappointed.

He pouts, and I roll my eyes playfully. Landon and I have been flirting—mostly through text—for weeks now but we haven't gone on an official date. He hasn't asked. Maybe he won't.

I've seen him be as flirty with other girls in our Chemistry class. And the one time I went to his frat house for that party, he was dancing in the middle of a *circle* of sorority girls. He didn't even notice I was there. This chemistry between us is likely a result of his personality, having nothing to do with him actually wanting to date me. And as cute as he is, I'm young and inexperienced. I won't turn eighteen until Christmas break and if he knew that fact about me, he'd probably run for the hills, or at least wait until January to ask me out. Besides, I don't want to "get experienced" with some guy who only sees me as a booty call or a side chick anyway.

I have a feeling that's how most fraternity guys work around here.

I sit up, brushing the grass from my clothes. "Well, I just wanted to say hello but I'd better get going. I've got to get changed before heading in to work."

I stand and he jumps to his feet, wrapping me in a hug.

"Go out with me?" The request is confident.

I still, my whole body rooted to the spot.

"Like on a date?" I sputter.

He laughs and releases me, stepping back slightly. I must look startled because he laughs again. "Of course it's a date. I really like you, Fresh. When are you free for dinner?"

I don't want to sound too eager, but I totally am. "I don't work on Saturday or Sunday night."

"Sunday is great," he says, one of his dimples popping in his cheek. "I'll pick you up outside of the freshman dorm at seven." He catches me in another tight hug and as he lets me go, I spot his friends laughing at us over his shoulder. I'm not even a little bit embarrassed. Because I, Hazel Forrester, have a date with Landon Freemount, one of the hottest guys I've ever met in real life. Not as hot as Dean Ashton, but we're not going there. Not today, Satan!

I practically skip back to my dorm to get ready for work.

"HEY, THERE BIG GUY," I say, reaching out my hand. "Are you okay? Where's your home?"

The dog appears to be a stray. It's black scruffy fur is matted and it's skinnier than it should be for its hulking size. The poor baby was digging through some trash when I found it.

"C'mere, boy," I say, walking closer. "I can help you."

He takes a tentative step forward, looking at me with big watery eyes, when he tenses. He barks, the sound echoing through the alleyway, before skittering off.

Disappointed, I resolve to look for him again after work. He could use some love and there's nothing I'd rather do than help him.

Something prickles along the back of my neck, a rush of grasping awareness. I freeze, listening intently, and the feeling only grows.

Someone is following me.

Not someone of the dead variety. I'm used to that. No, whoever this is, they are very much human and very much *alive*. I keep my head still but my eyes dart from side to side, taking in the alleyway, the red brick buildings on either side, searching for signs that I'm not alone. I will someone to come out of one of the back doors or to turn down the alley from Main Street, but nobody does. I fumble to get my phone out of my pocket and quicken my steps, gathering the nerve to look behind me.

There's nobody there.

Nobody that I can see, anyway. But they *are* there. I know they are. I want to release the breath caged in my chest, want to relax. But I can't. Because I can still feel them. The awareness is like a boa constrictor, wrapping itself around me, disabling my ability to reason. Glass scatters across the concrete behind me and I turn around.

This time, I see him.

He's tall, over six feet, wearing dark jeans and a black windbreaker that's zipped all the way to his chin. He's sporting a gray ball cap that hoods his turned-down face.

I can't get a good enough look to gather more, to get an age or coloring or anything identifying. I'm stuck in static indecision, wondering what I should do next. Am I being paranoid? Something dark and ethereal flashes above him and I squint, unsure what kind of spirit I'm looking at.

He pauses for a second, and then runs toward me.

It happens so fast, the feelings and thoughts that jolt through my mind. Part of me wants to be logical, wants to assume the best, that this man isn't a threat. But the bigger part of me knows all the way to my marrow, to my atoms, and the space in between, that he wants to hurt me. That he's already chosen to hurt me. That if I don't get away right now, he will succeed.

I whip around and run. Blood rushes through my ears, the soundtrack of panic.

Why did I come this way? How could I have been so naive? At night, after closing up the shop, I always walk along Main Street back to campus. It only takes a few extra minutes and from there I can follow the populated and well-lit walkway down the main part of campus back to my dormitory. There are always people around. I'm never alone. Never afraid.

I usually take this route during the day as well. And yet, today, of all days, I didn't. What was I thinking? Girls have gone missing. There's a killer on the loose! I never should have ventured off anywhere this remote, even if it is the middle of the afternoon. But it's a good shortcut and after flirting with Landon earlier, my mind became a flighty moth of a thing and before long, I was running late. I hate being late. So I took the shortcut.

Maybe today the long way would have saved my life.

The thought drips in panic and I run even faster. But his soft footsteps are closer, his breath a steady cadence growing near. And he isn't slowing down.

Neither am I.

It's only a few more buildings until I'll be out in the open. I'm almost there. I can get there. I have to. I keep fumbling with my phone but it's a useless weight. I don't have the ability to run for my life and use it at the same time. So I grip it, hang on for dear life, and push my body harder.

I'm frantic, praying for someone to see me.

"Help!" I yell, my voice high and reaching. I don't know if anyone heard. If they did, they don't come.

The footsteps behind me don't slow.

Something catches and scrapes. "Shit," the man mutters in a low, growly tone.

I glance back. He's lying on the ground but he's quick to scramble to his feet. I take off again, running at full speed for Main Street. It probably takes thirty seconds but it feels like a millennia, like I'm in a thickening dream and I can't wake up. Once I stumble onto the sidewalk, I brave a look back.

The man is gone.

The adrenaline is still electric in my veins and my lungs are on fire, but he's gone. He's gone. Tears prick at my eyes and I can't get my breath to slow. I hurry to The Flowering Chakra, trying to make sense of what happened. Wanting to pretend it wasn't real. Wanting to cry.

As I'm about to enter the shop, I look around one last time to make sure the man isn't still following me. My phone clatters to the pavement and I yelp.

The spirit dragon is perched on the roof across the street. The sunlight shines right through it, almost to the point that it's absorbed by the creature, like the ghost is a black hole for energy and light. It's ghastly and hulking with reptilian eyes that pin me down, watchful and intelligent. Their blue sheen stands apart from the black, unsettling my defenses.

The dragon is quick. It stands, unfurling two massive wings. They span ten feet on either side, a monument of power. And then it jumps, diving down first and then flying in a swooping arc, disappearing down the same alleyway I just came from. Is it simply a coincidence or is the dragon going after my attacker?

I don't follow. I'm never going back there again.

"Are you okay?" a gravelly voice asks, and I nearly jump out of my skin. It's Dean. "What's going on? What happened?"

He towers over me, his bare arms crossed over his white t-shirt. His eyes dart around before zeroing in on me. I don't know what to say, and when I do open my mouth, nothing but a frantic gargle comes out.

"Did you see the dragon again?" A long strand of black hair falls in front of his coal eyes as he stares me down.

I blink, trying to process what just happened, my heart still racing.

"Hazel! Where did it go?"

His forceful tone snaps me from my trance and I point toward the direction of the alleyway. Dean takes off running, charging around the corner and disappearing from sight.

SIXTEEN

KHALI

BRAM IS AS QUIET AND observant, as per usual. And even now, with so much happening that we could talk about, he hardly utters a word. I don't mind. I don't have anything to say to him either.

We've spent a few hurried hours on foot, but we can't continue this way. As soon as we're discovered to be missing, the King will send his army after us. I've seen them training. I know how fast they are, how skilled. There's little time to waste.

"We need to move faster," I say, my voice carrying over the flat landscape. Even through my velvet cape, a chill brushes along my spine. It doesn't help that my long black dress still leaves an opening for the chill to nip at my legs. "I feel so exposed out here."

"Agreed." His voice is soft.

I let out a breath, scarcely believing what I'm about to offer. "If I change into my dragon form, you can ride on my back."

He stops abruptly, his eyes shining under the moonlight. "Are you sure?"

That's one of the things about dragon shifters: under no circumstances do we carry *anyone* on our backs. We're not pack animals. We have pride and to be forced to carry someone is considered shameful. Some even say it's an affront to the Gods, though I'm not sure they care about us as much as we think they do. I've certainly never carried anyone nor has Bram climbed on a dragon's hide—they'd probably take his head off for such a gross offense.

"I don't see any other way." I run my cold fingers along my long braid and tuck it over one shoulder, trying to come up with the right words so I don't further embarrass myself. "If we don't take to the skies while it's still dark, we're not going to cover enough ground. The second your father discovers that we're missing, there will be dragons flying in all directions to find us. We need to take advantage of our early start while we still can."

What I don't add is that if they find us together, Bram will be in more danger than myself. Dean was exiled for a single kiss. What would they do to Bram for running away with their future queen? Without my magic, there is no guarantee the next line of royal children will be elementals. And what's he going to do when we return to the castle? I'm sure he has some sort of plan, but I don't ask him. Not yet, anyway.

I try to meet his eyes but he's looking down at the space between us, considering my offer. His gaze is hooded, hiding his thoughts from me. I don't try to figure them out. I've never been able to figure out the puzzle that is Bram Brightcaster, but then again, I haven't made much effort when it comes to him.

"Well, what do you think?" I ask, my voice catching. He'd better not make me beg because I'd rather leave him out here to fend for himself. "I'm fine doing whatever we need to do to make this work, just as long as we stay away from the water."

He nods. "I remember what the merfolk did to you. I'm sorry you had to go through that."

"Don't." I hold up a hand and push away the memories. "I don't want to talk about it."

He nods and looks away, then points. "Let's fly south but we'll have to take cover during the day. We should be able to make it to the Jeweled Forest before morning. Once we're in there, we can travel by foot and nobody will be able to see us from the sky. No water involved."

The Jeweled Forest? My stomach twists into a knot.

It's a brilliant idea, of course, but even if I don't know very much about the place, I do know it's dangerous and forbidden. I'm momentarily struck with gratitude for Bram and all his studies to have thought of such a great idea. I wouldn't have known where to go to hide along my journey to the border had I gone alone.

I walk a few paces away from him and shift. Turning into my truest self always feels like salvation, like slipping into a hot bath or taking off a too-tight corset. The magic's work is quick. The glimmer rises from within, growing around me in an orb of shimmery air. Then in a blink, the human part of me, and everything I'm wearing, vanishes and my dragon form appears.

My black hide gleams, and I stretch my wings out wide. The hum of elemental magic is stronger when I'm in this form and it calls to me as naturally as breathing. I hear the grass moving beneath my feet and the wind whispers an ancient song as it rushes past my ears.

There's something else there, too. Something… unwelcome. It nags at the magic, trying to weaken it. Like a physical sprain on my elements. I fight back, pushing it down, until it goes. Worry trickles across my hide but I push that aside, too. I'll deal with it later.

I crouch down and Bram doesn't hesitate. He climbs on

my long back in between my wings. Once I'm sure he's secure, I launch off the ground. My wings pump and carry us up, up, up. If Bram is afraid, I don't sense it. His heart rate doesn't speed and his body doesn't tense. It's strange that he's probably never had this experience before. He doesn't know what it is like to fly. Not for the first time, I feel bad for him. He grips me tighter as I press forward, flying south toward the Jeweled Forest.

The hours pass by in a blur of thoughts and the constant flapping of my wings. I'm faster than most dragons, but carrying Bram slows me down slightly. He might not know the difference, but I can't stop worrying. This will be a disadvantage to us but there's nothing we can do.

I grow tired but I don't allow myself to slow. Finally, the sun crests over the horizon and relief washes over me. Not far off, a forest sparkles like a rainfall of diamonds fell onto the trees and stuck to their branches. I dive low for our destination, grateful we made it in time, but also a little worried that this place is as dangerous as I've heard. I fly over the tops of the towering trees until the light is too much; it bounces off the jewels and blinds me. I force myself to keep from shielding my eyes as I bring us to a clearing and land. Bram jumps off my back and I shift back to my human self.

"Are you doing okay?" Bram asks. "You're not too tired?

We covered a lot of ground."

I'm too distracted to answer. "It's so much more beautiful than I imagined." My voice is wistful as I stare at the enchanted landscape. Seeing it from above was nothing compared to standing among its brilliance. The trees don't grow leaves here. They grow the most beautiful of jewels. They range in every color and shape, from red rubies, to white diamonds, to bright green emeralds and everything in between. I step forward, my fingers reaching out to touch a sparkling blue sapphire. It's mesmerizing. The size of an apple. If only I could have it…

"Don't!" Bram slaps my hand away.

I gasp and turn on him, rubbing the injury. "What was that for?"

"Did you not pay attention to your geography tutor at all?" he challenges, exasperated. "Anyone who takes a stone from this forest will be cursed to sleep for a thousand years."

I blink. "I guess I *might* have heard that." In all honesty, I am certain I did during some lesson or another, and I'm also certain I didn't pay attention as Bram has pointed out. I swallow my pride. "Thanks for looking out for me."

It makes sense. Nothing so incredible as this would still be here if it didn't have this kind of protection. There are enough people in the kingdom who would exploit it, if not just for the riches, then for the ability to ease their load, for the ability to fill their childrens' bellies every night.

The Brightcaster royals have a treasury of jewels, but *nothing* compared to some of these. If they could have taken them, they would have. They take everything they want, and damn the consequences to anyone they have to trample over in the process.

My eyes travel from gemstone to gemstone. Some are bigger than my head. This place isn't natural and it's not meant for me. The gemstones don't call out to my earth elemental, not even a little. I didn't notice at first, I was too drawn in by the sheer beauty of them. How could I have missed something so important? The realization makes me nervous.

"Let's get going," Bram says. "When you're tired, let me know. We can rest and I'll take first look out."

We walk until the sun is high in the sky but we don't move nearly as quickly as I'd have liked. We're too scared to touch any of the jewels with our hands. I'll have to make up for this delay once the night falls by flying us again. The forest is thick, which also doesn't aid our speed. And it is eerily silent. Save for the crunching our boots make as we navigate through the trees, there's no other noise. We don't even come across any animals. No water, either. It's as if the trees here are surviving on magic alone.

Perhaps they are.

My eyelids grow heavy and after catching me trying to cover a yawn, Bram insists we take a break. We find the tallest tree and settle beneath its generous canopy of glittering branches. The forest floor is littered with gems so we use our boots to clear a space, careful not to touch anything with our bare hands. I lay my thick, black cape out and curl on top of its velvety surface in a tight ball. Bram sits on a tree stump and turns away. My breathing slows and within a few minutes of closing my eyes, my mind drifts off to sleep.

SOMEONE SHAKES ME GENTLY, TWO steady hands of sunlight. Bram's hands. I blink to the setting sun and to him leaning over me. In an hour or two, it will be dark enough for us to fly. Red rims his eyes, brightening the green. He mumbles something about not letting him sleep too long and then he lays down, using his pack for a pillow and falls asleep almost instantly. I'll let him sleep until the second the sky is black, and then we're getting out of here.

I relax with my back to the wide trunk and root around in my pack, pulling out the block of cheese wrapped in beeswax cloth, one of the apples, and the heavy waterskin.

I started gathering supplies the day after I ran into Silas in the hallway. It was then I knew, I was leaving. Luckily, I don't have to ration the water because of my water elemental. Should I need more water, it will be easy to gather by calling it to me. But I only eat enough food to barely satisfy the hollow ache in my stomach. Food might be harder to find in the coming days.

"Khali..." a male voice sing-songs in tickling whispers. I whip around to Bram, but he's still fast asleep, his breathing steady and messy hair blowing slightly in the wind.

I still myself and listen hard, but several minutes pass by in silence. Maybe it was in my mind, a response to exhaustion.

"Khali," the voice whispers again, louder this time, and also seemingly from farther away. This is definitely not in my head and it reminds me of a voice I know as well as my own. But no. How could that be possible?

I hold my breath and listen harder, my heart wild in my chest.

"It's me," the voice says. "It's Owen."

I blink in disbelief. Could it be? My ears are playing tricks on me. Surely, that's all this is. I ignore it and busy myself with repacking my items, tucking the rest of the cheese at the bottom. The second I finish with the pack and everything falls back into silence, the voice is there again.

"Khali, come here. Come talk to me." It does sound like him.

This can't be real. And I can't move from my spot.

And there is that part of my mind, that logical part, which knows it's all a trick and I should wake Bram. We should leave this forest, sunset or no. Because something about this forest is utterly wrong. But that part of my mind fades to the other part, the part that is desperate to talk to Owen, pulled in by the enchantment like a moth to the flame.

I stand as quietly as I can.

I'll just go see what this is and come right back. Maybe Owen is speaking to me from beyond the grave. I've heard stories of the Gods allowing it. It's not impossible.

I leave my pack and cape where they are and creep through the forest toward the direction of the voice. The glittering gems don't entice me but I'm still aware of them and avoid them, even though they shine brightest in the setting sun. They have little hold over me compared to Owen. He coaxes me forward like nothing else would.

"This way," he says, his voice a feathery whisper on the wind. "That's right. Just over here. You're close."

I speed to match the thudding of my heartbeats. The more I walk, the more the need to find Owen overpowers me, pulling me forward. Soon it is the only thing that matters and I'm running.

"You're almost here," his voice says in that teasing, happy way of his. I smile. I've missed him so much.

My boot catches on a fallen tree and I stumble, going down hard. My momentum carries me over the rest of a hill and I'm rolling, branches and stones pummeling my exposed skin. I squeeze my eyes shut and tuck my arms in against the pain, fisting my hands against my chest. It all happens so fast. I'm spinning and then I'm not. I blink, the beginnings of winking sun momentarily blinding my vision. I find myself on flat earth and sit up with a groan to glare at the hill that I just tumbled down.

"Owen?" I ask, rubbing the side of my head. I pull my fingers away to find blood and wince. "Where are you?"

"Over here," the voice replies.

Once again, I'm confused if I'm hearing it in my head or aloud. But does it matter? It's Owen! "Over where?"

"Don't you see me?" the voice continues. "Look up. I'm right here."

I search the forest and then I see… something.

"Is that you?"

"Yes," he says, breathy. Eager.

"Why are you lying like that?" I rush forward to my friend. He's lying on his front, his face buried in the dusty ground.

And he's dressed funny, not in his normal princely attire, but in aged clothing that's practically rotting off his body. But his hair is that same dusty blonde curly mess and his skin is the tanned honey I know so well.

I kneel at his side and roll him toward me. "Owen?"

I yelp. The man that stares up at me isn't Owen. Before my eyes, his hair turns to orangish copper, and his face changes to that of an older man's. His brown eyes are glassy, vacant. But his skin is warm, his cheeks pink. A light breath of exhaled air tickles my arm.

"Who are you?" I growl.

Gripped in his hands are piles of gemstones and then I know.

I stumble away, scurrying across the dirt floor on my hands and knees until I can manage to stand.

"Where are you going?" the voice calls after me. It still sounds like Owen but I know that it is all an illusion. I don't know if it's the man somehow doing this, or the forest, but I'm not going to stay and find out.

"Khali, come back," the voice laughs. "It's not so bad here. You might like it."

Tears burn my eyes and I glance around the clearing. Horror overpowers me at what I find. There are *more* people here. At least ten more. And all are lost to a cursed slumber with shining gemstones clenched in their hands. The trees grow around them and over them as if they don't exist.

I need to get out of here.

I run back, trying to find the way I came in, fighting with the hem of my dress, climbing the hill, holding my hands in tight, fighting the barrage of panic. I'm almost to the top when I see a woman. She's flat on her back with a peaceful expression on her sleeping face. Her eyes are closed, and her raven hair curls around her in perfect symmetry. She looks to be young, my age. But her dress is of a style from centuries ago. Her bowed lips and cheeks are painted cherry red. Straight through the center of her stomach, a silvery sapling grows, encrusted with spiky rubies.

It's not magic that the trees feed on. It's not the elements. It's blood.

I scream.

SEVENTEEN

HAZEL

"YOU LOOK LIKE YOU JUST saw a ghost," Harmony says the moment I step into the shop.

I point at her. "So. Not. Funny." But I'm shaking, and even though I want to sound like my happy-go-lucky self, my voice doesn't come out even a little bit playful. The tone is akin to a strangled kitten. Not cute.

She wiggles her gray eyebrows but stops short when I shuffle closer. "No, really, you don't look right, Hazel. Are you okay? What happened?"

I swallow, not quite sure how to put it into words. "Someone followed me," I finally choke out. "He chased me down that back alleyway between Main and Crestmont."

Her eyes widen into milky-blue saucers and she closes the distance, wrapping me in a motherly hug. I sink into her, tears springing instantly.

"I can't believe I didn't see that coming," she mutters. "I'm *so* sorry. Paths can change so quickly, I don't always see these things in time. But I'm *so* glad you're okay. I don't want to think about what would have happened if you'd never showed up for your shift today."

"Neither do I."

She takes my hand in her weathered palm and leads me to the little back room where we do the readings. "I'm going to call the police. They can come take your statement in here."

I want to say no, want to put this whole thing behind me and pretend it wasn't real, that it didn't happen. But I also want the police to catch this guy, whoever he is, because he's still out there and it's very possible that he's the creep responsible for the missing women. He could come back for me. But why? What's the pattern? What am I missing? What am I forgetting? I can feel the truth nagging at me, so close to coming into focus, but I can't see it yet.

"I didn't get a good look at him," I mutter hopelessly, falling into the soft brown couch and sinking into its homey caress. I can finally breathe again, but it doesn't help. I can't stop shaking. I sit on my hands.

"That's okay. We still need to report it."

An hour later, the police have come and gone. I told them

everything I could. Of course, I left out the encounter with the spirit dragon—or any spirits—because I'm not a moron. The police were eager to write down every bit of info like it could be the missing puzzle piece. And maybe it could be. The head detective, a stout, balding man with a wiry mustache, left me his card in case I remember anything else or run into trouble. I hold the flimsy cardstock between my fingers, staring at the black ink: Detective Sanders. I quickly type the number into my phone, saving it to my contacts, then shove both items into my pocket.

The surreal terror of the afternoon has started to fade into the quiet of newly minted evening. I don't know when I stopped shaking but I'm calm now. And exhausted. My eyelids are anchors but I'm terrified that if I close them and sink into sleep, I'll end up reimagining the incident over and over again, unable to escape it.

Harmony pops her head into the back room, looking me up and down with pity. And I hate it. A fresh anger burns bright against my ribcage. How dare this guy take something away from me? I don't want to spend the rest of my life looking over my shoulder, let alone the rest of the school year. And the worst part is, there's nothing I can do about it. He was going to hurt me. No question about it. And if he was so brazen in broad daylight, who else has he hurt? What else has he gotten away with?

"I'll be giving you a ride home after work from now on," Harmony says matter-of-factly, snapping me from my torrent of angry thoughts. "Even if you're working the shop alone, I'll come back at closing and take you back to your dorm. And we have cameras here. Keep that detective's number on speed dial."

"You hired me to make your life easier."

She tilts her head. "So what? I don't want you out walking in the dark, at least not until they catch that man. Okay?"

I nod once. "Okay," I say, but in my head I'm thinking about the possibility of them not catching that man, or anyone. That whoever chased me today, and whoever hurt those girls, will get away free and clear. Free to live their sick life. Cora, the true crime-obsessed girl that she is, informed me and Macy that a third of the murders in the United States go unsolved. So that's a fun statistic to keep in my back pocket right about now.

I stare at the lavender wall, studying the way the plaster underneath creates the faintest pebbly pattern. The anger from moments before has been eaten by an emptiness, a hollowness that scares me. I spring up and brush myself off. "Enough of that," I say. "I'm not going to wallow in what happened or feel sorry for myself. It's over. I'm lucky to be here. And I'm not going to think about that creep anymore or let him stop me from living my life."

"Oh, honey," Harmony sighs. "I think we should close up early tonight--"

"No!" I cut her off so abruptly that she jumps. "I want to stay busy. I need it. Give me something to do, please. Let's just go on, business as usual."

She wrings her hands together. Her dreadlocks are piled on top of her head, like a basket of wiry snakes, but her eyes are kind and her rosemary and sage scent is a familiar balm to my emotional wounds.

"Are you absolutely sure?" she asks carefully.

"I'm absolutely, infinitely, utterly sure. Please, I need this. I need to work."

Harmony stares for a long second before her eyes become hazy, like she's seeing right through me. Probably to my "paths". Her eyes stay like that long enough for me to get nervous. But then they clear and she nods, relaxing into an easy smile.

"Yes," she says. "I have a new client who's interested in a reading. She's from out of town and called in last night. She'd like to meet you. And I think it will be okay. Despite what happened today, I see it as a positive path for you to take."

"Let's do it," I say, pushing down any lingering feelings of fear or worry. Time to move forward.

"I haven't met her in person yet," she continues. "So I don't know any specifics as to how the reading will go because I can only see her paths if I can get close. I see it going well for you, but I don't—"

"It will be fine," I cut her off like I have all the confidence in the world. I think back to Dean, and how I refused to work with him and what a disaster that whole experience was. But that was last week and that was different. Since then, I've done three readings for Harmony's best clients. Each one was just as she said it would be. Easy and natural. All I had to do was go into that quiet room with them, invite any spirits of the light to join us, and tell the clients what images I saw.

I couldn't always make sense of what the images meant, but that wasn't my job and nobody seemed to mind. The clients knew what to make of the images that came into my mind. And by the end of the hour-long session, all three clients left in tears. They would smile and thank me for a job well done and head over to the cash register to pay. It felt good. It felt like I was turning my curse into a gift, into a future, like Mom always said I could.

Maybe doing it again today will soften the empty feeling in my gut.

THIRTY MINUTES LATER, THE CLIENT arrives. She's polished and put together in the kind of "high-gloss" way that doesn't fit into an earthy place like The Flowering Chakra. But then again, Dean didn't fit in here either. I've learned not to jump to conclusions about who needs this woo-woo stuff. Everyone probably needs some version of it. Not that half of the population would even consider it. But then again, people can be full of surprises.

Surprises and secrets.

The client tiptoes into the shop like she's not meant to be here and is desperate not to touch anything, like the crystals might reach out and bite her. When her manicured fingers smooth out a sheath of crimson hair, a massive diamond ring catches the light. Her high heels click-clack on the wood floors.

I blink at her, worry sweeping wide. Will she believe a word I say?

Harmony greets her with a smile but after a few moments, she shakes her head and puts her hand on the woman's shoulder. "Are you sure you want to do this? It might be harder on you than you realize."

"What?" the woman sputters. "Of course! I came all this

way. I've been on standby to meet Hazel."

"No," Harmony continues. "I've changed my mind. Hazel had a bit of a scare today. She isn't in the right frame of mind to do this reading."

All my senses are alive, trying to figure out why there's a sudden change in Harmony. Her tone is protective, so it must have something to do with getting a look at this woman's future paths. But it doesn't matter. I want to do the reading. I want to be distracted, even if I'm not in the right frame of mind.

I hurry over to intervene. "I can do it," I assure them both, offering a pleasant, and totally fake, smile.

The woman's eyes soften when she takes me in, and Harmony looks like a ripened tomato, her face has grown so red. She keeps shaking her head. I know this is Harmony's shop, this is her thing, and I need to trust her. But right now, I don't care. I must take my mind off that alleyway and what could have happened if that man hadn't tripped.

"Right this way," I say brightly and lead the woman back into the lavender room. Before Harmony can stop us, I close the door. Now it's just me and this woman and the unknown of whatever's next.

If this lady were an animal, she'd be one of those million dollar race horses. Everything about her is power and money and winning at life. And her eyes are alight with so much gratitude for me that I don't know what to do with it. I don't want to let her down. I gesture for her to have a seat so we can get started.

"What's your name?" I ask, settling into my chair.

"Evangeline Connelly." She has a slight southern accent and there's an alarm in the back of my mind. Like I should know that name. Do I? I eye her again, but I've never seen her before today.

"I now invite any spirits, angels, or guides of the light to enter the room with me and Evangeline Connelly." I unclasp my obsidian necklace and place it on the side table.

They come. They materialize, surrounding her on all sides. Ancestors, and what I've figured out are guides by they way they glow like a nightlight is lit from within. And then there are the angels. She has two. They stand on either side of the room, stoic and massive.

I've seen all this stuff since I was a child. But the angels don't always show themselves, so when they do, it's hard not to stare. They look exactly like they're depicted in the Bible. Gigantic wings and warrior-like garb and massive energy. But they never say anything to me. They don't show me images. They don't interact. Ever. I'm sure they're here for a reason, but I can't say what that reason is. All I know is they're not *my* angels, they're hers.

It's the spirits, the ghosts of those who've lived here before, that I can connect with, that can send me the images. And it's one of them in particular that I now gape at.

Charlene Connelly.

She was that freshman girl who went missing two years ago. She looks exactly like the photos that popped up in the news over the weekend. They never found her body. Now I know why.

I look down at my hands. They're shaking again.

"Do you see her?" Evangeline Connelly asks gently, breaking the tension. "Do you see my daughter? Is she dead?" Her voice is laced with the kind of deep unresolved sadness that reaches into my soul and rips it wide open.

I don't want to be the one to tell her. But I have to.

I take a deep breath and meet her eyes. They're hopeful. They're broken. They're two years of living without knowing what happened to her daughter.

"Please, just tell me. I need to know. Is she dead?"

"Yes. I'm sorry."

She nods, the pain seeming to settle in deep, but also, some other emotion right along with it. Something I can't quite name yet. "Is she okay?"

I look over the woman's shoulder to where her daughter

hovers. Oftentimes I see the spirits caught in between this life and whatever comes next. I don't know where they go. They don't either, I don't think. They seem to be stuck here, trapped by the things that happened to them on Earth.

But not always.

Sometimes they come through from a far off place that I *can't* see, traveling to come to me. Sometimes they're happier than anyone walking this earth. And as for Charlene, her smile is genuine and she glows with the light of pure, unfiltered joy. And when I look at her, I don't see the pain, or the horror of what happened to her, or a young woman who had her life stolen away. I wish I could somehow allow Charlene's mother to see her this way.

"Yes, she's okay," I say. "Sometimes what I see is... disturbing. But with your daughter, all I see is her happiness. She's smiling. She's full of love. She's at peace."

Tears fall from Evangeline Connolly's eyes. Moisture instantly pools in mine, too.

"Do you know what happened to her?" she asks, so hopeful and needy.

I was afraid of this. I almost don't want to know what happened to this girl. I'm afraid of what I'll see. But I do ask because I must. For Evangeline's sake, but for mine too. Mine and every other young woman at Hayden College. I look up at the peaceful spirit hovering over her mother and ask the question that can only have a terrible answer.

I meet Charlene's gaze. "What happened to you? Will you show me?"

But she doesn't show me anything of her death. No water, like with Katherine's ghost. No death or screaming or terror, like with so many others. Instead, her spirit shows me a memory, a memory she wants me to share with her mother.

"She's seven years old," I begin. "Charlene is in first grade and she doesn't want to go to school because the other girls have become friends and have left her out. You and Dad don't let her stay home. Nobody is allowed to stay home from school unless they're sick. Not her two older brothers, either. It's the rule."

Evangeline nods along, mesmerized by the story, as if she's seeing it all again in real time.

"But on the drive to the elementary school, just as Charlene is about to burst into tears in the back seat, you look at her through the rearview mirror and you tell her that it's a girl's date day. Then you turn away from the school and the two of you spend the day shopping at the mall and go to the movie theater to see *The Emperor's New Groove*."

"She loved that movie," Evangeline says, tears streaming down her face. I hand her the box of tissues and she dabs at her makeup gingerly.

"She loved it because *you* made it special. After that day, the two of you kept the girl's date day a secret, a secret that became a yearly tradition. Once a year, you would ditch school and work and do the same thing, go shopping and then eat a bunch of candy and popcorn while watching a matinee."

Evangeline is ugly crying now. There's no other way to describe it. And I probably am too. This was not what I expected would happen when I saw Charlene's spirit. But I couldn't stop the tears even if I tried. It's not fair, what happened. She died with her whole life ahead of her.

"Thank you," Evangeline finally whispers.

"I don't know what happened to your daughter and she doesn't want to show me. Sometimes they do, sometimes they don't."

Her lower lip trembles. "I guess I can accept that."

"But I do know that her soul is at rest now. She's happy. And she wants you to move on and be happy, too. And she wants to thank you for being the best mother she ever could have asked for."

Evangeline wipes at her tears and nods. A smile cracks her face, a real one, this time. Not the fake glossiness from before. A peaceful feeling settles over the room and she stands, reaching for my hand, pulling me into an embrace.

"You remind me of her, you know?" she says against my ear. "Something about your eyes. They sparkle the same way hers did. And you're a helper. You care about people. She did, too. She wanted to be a doctor, cure cancer, save the world."

"She still cares about people. She cares about you."

"Thank you." Her hug tightens.

"You're welcome."

She steps back and gazes deep into my eyes. "Be careful out there."

"I will," I whisper.

She nods once but she's not convinced. "I'm leaving this town tomorrow and I'm never coming back. But you don't get to leave. You have years of school, but can you feel it?"

"Feel what?"

"There's something dark about this place. Something that killed my daughter."

My breath catches and fear builds up inside me like an incoming storm. I nod because I know what she's saying is the truth. There's something terrible happening in this town and for some unknown reason, it's only getting worse.

When I walk her outside, I forget to bring my necklace. I realize the loss of its weight around my neck the same moment Evangeline's warning is confirmed. Not only is Kathrine's spirit hovering over the sidewalk, ghostly water dripping down into a supernatural puddle, but so are the other women. Tessa is there, the girl who went missing last year. And the high school cheerleader. She breaks the pattern. She wasn't in college, she was only seventeen.

She wears her fitted white and red uniform, a large W embroidered over her chest, for Westinbrook High. Her long ice-blonde hair hangs plastered against her face, her mouth gaunt, her eyes bloodshot. All three spirits shoot images at me at once, images of their lives, of their lost hopes and dreams, and worst of all, of drowning, of water filling their lungs until their consciousness washed away. It takes over my vision, cold and final.

I don't stick around. I sprint back to the reading room and slap the necklace around my neck, falling onto the couch with choking breaths, as if I'm the one drowning.

EIGHTEEN

KHALI

"BRAM!" I SCREAM AND THEN force myself to be silent. I'm afraid to listen, afraid the cursed forest will mess with me again and confuse me with its ghost whispers. But I can't leave Bram here. I can't do this alone.

I stumble forward, battling wild emotions and wicked branches. The sun has almost set. My lungs burn against shaky sobs and my vision blurs behind a veil of tears. Where is he? I need to get out of here. I can't stay another second, especially not once darkness falls. My heart pounds and my hands shake and the trees press in around me. I need to shift and fly away.

"Bram, w-where are you." My voice catches and more tears erupt. I was never much for crying but ever since Owen's death and my father being hexed, I can't seem to stop.

More voices call out to me. Are they the voices of the dead? Are they linked to the trees, part of the enchantment of the forest itself? My elementals roar to life under my skin and I welcome them, tucking them close to my heart like a security measure. Panic races through me when I realize they're dimmed again, just as they've been on and off over the last few weeks.

What is happening to me? Am I losing my powers? As I get closer to my eighteenth birthday, I should be growing stronger, not weaker. I choke out a sob.

"Khali!" Bram yells.

I search for him, praying he's real.

"Bram?" I call louder. "I'm over here!"

And then he appears, fear etched into his face. Sweat beads across his brow and his eyes are frantic as they search me out. My sobs continue, but now in relief. What would I have done if I was all alone out here? Would I have taken one of the jewels and been cursed to the same fate as all those sleeping people? I stumble over the brush and send the Gods a silent prayer that I'm still standing. Bram's warm arms wrap around me, pulling me in close.

"Khali," he says, his voice hoarse. "It's okay. I've got you."

He tucks my body against his. The plane of his chin brushes the top of my head, and I turn my face into the hollow of his neck.

"It's okay," he says, over and over as I continue to cry.

I'm surrounded by scents of oak and cherries and comforting earth. He smells of life. The magic may have skipped him, but in this way, it clung to him. I've never been held like this before. A prickle of calm runs through me and I rub away the tears, feeling a bit foolish but also grateful. Then I untangle myself and tell him what happened.

He's quiet as he takes it all in, glancing around the sparkling forest of gems with a sour expression. It's not too far away that those bodies lie, twisted beneath the forest's grip. The sun has almost set, and in a few minutes we can leave. But I can't talk to him telepathically through the dragon link so we need to talk about this now.

"Why do you think that happened?" I ask.

His green eyes flash, and he runs a worn thumb along his lower lip as he thinks. "You're the most powerful Dragon Blessed on the continent. This forest won't be the only dangerous thing attracted to that. I knew the forest was enchanted but I didn't know it could speak to someone's mind. There are no documented cases of this happening in the history texts, probably because anyone who wakes up after a thousand years spent here has probably lost their mind. It could be that many who wake up here are trapped in the trees."

I blink, horrified. To be trapped within these monstrous trees? A soul should be free after death. How can something so beautiful be so misleading?

He clears his throat. "I'm so sorry, Khali. I shouldn't have—"

"It's not your fault," I quip.

His lips press into a flat line, jaw popping. A lock of chestnut hair brushes his cheek and shines golden in the sunset. The planes of his face are cut almost as sharply as the gems surrounding us. He suddenly looks much older than I remembered. He almost looks like Dean and that makes my heart ache.

"Come on," I say. "Let's get out of here. How much farther do we have?"

He searches the last bits of coral sky flashing through the jeweled canopy. "We're close. Maybe a few hours flight," he says. "But we need to be careful. No doubt the army is out in force searching for us."

We start to walk back to our spot under the tree where we left our packs.

"That's true, but once we cross the border, they won't follow us," I say confidently. We'll be faced with other issues, but at least this one will be over and done with for now. Keeping inside our borders is part of why the Brightcasters' have been so supported in their reign. The kings might have had their spies over the years but the wards keep our enemies from coming in and we don't risk leaving. Save for the merfolk, who tend to keep to themselves, our people are the only ones inhabiting this land.

"They won't risk the army and weaken the wards, not for my sake."

"I wouldn't be so sure about that," Bram laments. "Do you forget how important you are to this kingdom? To my family?"

I bite my lip and look away. I've heard this kind of talk my entire life. I don't need to hear it now, not when my mission is so important. Father is counting on me. And besides, it's not like I won't be back. I still have to take down Silas!

I rub my boot into the dirt and fight the thought, the wish, to never come back.

"We just need to leave," I say. "Now."

He studies me carefully and then continues walking. "After we cross the border, we will be in Fae territory. You know what to expect?"

"I think I do."

"You need to be prepared for anything. The Fae are immortal beings comprised of different races of faeries and elves and the like. They can be killed but their ageless existence has made them extra cunning and equally dangerous, especially the High Fae." He sounds like he's reading from a textbook. He sounds like the Bram I know, not this new one full of adventure.

"But their magic is elemental, like mine, so shouldn't they be similar?"

He twists his mouth, thinking for a while, before speaking. "We don't know the full extent of what they can do. They had their own secretive courts and kings until the Sovereign Occultists conquered them, killing off all the royal lines in one swoop. There are barely any High Fae elves left as far as I know."

I bite my lip. That could be our kingdom next if we're not careful.

"We're heading into unknown territory, occupied by the most ruthless empire ever to rule in Eridas, so we need to be careful. Anything could happen."

His words leave me hollow and I suck in a breath, trying to fill myself back up. Even though I want to take to the sky right now, we need to have this conversation first.

"You're right. I didn't know all the rules to this wicked forest and I won't make that mistake twice. So remind me of what I might need to know."

"You can eat the food and drink the wine," he says, "but since my blood isn't magicked, I can't. And if we come across anyone, we do not want to make enemies, but we absolutely can't make any deals. Their magic is far more binding than ours. If we make a deal and we break it, it could kill us."

We fall silent, letting that truth settle over us.

"They can't tell lies, though," I add, remembering that part. I always thought that would be odd, but also useful for a court such as ours. "That's to our advantage."

"But they can tell half-truths," he says. "They are shifty. Don't trust any of them."

I gulp. "Okay. And you know where the ley line to get to Dean is?"

"I have a pretty good idea," he says, but he doesn't add more and I don't press him. If anyone can find it, it's Bram.

I'm not sure what to expect. Ley lines can't be seen, they can only be felt. Three realms sit on top of each other but operate independently: the magic, the spirit, and the non-magic. The ley lines are energetic lines connecting significant places and sometimes where they cross, the energy is magnified so much that those with elemental magic can move between the realms. It would make sense that when Dean was exiled, my father helped him cross through to the human world where he would be able to live in safety. My father doesn't have dragon magic, so he couldn't cross into the human world alone; Dean would have had to have helped him as well.

There *are* a few advantages to being nonmagical in this world, mainly that magical beings can't sense the nonmagical, nor do magical beings really care to be bothered by those without magic. Maybe that's why King Titus sent him.

The thought of crossing realms gives me pause. I remember Owen's words at dinner the night he was killed, finding the hole in his ideas. "Why would the Occultists need us to cross if they've conquered the Fae? Couldn't they have crossed into the human realm with Fae magic?"

"I've been wondering the same thing," he says. "And I'm afraid I only have a flimsy theory. They must have tried, but they might need all of us. Why else would they be moving from kingdom to kingdom, conquering every magical race?"

The thought hardens my stomach. "We can't get caught," I whisper.

"No," he replies. "We can't."

His theory solidifies why King Titus would be using my nonmagical father to cross into Fae territory instead of one of the Dragon Blessed. My father, the bravest man I know, would have agreed.

I need to draw on his strength now. I need to be like him.

I hold Bram's gaze for another long moment, taking in the intensity of his green eyes until I can't handle another second and look away. We've reached the place where we rested, our packs untouched and waiting for us. I wrap the cloak around my chilled body and drape my pack over my shoulder, Bram's too, then shift into my dragon form. When I shift, the clothes and packs disappear and shift with me, held to me by some unseen force.

Bram isn't shy this time as he climbs onto my back.

I'VE NEVER SEEN THE BORDER before. I've heard the stories, seen artists' depictions, but as we get closer, my heart speeds in anticipation. I didn't expect to be able to *feel it.* Even from here, miles away, the energy buzzes through me and pulls me closer, like gravity. The magic of the wards are the same magic of my four elementals, but I've never heard of this happening to anyone else. I long to ask Bram but I cannot in this form and we can't stop.

Firelight twinkles in the distance. A nearby village. I'm careful to steer clear. Since there are less villages and people this close to the border, I'm able to fly low, but those lights leave me uneasy. With the wards' energy crackling through me, I feel safer down here, more grounded. I want to be as close to my land for as long as possible. I want to turn back. To stop. To keep going. I want everything and nothing and the riot is maddening.

Finally, the border rises up in front of us, an iridescent wall of fog reaching too high to fly over. The warring energies settle into one smooth thought: I cannot pass through.

But I must.

I land us in a field of grass, a dozen paces from the wall. Bram jumps off my back, and I return to my human form.

He must see the fear in my eyes because he takes my hand.

It would be so easy to turn back. I'm safe here. I matter here. I'm going to be the next Queen and even if Silas ends up as my husband, I could live a semi-happy life. My people need me. They need me to bring them more elemental royal heirs; for it's only the elemental magic that keeps these wards strong. Dragon Blessed is not enough on its own. If that magic was lost, the wards would fall and we would be thrust into war. If the Occultists conquered everyone else, what would make us so different?

I swallow my fear and think of my father, lying in his deathbed. I think of Dean, living a new life because of my choices. I think of Bram, who has come so far and risked everything to help me. These thoughts, they urge me forward.

I squeeze Bram's fingers tight. "Let's go."

Together, we walk through the fog and into an uncertain future.

NINETEEN
HAZEL

"I CAN'T BELIEVE YOU'RE DOING this," I mutter to myself. Just yesterday I was chased down an alleyway and giving a statement to the police. And today? Today, I'm skipping anthropology class to go sneak around Dean Ashton's house.

Alone.

Because he knows something about that dragon spirit, the same spirit I saw go after my would-be attacker, the spirit he was desperate to find. There's a connection. I don't believe Dean is the murderer, my instincts tell me not to fear him, but there's more going on than meets the eye and if he won't tell me, I'm going to figure it out myself.

I don't meet Cora and Macy at the dining hall to eat breakfast before class like we've been doing all semester. Instead, as I leave the dorm building, I text Macy a quick excuse and veer in the opposite direction, tugged toward Dean's neighborhood. The gray sweep of clouds and gusty autumn wind add a wintery bite to the air, sharpening my senses.

Nobody seems to notice me in the midst of their morning hustle once I'm walking down the suburban streets. Sleep-rumpled parents are busy ushering bright-eyed children onto overheated school busses. Commuters pull out of garages, strapped into shiny vehicles, already tuned in to their favorite radio stations and podcasts. It doesn't take long to locate Dean's house, but I walk right past the brick cottage and wait much further down the street until the man himself comes through the front door, locking it behind him. He doesn't see me or even look my way as he heads toward class.

A couple of minutes after he's gone, I stroll back to the house, keeping an eye on the neighborhood. The morning rush has come and gone in a mad dash and once again, the street is empty. No cars. No kids. No parents. But it might not last. I need to be quick.

I saunter up his driveway like I'm a regular guest of Dean's and go for the garage. I don't know the code to get inside, but there's a gate along the white vinyl fence that's my target. If there's a padlock, I'm screwed. But sweet mercy, there's nothing but a latch. I slide it up and open the gate just enough to slip into the backyard. This guy must not be too worried about security if he doesn't even lock his gate. I wonder why not? That in and of itself comes with its own suspicions.

It's as well kept back here as it is out front. No surprises there. I hurry past the aging trees, heavy with their dying leaves, my shoes crunching on the yellowing October grass. My lungs inhale steadying breaths, the brisk scent of the morning filling me up. The back porch is covered. None of the back neighbors will be able to see what I'm about to do, thank God.

I try the sliding door first but it's locked, as expected. I go for the adjoining window next and press my face against the large pane of glass, eyeing the modern living room and kitchen inside. I don't see signs of a security system anywhere, no cameras or monitors or anything. Is it really worth it? Breaking and entering is a crime. I could get caught. If I do, what will happen to me? Will Dean press charges? Will I get expelled from school? All my dreams of vet school and a career helping animals heal could be washed away.

Hopefully, Dean was telling the truth when he said he lives alone.

I palm a nearby rock before I can talk myself out of what I'm about to do and throw it squarely at the window. It crashes through, the glass splintering and falling to chaos.

The wind is almost enough to drown out the noise. Not quite. I pray nobody heard it but me. Adrenaline storms through my veins. My nerves kick into overdrive.

I can't believe I'm doing this! I am acting like a crazy person right now!

There's no turning back. It's time to find out why Dean knows about the spirit dragon, what his fiery eyes mean, why he was so horrible and territorial when he first met me, and most importantly, why these things have anything to do with me.

I pull my hood over my ponytail and hug my arms in close. The beloved burgundy Gryffindor hoodie is all I have to protect myself as I shimmy my arm through the hole I made, trying to avoid the sharded glass, to unlock the window and pry it open. I swear, if I accidentally cut this hoodie, I'm going to cry.

I look around, taking in the clean lines and spotless decor. If I was hiding something in this house, where would I hide it? Heck, *what* would I even be hiding? I start with the kitchen drawers, tearing through them in a mad dash, but find nothing but perfectly organized cooking utensils. Dean is a clean freak. And he cooks. Who knew? But spatulas and measuring cups definitely aren't what I came here for.

I release a puff of air and go for the stairs. Considering this place isn't massive and the main floor is designed for open living, Dean's bedroom must be upstairs. There's bound to be something in there that will help me make sense of it all. With him in class, I should have a full hour to look, but I don't want to dawdle. The faster I'm out of here, the better.

The stairs are one of the only things left inside the house that have been restored with the original design. They're dark hardwood and narrow, polished and quant. I'm hurrying up them when I notice a tingle at the nape of my neck. Almost like the beginnings of a sunburn. I grip the railing and take another step, brushing it off as nothing and continue climbing.

But then all at once, it grows and heats, spreading around my neck like a burning noose, reaching up and over my head, pouring down my limbs like lava.

I drop to my knees.

All thoughts fall from my mind except for the need to make it stop, but I can't. I'm immobilized. I'm unable to do anything but lie on the stairs and pull at my clothing with fumbling fingers. *I'm burning up.* I'm being seared alive from the inside out.

Suddenly, I can't move anymore.

Somewhere in the recesses of my mind, I hear the screeches of agonized screaming. It's animalistic. And then

I realize where those primal sounds are coming from—me. Tears pour down my face, the salt streaming into my mouth. I'm coughing in between my panicked screams. The burning is relentless. I try to climb back down the stairs, but it's all too slow. Nothing is working. I'm not moving.

And none of it makes sense because there's no actual fire. My skin isn't blistering. To my eyes, nothing is happening. And yet, all my other senses are firing and the pain goes on and on. I'm sealed in place, sealed right in the middle of a hell that stretches on for eternity.

My vision blurs and my eyes flutter shut. I'm lost to the agony, ready to surrender to death. That's better than this. Anything is better than this endless torture.

"Hazel!" The voice is far away, a figment of my imagination, a ghost on the wind or the beginnings of a dream.

But then arms are lifting me, dragging me further up the stairs. I keep screaming. I can't stop. I can't think. I'm nothing. Nothing but pain.

A door slams open and metal clicks against metal and the sound of falling water penetrates my mind. My eyes pop open just as I'm being thrown into a cold shower.

Blissfully, mercifully, the heat is washed away. It melts off of me as quickly as it came, and I lie on the shower floor like a newborn baby, grasping at life. I'm traumatized and born again, and reality sinks back into my consciousness.

"Hazel!" The voice shouts again and this time there's no hiding from it, I know it's real—he's real.

I look up at Dean through the pummeling water. The glass shower door is open and he's standing, fully clothed at its entrance, glaring down at me. I'm also fully clothed, drenched from head to toe, but I can't get enough of the water.

I close my eyes again. The cold is pure bliss.

"Oh no, you don't!" He shuts off the water. "What the hell are you doing breaking into my house?"

Well, I guess it's time for me to face this. I blink and peel myself off the tiled floor to stand. All the burning pain from before has gone. I run my hands over my body, my eyes trailing down, looking for proof of what I endured. But there isn't a mark on me. Water drips down my face. My long hair is matted to my head and shoulders. Somewhere in all that, I lost my ponytail. My hoodie and jeans weigh a ton, and my tennis shoes are filled with water.

But I'm alive. It wasn't real. How is that possible? I don't even have a headache. I'm not even tired. There's literally no trace of what just happened.

"I should call the cops on your ass right now," Dean continues, so fuming mad that his hands are clenched and once again, his eyes are ringed with sparks of dancing fire.

"You have some explaining to do."

I fold my arms over my chest and glare right back. "Actually, Dean," my voice cracks, so hoarse from all the screaming. "I think it's *you* who has some explaining to do."

Because what in the world just happened to me?

He rocks back on his feet, his jaw tense, as he holds my gaze. The air between us crackles, neither one of us willing to give in to the other's demands. The tension grows taught until he finally turns on his heel and storms out, slamming the bathroom door behind him.

But he's not getting off that easy. I ignore the wet clothes and the thought that he could be calling the police at this very moment and go after him.

"Dean Ashton," I yell, storming into the hallway. "Don't run away from me. We need to talk, buddy!" I go from room-to-room, bursting from door-to-door, tracking water everywhere, but don't find him straight away, and that bothers me even more. "You've been weird since the day I met you, Dean. Don't even try to deny it. I'm tired of all these unexplainable things happening whenever you're near."

I locate the master bedroom and push my way inside, continuing my tirade. "What is going on? You want my help? Well, it's like I said, you need to help me understand this."

It smells like him in here and I stop, letting water pool

onto the hardwood. The bed is perfectly made, the corners of the slate gray bedding tucked in tight. The walls are eggshell white and the furnishings a mix of light and dark grays. There aren't any photographs or really anything personal in here. The rest of the house is the same way, but I figured he'd have something in here that spoke of his past. But it's like walking into a museum for minimalist design.

If it weren't for the faint woodsy scent that is distinctly Dean's, I wouldn't have any way to know this was his bedroom, let alone his home.

"Did you have to drip all over my floor?" He steps from the door on the far end of the room, which I presume leads to the closet or bathroom. "You already owe me a new window."

The sunlight streams in through the opened curtains, lighting him from behind so that his expression is in shadows. I glance down to where I'm leaving a puddle on the dark floor. These floors are old and restored; I'm sure they've been through worse. But hey, he was the one who threw me in the shower and then left before explaining himself.

"Give me a towel"—I shrug—"and I'll clean it up while you explain to me what's going on."

He sighs ruefully, raking a hand through his disheveled hair. He returns back through the door for a second, holding a fluffy white towel and a pile of clothes that he promptly throws onto his bed. Our gazes collide and his is still hard as steel, but something has shifted the tides of our tumultuous relationship. There's a gleam of defeat somewhere in those blackened eyes, a gleam that sends a shiver of triumph through me.

"Hazel, you are so damn annoying."

I smirk and stick out my tongue.

He walks past me. "Get yourself cleaned up so we can discuss this like grown ups." And then he's gone.

TWENTY

KHALI

THE FOG DOESN'T WANT ME to pass through to the other side. Its magic yanks at my emotions, demanding my elements to keep me in Drakenon. I'm powerless to refuse. All I can see is a thick cloud of gray. The iridescent shine must have only coated the outside because in here, everything is void of color. My body shakes and Bram's hand tightens around mine.

"I don't think I can do this," I say between gritted teeth. I am speaking to Bram. I am speaking to nothing. I am nothing if I leave Drakenon.

"Yes, you can," he urges, his tone doubtless. "Don't you dare let go of me, Khali."

But letting go? It's all that matters.

The need to rip away from him and run back is so strong

that I can hardly think of anything else. Bram must sense what is about to happen because his arms wrap around my torso and he lifts me off the ground completely. I shriek. I want to fight him, want to hurt him for this. And I could. I am powerful. He wouldn't stand a chance against me. I could burn him to cinders or drown him with his own saliva. I could call upon the winds to suffocate him or raise up the earth to bury him alive. Well, truthfully, I don't know if I can do these from actual experience, but I can feel the power within me, just waiting to be unleashed.

He rushes us through the last of the fog, bringing us out the other side. My malice evaporates into gratitude. Thank the Gods for Bram. If it wasn't for his lack of magic, if it wasn't for his quick wit, I never would've made it out of Drakenon.

"Thank you," I whisper softly. He's holding me so close that my lips brush against his warm neck as I speak. We both still and then he sets me down carefully. I take his hand again and squeeze. "No matter what happens," I say, "we stick together from here on out."

"Deal." He squeezes back. He looks different to me, somehow. And the same. And my stomach does a little squeeze.

Then we turn and stare, wide-eyed, into a new kind of danger.

The elementals connecting within me feel the same as our

kingdom, but the horizon is much different. Where we have fields of grass that roll into mountains, this area is flat and covered in a thick, mossy forest that is both unfamiliar and unnerving. It's darker here at night than in our home. And while there doesn't seem to be anybody around, that doesn't stop the sensation that we're being watched from washing over me like a July breeze. Something about the warm temperature feels off.

"Why is it so hot here?" I ask. I remove my cape and stuff it into my pack. "It's late enough in the year that it shouldn't feel like mid summer." Or maybe we came much further south than I realized.

"The magic is different," Bram answers. "The seasons take on a life of their own in Fae territory."

I'm not quite sure what that means but I think it's something to do with the way the Fae Courts operated before the Occultists conquered. A flying insect of glowing white hovers near my left ear, buzzing louder than the bugs back home. I swat it away. The air is thick with water and it settles on me like a second skin. Owen would have loved that. The shadows are long and unmoving underneath a sky animated with winking stars.

"There is no moon tonight." I peer up and sigh, not sure if that's a good or a bad thing.

"Come on," Bram says, pointing toward an indent in the forest. "There's a road."

"Aren't we going to fly?" Fear sparks in my voice. The thought of walking into that unknown forest makes my skin crawl. The trees are different here than in Drakenon. More alive, somehow.

"There are no dragons here," he says. "Who knows who, or what, will see you if you shift. We can't risk it."

"But won't they know me by my eyes?"

"Not until morning," he says.

I swallow and nod, stepping through the tangled grass toward the direction of the road. Bram pulls up his hood as well. We need to blend in and travel unnoticed for as long as we can—he's right about walking.

"How far do we have to get to the ley line?" I ask as we hike side by side through the waist-high grass, my palms brushing along the wispy tips. I breathe in the sweet, leafy scent, and try to relax.

"To travel between the realms, one would need to find where the lines intersect in both our world and the human one. I only know of a few places that could be. The land takes on energy in significant places."

"Like at churches?" I ask, thinking of the centuries old chapels back home and the reverence they hold inside their walls.

"Could be," he says, "but it would have to be a place where people have been going to worship for centuries if it was a church."

I bite my lip. The Occultists are also religious but I've never heard that of the Fae. They worship the earth, the elements, the seasons and stars. I don't think they have actual churches like we do.

We're at the edge of the forest now; the thick line of trees feels like a threshold into a new life. I don't want to go in, my senses rioting at the very idea of it. We stop and look at each other, and I sense the same worry on him, even in the darkness. Either way, neither of us wants to continue this conversation in there which is probably for the best.

"I have been looking into this ever since Dean left," he admits. "When he was banished, I lost my mind and demanded my parents intervene."

"I remember you two were close." My eyes were always on beautiful Dean, barely noticing little Bram in the background, but he *was* there.

He nods. "You always had Owen, Silas did his own thing, but Dean and I, we got each other. I don't know how to explain it."

I hold my tongue, not wanting to say the wrong thing.

"My mother promised he was going to be okay, swore

that they had a plan for him. She wouldn't give me details, but she said he was going somewhere that nobody from the other courts could get to him. Where else could that be but in the human realm?"

The unfairness of it hits me harder than ever, that something as small as a kiss with me could lead to a man being banished from his kingdom. The dragon clans agreed long ago that it was the best way to keep things fair for princes before one would be chosen as king. Do the Brightcasters really have so many enemies within their own court that they couldn't change things for Dean?

"I'm sorry," I whisper. "I'm sorry you lost your brothers because of me." I'm not just talking about Dean. Owen's face floats to my memory and my heart hurts.

He reaches out and squeezes my hand for a moment. "You didn't choose to be born with all that magic, just as I didn't choose to be born without any."

I think on what he said about Dean being taken to the human realm, where he'd be safer. It *was* strange when Dean left. His parents followed the law without question, but they didn't mourn him either. Not as I expected. They acted like nothing just ripped their family apart by the seams. They acted like Dean's future wasn't their concern anymore, loyal to Drakenon only. Maybe this is why.

"It makes sense," I agree.

He stops, dropping his pack and rummaging in it. He pulls out a map, worn with use and marked up by what is, most likely, his own hand. Of course, he would have a map, because who doesn't carry a map with them when running away? Oh wait, that would be me. He looks at it for just a few seconds before rolling it back up and returning it to its place in his bag.

"We're on the right track."

"Where are we going?"

"There's a place not far from here where a human battle occurred during a civil war. It was many years ago in their realm, but it was brutal. Brothers killed brothers." His voice grows hoarse, and I can't help but wonder if he's thinking of Silas and Owen. "They said the land was stained red with rivers of blood. Anyway, that kind of energy doesn't just fade away. It gets absorbed, especially if what happened is what was recorded. The humans have since created monuments to the battle. That alone will hold the energy over the years."

"And the Fae?" I ask.

"That area just so happens to be the same place the Fae has had their Summer Solstice rituals for centuries before they were taken over by the Occultists."

A place like that with so much energy in one spot could

create a fold in the ley line and a place where an elemental like Dean could slip through. The realms are layered on top of each other. We all share the same planet even though we walk different planes.

"How far?"

"A few days by foot," he says. "Faster if we can get horses but I'm not sure I trust Fae animals."

I study the mossy black forest. The road is narrow and surrounded on all sides by trees with monstrous qualities in the darkness. "What do we do once we get there?"

He doesn't say anything at first, so I turn and study him just as I studied our surroundings. He swallows hard. "That's the thing I don't have an answer for," he says reluctantly, "but if your father could travel through the realms to visit Dean, I'm certain you'll be able to do the same."

I frown. "But what about you?"

"I'm not sure if I'll be able to come or not," he says. He sounds so brave, so certain that this is the right thing to do, but how can he face all of this without worry for his well being? He came with me because he wanted to see his brother, but what if Bram can't get out of the Fae realm? What happens when we have to go back home? What if he has to go without me, won't they send him into exile as well? Could the Brightcaster princes dwindle down to only one?

Bram coming with me suddenly doesn't make sense. The questions build upon another like bricks.

"Why are you here?" I press. "Seriously, why are you taking this risk?"

He cocks his head, his eyes unreadable in the shadowy darkness. "I thought it was rather obvious."

My chest warms. I let out a breath and look away, putting the questions away for another time. I rummage around in my pack, find my waterskin, and take a quick drink and then pass it to Bram. I also find the last of my food and hand that over to him as well.

"What's all this for?"

"I can get more food and water," I say, "You take the rest of mine. You need it more than I do."

His smile is barely there. I can't tell if he's grateful or embarrassed or something else entirely, but it doesn't matter. We're in this together and if he's going to look out for me, I'm going to do the same for him. Hopefully there's enough magic in my veins for the both of us to survive this place and travel to the human realm.

"Come on," I say, leading the way. It's time to put the bordering wall of thick fog behind us and head into the canopy of trees.

Save for the occasional glowing insect with their buzzing

wings and our boots trudging across the rocky dirt road, the first few hours are met with silence. I find that worrisome, but what can I do but stay alert? The smells are more vibrant here, more earthy and alive. The magic feels stronger, too. In Drakenon the magic is mostly reserved for the Dragon Blessed. Sure, we have the merfolk and the occasional enchanted relic or forest, but the elemental powers stay inside the bloodlines of a select few families. The only randomness of our magic is which baby girl, with all four elementals, will be born to the newest generation.

But here? Here it's different. It's as if the land itself, the trees, the thin blades of grass and the pebbles embedded into the earth each have their own kind of magic. Is this where the Fae creatures get their power? Perhaps it's not passed down through bloodlines but rather offered up from the land itself. I wonder if Bram can sense it too but I don't dare ask.

The morning sun begins to rise, turning the sky a blue that will soon transform to pink. It lights up the forest, transforming it from menacing to enchanting. But I know not to trust what I see. Looks can be deceiving.

"Hello, good sir." A woman's cheerful voice echoes up ahead and we freeze.

She appears from between two trees, slipping through their opening as fluid as water running down a brook.

Dressed in nothing but a sheer white dress, her nakedness is on display. I try not to allow a horrified reaction to show on my face because this is truly shocking. Are all the Fae like this? Her long raven hair trails to her feet in luminescent waves. Her mouth and cheeks are perfectly rosy, her smile seductive, her golden eyes latched onto Bram.

"Can you help me?" she asks sweetly. "I seem to have gotten lost."

Bram's eyes are shifty, his cheeks flaming. "Um..." He mutters a few incoherent words.

"I'm sorry," I offer, stepping in front of him, "but we are in a hurry." I can sense the magic about her. And the menace.

The woman ignores me, never looking my way. But is she a woman? Something about her doesn't feel human. She's certainly not like us and she doesn't have the pointed ears of higher Fae. So who is she? *What* is she? My muscles pinch with tension.

Outstretching a dainty hand toward Bram, she speaks again, "Please, young man. I need your help. If you'll just escort me home then I'll be safe."

"I thought you said you were lost," I deadpan.

Bram's eyes are on her now, both unfocused and focused. A glossy shine has fallen over the green of his irises, the black pupils narrow with intent on this woman.

"Bram?" I whisper. "Are you okay?"

He lifts his own hand toward hers.

"Don't touch her," I growl, pulling him back. The woman hisses at me, giving me an enraged glare. Her pretty eyes turn deep purple and inky lines of scarlet bulge in her face.

Something shoots through the air with a snap and slams into her shoulder, knocking her down. She howls, rips the arrow with blue feathers from her skin, and scampers back into the trees. As she turns away, I flinch. Her backside is nothing but hollow blackness, a void.

"What was that thing?" I wonder aloud as I look around for the source of the arrow.

A man drops silently from the canopy of trees, landing like a cat a few feet from where I block Bram.

"That was a huldra," the man says, looping toward us on silent feet. He raises a sly eyebrow, the color of spun gold. "Cousin to the siren. She and her sisters lure men to their deaths."

I gulp, terrified of what could have happened to Bram. I know of the siren, though I've yet to encounter one, but not the huldra.

The man skulks closer, his movements as feline as some of his features. I study this new threat and widen my stance. He is tall and thin, with a beautiful face of high-cut cheekbones and cat-like blue eyes. Even his pupils are long slits. Dressed in finely stitched clothing, his golden hair tied back, his pointy ears framing his perfect face. A large bow with a quiver of thin arrows hangs over his shoulder.

Bram places a gentle hand on my arm and eases me back to him, the glamour having lifted from his eyes. "I know of the huldra," he says slowly, "but that one caught me off guard."

"You can't look them directly in the eyes," the man says, his own eyes sparkling with mischief. "I'm Terek." He extends his hand to me. "But don't worry, Princess, I'm not going to bite you." He winks. "Unless, of course, biting is your thing."

I freeze. *Princess*. He must know me by my eyes. Of course he does. The Drakenon tradition has lasted ages.

Bram and I exchange a guarded look, unsure of how to proceed. He is an elf, meaning he's one of the High Fae still alive. Someone was bound to recognize me. But the elves used to rule this territory and if anyone can help us navigate it, it's them. Or they could just as easily be our demise. Before the Occultists, the elves were our greatest enemies. This one not only knows my identity, but he intervened and saved Bram's life.

What does he want?

"I'm Prince Bram of Drakenon," Bram says, surprising

me by shrugging off his earlier hostility and shaking Terek's hand. "And you're correct in assuming this is our Princess."

I quickly run through the list of rules Bram and I talked about before walking through the border fog. We aren't to make any deals but we also aren't to make any enemies with the Higher Fae, and we certainly can't be caught by the Sovereign Occultists. I eye Terek. I can't trust him, but I decide to try, to see where this could lead us.

He may be powerful, but so am I.

I pull off my hood, shaking out my mane of dark hair. Then I bring the most dazzling smile to my lips and take his hand. His nails are long and pointed, like a cat's. I don't let it bother me. "Hello, Terek," I say, all confidence. "It's a pleasure to meet you." I glance around the forest, assessing its beauty like it's a part of him, like I'm a guest in his home. "I think, perhaps, you and I have something in common."

"And what is that, Princess?"

I hold his gaze with mine. "We share a common enemy."

TWENTY-ONE

HAZEL

I TAKE MY SWEET TIME getting ready because it will piss Dean off—which is an added bonus for me—but also because I'm nervous. Deep down, I know that whatever is about to happen could change the course of my life. But this is what I wanted. I came here, came to him. I broke in. I did this. And I am not going to chicken out now.

So I pad into his ensuite bathroom and sneak a look into the closet at the back. As far as I can tell, there's nothing out of the ordinary. Just a chest of drawers and two rows of hanging clothes. His closet is boring compared to mine, which Cora has lovingly named The Land of Misfit Toys. I snoop in the drawers as well, but it's just underwear and pajamas and workout gear. Since when did I become the creeper who goes through someone's underwear drawer? But more importantly, what kind of person doesn't have a single nostalgic item hidden in said drawer? Or in his closet, for that matter? Heck, I brought my favorite stuffed animal to college with me—a floppy rabbit that's seen better days—a blanket Mom made with pictures of us printed on the fabric, and a stack of ratty old t-shirts that mean the world to me because of the memories attached to them. I'll never part with my oversized middle school band t-shirt, thank you very much.

As far as I can tell, Dean has nothing cool like that. Not one single thing.

I grumble and go back into the bathroom to undress, toweling myself off, and slip into the dry clothes he offered. The black sweatpants and cotton v-neck are super soft and way too big for me but they are clean and comfy and melt away my defenses. They smell like the same lavender fabric softener my mom is obsessed with, which makes me chuckle. I roll my eyes because of course, Dean uses this stuff. I fish my phone from my wet pants pocket, figuring I'm going to need to stick it in a bag of rice and pray for mercy. But miraculously, the phone is still alive. I shoot Mom a quick "I love you" text and then pull up the message waiting for me. It's from Cora.

You're sick, huh? This illness wouldn't happen to have anything to do with why Dean took off ten

minutes into class like a bat out of hell?

Maybe, I type back.

What's going on with you two? Her reply is almost instant. **Are you hooking up and trying to keep it a secret? Cuz you can't keep that shit from me!!!**

I snort and text her again. **Not hooking up with Dean or anyone. But I am with him right now, actually. If something bad happens to me, you know who to blame ;)**

She replies right away. **Don't even joke about that…**

Well… I'm not really joking. BUT I'm fine.

You better be! What the heck?

Don't worry. I'll see you later. XOXO

You have to tell me EVERYTHING.

I drop the phone into the pocket of the sweatpants and run the towel over to the floor, mopping up the mess. I head out into the bedroom and then the hallway, cleaning up the trail of water that leads into the other bathroom where Dean threw me into the freaking shower! That experience was definitely not a *steamy* one to remember, dang it.

I hang the towel on the bathroom door and hurry downstairs, ready to face whatever is next with a mask of confidence.

I find Dean in the family room. He's already swept up

the glass and is busy taping up a flap of cardboard over the broken window. The wind outside isn't helping matters. It keeps blowing the board into his face and while part of me feels tremendous guilt, the other part wants to point and laugh. Maybe take a video. Post it to YouTube. Start a channel. Strike it rich. *Anything is possible, right Mom?*

But I'm going to be a grown up about this. So I hurry over and help him finish the job, neither of us saying a word to the other.

When it's finished, he steps back and turns on me with an annoyed groan. His eyes have settled back to their unreadable charcoal gray and he runs a hand along the stubble on his chin.

"You really want to know why that happened?" He nods to the stairs, his mouth pressing into a grimace.

"I have to know." But my palms are sweating and my hair is cold against my cheeks and suddenly, I'm not so sure of anything except that I probably shouldn't have ever come here today. A smarter girl would have left it alone.

"First of all, you're not as stealthy as you think you are," Dean says, raising an eyebrow. "I have a silent alarm in here. *And* I have three hidden cameras set to monitor the outside of the house. I knew you were here the minute you walked into my backyard and one of them alerted me on my phone."

Blood rushes to my cheeks. Well, that's not embarrassing or anything…

"And what about the burning?" I ask. "How is that possible? Because nothing was really happening but my brain thought it was. I felt it. It was…" my voice catches, "horrible."

"That was my ward doing its job."

"Ward?" I'm stuck on that word, like a *real* muggle would be. Holy crap! "So what are you, like some kind of warlock? Are you a wizard, Harry?" I make my best attempt at the Hagrid voice but inside I'm reeling.

"Who's Harry?" he asks, a worry line appearing between his eyebrows.

I blink at him. Has he been living under a rock? The poor, poor deprived man. But I can't get into Harry Potter with him now. This whole wizard thing wasn't what I was expecting. I don't even want to say what I was expecting considering it had to do with dragons, shifters, trainers or something even more impossible. I guess the wizard thing makes sense if really I stop and think about it logically. Magic is a better explanation for what happened to me on those stairs than temporary insanity, which, let's be honest, that isn't out of the realm of possibility. I do see dead people. Not quite magic. But close.

"I'm not a warlock," he says, with a slight sneer. "But I can cast a fire ward with my elemental, given what I am."

I bite my lip. I have to ask the question. I have to know. "What are you?"

"Are you sure you can handle this? You're positive you want to know?" His eyes are glued on mine and there's a vulnerability there I've never seen before with Dean. My heart skips and I nod.

"I can show you right here, considering you've just about figured it out on your own," he says. "But you have to swear never to tell another soul. Not your friends, not your family, not even Harmony. And you have to swear to help me because I need your help. I need you to do that mediumship reading for me."

Again, I nod. This is what I wanted all along.

He points to a chair tucked into the far end of the living room. "You'd better take a seat for this. Keep in mind, it's not going to be as impressive as if I were at home."

Ummm… okay?

I stride over to the chair on shaky legs and plop down. My hands are shaking, too. I squeeze them together in my lap and take a deep breath. Whatever he is, I'll deal with it.

Dean stands in the middle of the room for a long minute, staring at me, as if considering his decision. The black sleeves of his shirt are rolled up to his elbows, his tanned skin popping against the fabric. His dark eyes glow with intensity and his perfectly disheveled hair falls around his cheekbones. *It's hot. I have to admit.* Finally, he exhales and rolls his broad shoulders back.

And then, he transforms.

One second, he's Dean, dressed in that standard attire of dark washed jeans and a snug cotton top, smirking in that exasperating way of his. The next second, there's a glimmer of light and shadow, almost like what happens right before a spirit appears. And then, standing before me is something no longer a man, no longer a human. And it's no spirit, either.

It's a dragon.

A flesh and blood, living and breathing, real-life dragon.

It's so large that it has to crouch so it doesn't hit the ceiling. It looks so much like the spirit dragon that I almost believe that's what I'm seeing. Except that creature is of another realm and this one is most definitely part of this world. It's black and scaled like the other, but where that spirit dragon has blue eyes, this one's are orange and red, swirling like fire.

"Dean?" I whisper.

The dragon nods its head.

His head. *Dean's head!*

Somehow, I'm not afraid. And I know that's crazy. I should be terrified, not believe my eyes. I should run for my life, hide away, never come back here. But instead, I stand and walk forward, my hand outstretched. His wings are wrapped in on himself and his claws look like they could kill me with one swipe, but I continue until I'm close enough to touch. As I'm about to press my finger to the scaly skin, he shifts again.

And it's Dean standing before me, dressed exactly as before.

I pull my hand back.

"So now you know," he says, narrowing his eyes. "And like I said, you can't tell another soul. If you do, you'll be putting innocent people in danger. And I'll have to silence you."

I gulp. "Is that a threat?"

He smirks but I know he's serious. "You bet."

"I won't tell. Besides, nobody would believe me if I did."

"Don't be so sure of that, Hazel. There's a lot to this world you don't understand."

I let out a breath, trying to open my mind to what he's saying. "What does any of this have to do with me? Why did you tell me to get off your territory?"

"I'm sorry about that." He moves to the couch and I sit on the other end. "When I first met you, I felt that you were different, too. I thought you were here to spy on me."

"Why would I do that?"

"It's complicated."

"Try me."

"Let's just say, this place isn't exactly my natural habitat. Where I come from, is much, much different. But I *have* to be here. I can't go home. So I've made myself comfortable and I don't want to leave. If the wrong people find me here, I will have to leave."

"You thought I could be one of the wrong people."

"I did," he replies. "Now I realize you know very little about your gifts or lineage. You could be dangerous to me. But for now, it's probably the other way around."

"Gee—thanks," I scoff, but inside my curiosity is piqued. And also, I'm a little bit freaked out. I don't think I'm ready to ask him about my *lineage* because this is too much to process right now. And then I blurt out the next part before I can think like a logical person, "Did you have something to do with those missing girls?"

"Of course not!" His entire body tenses. "I'm a dragon shifter. Not a monster."

"Glad to hear they're not the same thing." I raise my hands in surrender.

"Not at all," he retorts.

"Because I saw that dragon spirit again yesterday after almost being attacked."

"I know."

"Yeah. I know you know. I remember. So why did you go after it?"

Dean's body is a coiled spring, tension tight and ready to explode. "The dragon must be here for me. He has to be one of my kind who's passed on and I need to know what he wants with me, especially after he sent you a vision of Khali in trouble. It's why I wanted to do that reading. I can't see him like you can. I can't talk to him. Only you can do that."

We fall into silence for a moment.

"Hazel, if you see him again, you must call me."

"I've only seen the dragon twice," I mutter with a shrug.

"Not the dragon. The dragon won't hurt you," he presses. "I'm talking about the man who tried to attack you. Do you feel safe? You can't go around by yourself anymore. He might be targeting you."

My heart rate picks up as the PTSD washes over me. And to think, it could happen again. It could end much worse. But if Dean's right, *why* is he targeting me? There has to be a reason.

"I know," I grumble, disheartened. "You don't need to remind me."

"Apparently, I do." He reaches out and takes my hand in his. Warmth floods my body. "I need you safe."

Dean is a dragon shifter. He's not even human. But he's the

least of my worries, it seems. Because even he doesn't know who tried to attack me and I believe him when he says he had nothing to do with the missing women. If Dean isn't the one out to get me, if he's not the enemy, then who is?

TWENTY-TWO

KHALI

"WHEREVER YOU TWO ARE GOING," Terek says with a conspiratorial grin, "I'm coming along for the ride." He flits a hand about the air nonchalantly but, with those nails filed into clawlike points, I have to force myself not to jump back. "It's been so *boring* around here lately," he whines. "I'm in dire need for an adventure."

"But we just met," Bram interjects. "Why should we bring you along for anything?"

"I saved your life," Terek's reply is smooth but full of metal. "That means you owe me a debt."

Silence stretches between the three of us because like it or not, Terek makes a good point. The Fae are notorious for this kind of trickery, and we can't afford to argue ourselves into a worse position. And if this man's mind is anything to match the feline features of his appearance, it is going to be hard to best him. I'll play along with his game—for now.

"We don't need a tagalong," Bram continues, his voice hardening into accusation.

"It's fine," I interject and elbow Bram in the ribcage. "But we're not telling you where we're going or why. You're just going to have to trust *us.*"

Terek grins, and a long, thin tail wraps around his body, dancing between us. I try not to stare, not wanting to appear rude, even though it's one of the strangest things I've ever seen. "Oh, darling," he says, "I don't trust anybody but myself, and even *that* is questionable at times."

Bram grumbles but there's nothing more to be said about the matter. I trudge forward and the three of us set off, an odd trio if ever there was one. Terek seems to be a mix between cat, man, and elf, and he's a ball of energy, constantly moving, graceful but wild. He loops through the trees, and a few times hisses at threats unseen to us. Bram and I try not to stare but it's hard not to watch him, especially with the strange hissing. I knew the Fae often took on animalistic qualities, but this is beyond what I'd ever imagined. It's a little terrifying. Was he always like this? Or did something happen to him? Terek might tell me if I asked. And Bram might already know. But I don't ask.

After what feels like hours of traversing along the quiet road, Terek finally speaks, "So how far is this mystery location?"

I clear my throat. "A couple of days walk." Maybe that will put him off.

"Wonderful," he says, happily. "Just so long as we aren't going to Highburne. It's such a dreadful place these days. I'd rather swallow thorns than step foot there."

Curiosity gets the better of me. "Why is that?" Of course, I think I already know. Highburne is where the Occultists have set up residence. They're known for their brutality. I can't imagine it's a joyful place for any of the Fae.

Terek pulls a bow from his quiver and twirls it around his wrist like a baton. "Oh, you already know why Highburne can burn, Dragon Princess. Common enemy and all that."

"Have you been there?"

He stops abruptly, causing Bram and me to stop, too. The forest is quiet, but not the kind of quiet of predators nearby. Then again, what would I know of it? I widen my stance and pull my elements to the surface where they sizzle just under my fingertips, ready to fight. Should I need to shift as well, my dragon is ready.

The forest grows deathly silent, holding its breath.

Terek is quick. He strings the arrow into the bow, points

up into the canopy of green, and shoots. Seconds later, a flutter of movement is followed by the arrow fumbling back to the earth with a dull thud. A large bird, much like a hawk, lies bloodied and dead at our feet, the arrow centered through its heart. My nerves slowly uncoil. This is not what I was expecting.

"Lunch." Terek practically purrs, picking it up. I almost expect him to bite into the raw meat by the way he's looking at the fowl, as if it's the tastiest treat he's ever seen. But luckily, he doesn't. "Shall we stop soon?" he asks, eyeing me and Bram with utter delight. "The Princess can conjure up a fire for us and I can cook this beauty to perfection in no time." He licks his lips and I'm stuck on the fact that he knows I can conjure fire. He must know about my abilities.

Bram and I must appear to be shocked speechless because Terek grins savagely.

"Come," he says, veering off to the side of the tree-lined dirt road. "I know of an excellent spot for a picnic. We ought to get off the road for a while anyway. We're nearing a village and the merchants will be on the road soon. Best not let anybody else see you two." He winks. "Not everyone would be as kind as myself."

"That remains to be seen," Bram grumbles but if Terek hears, he doesn't react. I elbow Bram yet again and he widens his eyes at me, his mouth set in a determined line. He doesn't trust Terek. He knows too much about the Fae to trust any of them, I suppose. And I get it, I do, but I also want to survive this place. So far, Terek has proved useful.

The cat-like elf leads us down a path so thin and overgrown, it must be the kind of trail made by deer hooves and not meant for larger human feet. Unease washes over me. This time, it's Bram's turn to elbow me in the ribcage. I shrug and keep going because I don't know what else to do other than to follow Terek farther into the forest.

"Seriously, what have you gotten us into?" Bram whispers from where he walks close behind. His breath is feathery warm on my neck. His accusations feel like barbs. "What's the plan, here?"

"I don't know," I bite back, annoyed. "But will you relax for two seconds, please?"

"I'm trying to keep us alive."

"Yeah, so am I."

Bram huffs but doesn't say another word but I feel his glare hot on my back.

Terek leads us deeper and deeper into the forest until we come upon a clearing. We walk into its center and he motions around us with the widest grin. "You're welcome," he says.

Above us, the sun hangs high in a swath of azure sky. Below us, the grass lies soft as crushed green velvet. All around the edges of the clearing are the same mossy trees, but also, tall flowers of every color and shape. I breathe in long and deep, letting the floral aroma carry me away. For the first time in weeks, my body melts with relaxation.

"It's so beautiful." I'm breathless. Enchanted. And definitely cautious, but that feeling seems to be fading on the breeze.

"What is this place?" Bram asks. "And those flowers," he points a curious finger, "what are they called? I think I've seen them depicted before in one of my books." He seems to be shuffling through the encyclopedia of information in his head and for once, unable to locate the answer. I don't know if that's a bad thing but it makes me giggle.

"What are you laughing about?" Bram's voice is teasing in return.

Bram catches my hand and pulls me to him. I laugh again. My palm spreads open against the flat plane of his chest. He's so much more manly than I realized. He's grown up.

"I can feel your heartbeat," I say softly. But I don't find the speed at which it's pounding to be funny. Neither of us are laughing anymore.

We're standing so close now, closer than *ever*. The floral aroma of jasmine and lilac, rose and juniper, and so many others I can't name, marry into the scent of the wonderfully warm earthy scent of Bram. I gulp, a shudder running through my body. When did he get so tall? When did he fill out like his brothers? How did I not see this before?

He shifts closer, his eyes leveled on my face. It takes courage, but I find it within me to look up and meet his gaze. They are ablaze with a galaxy of sparks, layered with depth. They brighten in intensity as I stare, matching the green surrounding us. I can't seem to focus on anything but those two bewitching eyes.

His hands circle my waist, drawing me in so we're not just standing close anymore, but our bodies are flushed together. Then he runs his smooth hands, ever so slowly, up my arms to cradle my face. The feeling is complete bliss, sending shockwaves over my skin. His thumb brushes a loose strand of hair from my cheek, lingering for much too long. My eyes flash to his cherry lips, so full and inviting.

What would it feel like to kiss those lips?

I don't have to wait to find out. He presses them to mine with that perfect intensity that is unique only to Bram. His is the kind of focus that takes souls, and he takes mine without caution. I surrender, closing my eyes and opening my mouth and my every emotion to him. I never knew a kiss could be like this. I never knew *anything* could be like this. My heart burns in my chest, my every sense tuned into Bram, to the feel of his muscles under my hands, his scent in my nose, his taste in my mouth. If I am lost in him, then I don't want to be found.

Terek's insidious laugh breaks us apart. "Wow, that was quite the response!"

Bram shuffles back from me, his cheeks splotchy and eyes shiny with the impact of what just happened. I exhale, lifting my hand to my swollen lips.

"What the hell was that?" Bram growls, turning on Terek.

"Don't blame me." Terek holds his hands up in surrender but his expression drips in satisfaction. "Blame them!" He points to the tall flowers. A breeze rushes through the clearing, sending a few of them swaying and more of their otherworldly floral aroma into the air.

"What do you mean?" I ask, trying to make sense of it. My heart is a wild beast in my chest, and even though I know better, all I want is to crawl back into Bram's arms and surrender.

Terek's grin is wicked. "This isn't Drakenon, Princess. How am I to know that you and your little prince would react so strongly to the flowers? They *are* magic, you know. Everything in this land is here for a reason."

I don't have a reply to that. I don't even know what I *could* say. Was the kiss real? Was it the result of the flowers and nothing else? I want so badly to know but I can't go there, can't think it. Because either way, that kiss with Bram can *never* be repeated.

"Nobody can know about this," Bram says in a rush. "It could be dangerous to us both and anyway, it wasn't our fault. We didn't mean it."

I hold my breath. He's right, surely. But I can't speak.

Terek smiles at us like we're his best friends. I take in his pink lips, slightly pointed teeth, and the thick golden hair framing his face. Somehow, I highly doubt that we're anything close to friends, especially after he brought us into this meadow. He's playing a game of cat and mouse. At first I thought he had a reason for toying with us, but now I wonder if he wasn't lying before, and if the elf actually is just bored.

Actually, I know he wasn't lying. Elves can't lie.

"Consider this already forgotten, please?" I ask through my most charming smile. I've had seventeen years to perfect my fake smile, but I wonder how many years Terek has had to perfect his. He could be centuries old, for all I know.

He holds up the bloody dead fowl and waggles his blond eyebrows. "Who's hungry?" When we don't answer, he clarifies with a teasing laugh. "Hungry for *food*, I mean."

I want to sink into a puddle of embarrassment right then and there. Once again, Terek laughs at our expense. He never agrees to keep our secret. Of course he doesn't. He can't. *That* probably *would* be a lie, afterall.

"Welcome to Fae territory, where we trade in lust and traffic in secrets."

TWENTY-THREE

HAZEL

"I SHOWED YOU MINE," DEAN says. "Now it's your turn."

My cheeks flush and I clear my throat. "I'm assuming you want me to do that reading for you now?"

He raises an eyebrow. "That would be correct."

"Right now?"

"It's only fair."

I have so many questions for him but I know those will have to wait, so I start how I always start, by inviting only the spirits of the light into our space. As I speak, embarrassment twists in my gut. I feel so weird doing this in front of Dean but then again, if he thinks I'm weird, then he'd be one to talk. He's a dragon shifter, for crying out loud! That, my friends, is the opposite of normal. I've never met someone who's stranger than me, and as much as I hate to admit it, I like this new revelation. I like him. And I shouldn't. I should be focusing on my feelings for Landon. He's the kind of person that will keep me sane. He's what I should want. He ticks all the right boxes… I think. At least, I'm pretty sure he ticks off the "normal" boxes.

As Dean and I wait for the spirits to reveal themselves, I run my index finger along my obsidian necklace. I know I need to remove it. I always keep it on, even when I'm showering or working out. The only times I remove it is when I'm doing readings at The Flowering Chakra, so I can allow the spirits to fully come in. For some reason, I'm too afraid to do that now. The little circular stones lay warm against my skin, a protection.

Dean's secret scares me, but it also draws me to him. Maybe I should take off the necklace.

"Anything?" he asks, his eyebrows drawing together in concentration. This is important to him.

I bite my lip, knowing I'm about to disappoint him. I mumble, "No, there's nothing coming through yet."

My heart is racing. *Take off the necklace!*

I'm so used to him getting angry at me that I expect anger to be his immediate reaction. But it's not. Frustration and sadness filter across his face, even as he holds his composure.

Then his eyes dart to where I'm playing with the obsidian necklace and an idea sparks.

"Maybe you should take that off," he says, nodding toward the necklace like he can read my thoughts. "Those are protection stones, right?"

"Right." I sit back, revealing my own vulnerability. "Truth is, I'm afraid if I take it off, the unwanted spirits will come. You're different than other clients. What will happen? And anyway, both times the dragon spirit came through, I had this on. I don't think the stones protect against that spirit, just other ones."

He lets out a breath, laying it all out there. "Please, Hazel. I need your help. I'm the only dragon shifter here. Something happened and I had to leave my home. I can never go back."

There's a vulnerability in his dark eyes I haven't seen before. I want to help, I do. But to take off my necklace?

"Who's Khali?" I ask. Her name has been rolling around in my brain since the moment he spoke it. To say it aloud almost feels like I'm admitting to the crush I've developed for the guy, because I'm illogically jealous of a girl I've never met.

"She was my friend and the reason I had to leave." He frowns and rakes a hand through his hair. "I've been worried about her ever since that dragon sent you her image. I need to know more because I can't go back. Was the dragon her or someone else? That night I left you with my car, I was trying to get more information, but I couldn't get anything. I have no idea what's going on back home and it's killing me."

Is he being purposely vague about this? Probably. Is he in love with this Khali girl? It sounds like it. I don't blame him. I saw her, she's drop-dead gorgeous. They match in so many ways. They would be perfect for each other. And that thought makes my heart pound even more.

"Okay," I say and before I can second guess myself, I unclasp the necklace. It drops into my hands, and I ignore the icy fear creeping up my spine as I set it on the nearby coffee table.

And then all at once, I'm surrounded. The spirits come from all directions, but it's one that sends a terrified gasp to my lips.

Katherine.

She's still dripping wet. She's still gagging on the water, her hair stuck to her face, her eyes vacant and bloodshot. She's still trying to speak to me, even though I know it won't work. She seems to realize it too, because suddenly, she rushes at me and grabs hold of my arms.

I know it's not real, know she can't actually touch me or hurt me, but I scream anyway. And then everything goes black. I fall back against the couch, my eyes fluttering shut, as the images wash over me, one after the other, so fast they consume me until I am her and she is me and I can't get away.

IT'S THE FIRST DAY OF *classes. There's not much to it, no real assignments yet, so when I see the flyer for the party at the fraternity house, I decide to go. Maybe there will be some sorority girls there and I can get a jump on recruitment week. I dress up in a black silk blouse, tight ripped jeans, and black heels. I don't want to go overboard but I still want to look good, so this seems like the perfect compromise. I don't know any girls in my dorm yet, but I should be fine to go alone. Greek row isn't far from here. And I'm sure I'll make friends when I get there. I wasn't all too good at making friends as a kid but I have improved and these days, it's easy for me to strike up conversations with strangers.*

And that's exactly what happens.

When I arrive at the party, I make polite small talk with the girls and flirt with the guys. It's really fun! There's this one guy in particular that catches my eye the moment I see him. Honest to God, it's like time stops when our eyes meet. And he walks right to me and introduces himself. He's the fraternity president but he seems so serious and smart, too. I like that about him. Plus, he's really cute. We dance and hang out for a while, but he never makes a move which makes me like him even more. He's respectful and that's what I look for in a guy.

It gets late and soon the party empties. I'm getting tired and have a 7a.m. yoga class planned. It will only be a ten minute walk back to the dorms, five if I hurry. My new friend says he wants to walk me home but I know if he does, he'll kiss me. I can tell just by looking at him. And I want to keep him waiting. Not too long, of course. But I don't want to give him the wrong impression about me. So I leave alone, sticking to the lighted paths as I walk back. A few students mill about, but I mostly ignore them.

I'm still thinking about him, a huge smile plastered across my face, when it happens. It's so fast. Footsteps rush and someone grabs me from behind. They push me to the concrete and my face hits it first. Pain explodes along my jaw. A hand quickly locks over my mouth and another hand wraps around my waist. I try to scream, but I can't get much sound out. I can taste blood on my tongue. And the skin of this stranger's hand.

Terror pours through my every cell as I'm lifted and blindfolded. I'm kicking and arching and desperate to get away, but whoever this is, he's so much bigger than me. And I can't see a thing. For the briefest of seconds, the pressing hand lets go of my mouth. I scream. But something is stuffed into my mouth and then duct tape is pressed on top of that. Tears stream down my face. My heart pounds out of my chest.

This can't be happening. This can't be real!

I'm carried away. Thrown into the trunk of a car. Just as he's shutting me in, I catch sight of his eyes. They're black--dead black--like his pupils have blown all the way to the edges, covering any trace of white. I can't understand it. I've never seen anything like that before. It's evil. Pure evil.

The rest? It's forgotten. A stain on my memory. When I wake up, I don't have a body. I'm a spirit, floating over a lake, confused, angry, and panicked. And there's nothing I can do about it. I stick around for a while, until I finally get the nerve to roam the nearby town where I was supposed to spend the best years of my life. I go back to the lake and I watch as they pull my body from it days later.

And still, there's nothing I can do. I'm stuck in a loop of the terror. It's all I can think about. The images consume me. I don't know what I'm supposed to do next. I don't know where to go. I don't know who murdered me or why or what those black eyes meant.

"HAZEL!" HANDS ARE WRAPPING SOMETHING

around my neck and a voice is yelling my name over and over again. I cough and wake up. My face is wet. I wipe away tears with shaking hands, hands that I can't control. I don't think. I just crawl into Dean's lap and sob.

"What happened, Hazel? What did you see?" He runs a warm hand over my hair. My mind is blank. Everything is numb. I don't even want to think about it. I can't go back there. I'm so cold, like I'd been the one stuck at the bottom of the lake. Dean's inner fire is the only thing I can cling to for warmth.

"Did you see Khali again? Is she okay?"

Reality settles over me, and I crawl off him to sit back on my end of the couch. Dean is so eager, and I hate to disappoint him, but I am never taking the necklace off again around him. He must have put it back on when I was in the middle of that horrid experience, because it's once again secured around my neck. I grip at it like it's my lifeline to sanity. Which at this point, it basically is. When I took it off at The Flowering Chakra, I never got any sort of reaction like this.

"I'm sorry," I say between ragged breaths. "I didn't see anything of Khali or dragons."

"Then what did you see?" he asks, confused.

I don't want to say it. My eyes well up again, and the memory is so alive in my mind that I can't shut it off, but I force the words out anyway, "I saw that freshman girl who died the first week of school. No, I didn't just see her, I was her. I felt it all. She went to a party and walked home alone. While she was walking, she was attacked from behind. The man"—the tears are heavy now—"he bound and gagged her and then put her in his car. She never saw or heard him. And then she was dead, her body thrown into that horrible lake."

All color has washed from Dean's face as he stares at me. "You said you were chased in broad daylight yesterday? Do you think it could have been the same guy?"

I want to say no. But I can't help but wonder if this is part of why Katherine keeps coming to me. "It could be. This guy had black eyes and I couldn't see my attacker's eyes."

"What do you mean?"

"I mean that his pupils were completely blown, like he was on drugs or something. But it was more than that. The black covered all whites of his eyes, too. That's not possible, right? Could it have something to do with magic? Or your dragons?"

"I'm taking you home," Dean says. "You've had enough stress for one day. We can worry about my stuff later. Besides, you have a class this afternoon to get to and so do I. Midterms are coming up next week so I just want you to worry about staying safe and I'll worry about finding this guy." There's something more he's not adding and I think it has to do with the blacked-out eyes and my questions. I want to scream at him, to demand he tell me what he knows. But I don't because I'm afraid of what I might hear.

My voice sounds hollow and far away when I say thanks and stand. I doubt I'll be going to any more classes today.

"Wait, don't you want me to try again? Try to find out who that dragon is?"

He shakes his head. "Not right now. I can't do that to you again." He points to my necklace. "Keep that thing on."

Dean drives me to my dorm. It's not far, but I'm still shaky and he insists. He doesn't tell me anything more about himself. Just before I get out of the car, I asked if there were more dragon shifters like him. I've been wanting to ask him about it since the second he shifted for me.

"Yes. But they are not here in this human realm. Like I said, I'm the only one."

Human realm? I'm not sure what that means exactly, but just the thought of other realms makes me shiver.

I want to see him shift again, want to know more about him and the shifters. I want to know what he thinks about the black eyes. I want to know everything, but it feels like as soon as I get one question answered, a dozen more pop up. I realize that I'm basically living in my very own young adult novel at this point, and I need to find out what's going to happen next. But it's true that midterms are coming up and Dean and I both need to study. Not to mention, I need to get those horrible images scrubbed from my mind. Katherine wants me to help her, but I don't know how I possibly can. I don't know who attacked her. I don't know how to send her to the next life. I don't know anything.

I STAND IN MY DORM room, staring at myself in the mirror, failing to drudge up the motivation needed to get my butt to my afternoon class, when a knock sounds on my door.

"Open up, Hazel." Cora's voice filters in from the other side of the wood. "I know you're in there. I can see your shadow."

"I'm worried about you," Macy adds in a softer voice.

"And I'm wanting the dirt on what happened with Dean." Cora laughs.

I pad to the door and open it. I don't know what I'll say to them. They'd never understand if I told them everything. Besides, there's so much about me that I've kept from them. I've been so fearful that if I told them the truth about what I can do, they wouldn't want to be friends with me anymore. That's always what I experienced back home in Ohio. They know I work at The Flowering Chakra, but they don't know I

293

do anything besides stock shelves and ring up customers. If I tell them the truth, will they still love me?

The second they see me, they must know something is wrong, because they rush in and hug me on both sides. I sink into them, trying not to cry.

"Oh, hon, it's okay," Cora mumbles into my hair. Her vanilla scent wraps around me.

"What happened?" Macy asks gently.

I step away and close the door, ushering them to sit on my bed. My room is a tiny box but at least it's private. The bathroom and showers are shared and down the hallway. All that's in here is a tiny closet and a chest of drawers, a twin bed, and a desk. But I've decorated what I can in my favorite colors, forest green and lilac. And being in the familiar environment settles me enough to tell them the truth.

I leave out Dean's secret, of course, but I tell them all about my gift and about Katherine. I explain what happened today, that I sneaked into Dean's place but didn't find anything. That he caught me on his security camera and confronted me. But that after we talked, I trust him and I don't think he's responsible for the missing girls. I tell them about how I took off my obsidian necklace and got flooded with images, and how Katherine came to me and showed me what happened to her.

By the end, their jaws are practically on the floor.

But they don't mock me or doubt me. They don't leave or laugh. They believe me. And that alone makes me love them even more than I already do. I've always wanted friends like this. Now that they're mine, I'm terrified I'll lose them. So I take a deep breath and tell them all about almost being attacked yesterday. Macy starts crying. Cora cusses and stomps her foot.

They get it. They understand why the fear is so real for me.

I beg them not to go to any more frat parties, not to go *anywhere* alone, and to be extra careful. When they agree, it's my turn to start crying. Again! It feels good not to have to keep this to myself anymore, to have more people to share my burdens with. But somehow, even with the cathartic crying and the confessions, I still don't feel any better. Because somehow, I know this is far from over.

"Hazel, we have something to tell you," Cora says. She looks as if she's about to cry.

"What is it?" I ask. When they hesitate, I fold my arms and raise my eyebrows. "Just tell me. I can take it."

Cora and Macy exchange a worried look but then Cora finishes her thought anyway, "Another one of the freshman girls went missing yesterday. They already found her body. She was murdered."

The world crashes in around me and my breath is knocked

out of me. This is number five in two years, but these deaths are occurring at a much faster rate and whoever is killing people isn't afraid to keep acting. I pull my friends into a tight hug, the three of us a tangle of limbs and shaky fear. How much longer until it's one of us?

TWENTY-FOUR

KHALI

"TRAVELING WITH YOU IS PROVING to be an education at our expense." Bram glares at Terek.

"That's an interesting way to put it," Terek retorts coolly, "because it seems to me that you rather enjoyed kissing your pretty, pretty Princess."

"Enough," I cut in sharply. "We don't have time for this. Let's eat and get back on our way."

I expect them to argue, but Bram looks away and Terek busies himself with defeathering the bird. Bronzy feathers go flying, and I try not to gag at the sight of it. I occupy myself with starting a small campfire for Terek to cook on, all the while avoiding Bram's loaded gaze. I don't have to be in my dragon form to access my power so I draw on the spark of life within me, pulling it forward and creating a slow burning flame in the palm of my hand.

"That's not something you see every day," Terek remarks gleefully.

I shrug and light the kindling and wood, and ten minutes later, lunch is ready.

Terek waves the cooked bird around like a trophy. "You're welcome!"

"And I can trust it's safe to eat that?" I raise an eyebrow.

"This is absolutely safe," Terek purrs. "I wouldn't lie to you."

Ha! More like he *can't* lie to me.

I lay out my cape again, sitting on the black velvet. The poor cape is starting to look tattered. The juices run over my fingers and it smells like heaven compared to what I've been eating the last few days. I take a bite and groan, it's so good. Terek also found some purple berries to round off the meal so I plop a couple of those in my mouth. They are sweet as sugar and stain my fingers and lips. I don't bother with the canteen since I gave it to Bram. All I have to do to get water is draw it out from the petals of nearby flowers with my water elemental. Little watery balls float to me, landing gently on my tongue.

"Such a show off," Terek teases, but from the way his eyes stay fastened on me, I can tell he's fiercely intrigued.

Maybe it's foolish to let him see my magic in action, but Bram needs that canteen of water more than I do. Bram, of course, doesn't eat the elf's food. He sticks to the provisions we brought from home.

We finish and clean up, and I try not to look at the flowers or breathe them in too deeply. My heart still feels like it's a feather floating on the breeze. We set off again and this time Terek leads us along a forest path that he promises will veer us around the village so we won't have any run-ins there. It adds an extra hour onto our journey, but according to Bram, we're going in the right direction, so neither of us offers any complaints.

All the while, the feel of Bram's lips lingers on mine, an imprint, a tattoo that won't go away, devouring my every thought. His scent lingers with me, too, even though he's not walking close enough for that to be why it follows me. We don't look at each other, don't make eye contact. It's too strange, everything between us has changed and I don't know what to do about that. Questions whirl around in my brain, a cyclone of them that are better left unanswered. Bram can't be caught kissing me *ever again*. And besides, it's not like that. I don't have romantic feelings towards him and he isn't interested, either.

Terek's odd feline tendencies continue as we travel, and I

can't help but wonder if they have something to do with the Occultists. Fae shouldn't act like this. They might be born with some animalistic features, but their behavior has always been reported as being just as human as the dragon shifters. As I'm considering how to ask Terek about it, he crouches and growls, pulling out his bow.

The fire burns under my palms. In the space of a breath, I'm ready to fight.

"There, there, little kitty cat," a silvery voice whispers from behind the thick trees. "I'm not here to hurt you, as much as I would enjoy it."

Terek hisses, primed to release his arrow.

"You are a hard one to track." The man attached to the voice steps out from hiding. "But I would expect nothing less."

I immediately recognize him as a Sovereign Occultist from the heavy crimson robe with black embroidered symbols that hangs off his thin frame. His face is ageless and white as porcelain. And his eyes, they glow red as freshly spilled blood. His appearance blends right in with everything I've heard of the powerful cult of warlocks that have terrorized Eridas. I've never seen one in person and never wanted to. Needle-like terror prickles over my body. Their magic is unlike mine, but just as powerful if not more so. Where

I draw from the elements of nature, the occultists deal in black magic, ancient oaths, and blood sacrifice.

"And I see you brought some friends." He sounds pleased. Pale, long fingers remove his hood, revealing his sickly smile. He could be my age, or middle aged, or he could be a thousand years old, there's no way to tell. The warlock's features drip in agelessness and eternal damnation. His red eyes travel from me, to Bram, and back again.

"Leave them out of this," Terek snarls as he loosens the arrow. It shoots straight at the man, swift as a heartbeat, but with only a flick of the Occultist's eyes, the arrow turns at a ninety degree angle and embeds into the trunk of a tree.

"Uh, uh, uh," the man chastises. "Do that again, Catboy, and I will turn your little arrows back on you."

"Your quarrel is with Terek, not with us," Bram speaks up, his voice strong but cordial. "Please, let my friend and I pass and we will be on our way."

Terek shoots Bram a hurt glare, and once again, the Occultist smiles that sickly sweet grin. A long row of perfectly white, square teeth glint in the afternoon sun. He looks so human, almost normal. A chill runs through my bones. Something isn't right about him. I can sense an evil darkness radiating from him and I don't know what to do. I call on my magic, bringing it under my surface, should I need to use it.

"I would be remiss if I didn't introduce myself to a Prince of Drakenon," the devilish man says, drawing the words out like a sharp dagger across a soft throat. His eyes land on me. "And to Khali, the future queen of Drakenon."

We fall into silence, the pressure building.

It was one thing to be recognized by a Fae, but by an Occultist? This won't end well.

"Then again," he says, gliding forward, his height seeming to grow. "I have met Khali once before." Those bloodied eyes lock me in. "Not that you would remember." My mind is whirling, trying to grasp what this could mean. "You were an infant." A cruel shadow passes over his eyes. "And I spelled you to sleep through it. Tell me, Princess, have you noticed anything strange happening to your magic recently?"

I suck in a breath, memories of my magic failing me coming to mind. Is it possible I've met this horrid creature before? And if so, what does it have to do with my magic? I let the possibility of it settle in. A strange sense of déjà vu and a keen awareness that I can't quite place takes over. Deep in my bones, I know he speaks the truth.

"I must say," the man laughs, "this is quite a fortuitous meeting. I've been tracking young Terek here for weeks. I was rather annoyed with him for escaping me the first time but now I can't say that I'm anything but delighted with how things have turned out."

Terek pounces.

"Run," he yells, as his claws rake across the Occultist's face, who immediately throws him off with a roar.

Bram and I explode into an all-out sprint. My dragon ignites and I welcome her forward, shifting in an instant. Bram jumps onto my back, his grip tight. Good thing, too, because I have to fly straight up through the canopy of branches.

"Head south," he calls into my ear against the rush of wind, "as fast as you can. Look for the part of the forest where there are many lakes. That's where we're going."

My wings lift us higher and higher. The road cuts into the thick forest below, though it is peppered by the occasional village or estate, and most of the land is a picture of wild green. Adrenaline runs through my body, and my dragon gains speed. I have to get us out of here. As far as I know, the Occultist can't fly, but he also can't be far behind, not with his level of magic. If we're caught, we'll never make it to the human realm, let alone back to Drakenon.

A wall of dominant energy slams into me with such force that the air is knocked from my lungs. Bram's hold on my back disappears. I whip around, horrified as his body pinwheels toward death. We're high enough that there's no way he can survive a fall like this, his body would explode on impact. I race after him, pushing every muscle in my body to the max. But it's not fast enough.

The trees grow closer. There's no time left. I can't lose him, too.

I draw on my elementals, bringing a giant gust of wind up underneath Bram. It wraps around him, slowing him enough to break the fall. Relief is quick. I fly toward him but another wall of invisible energy blocks my path. I slam against it with a thud and fall. A screaming pain pummels through my right wing. I tumble into the trees, branches attacking, while desperately holding onto my dragon form. I'm stronger this way, my scales creating a thick hide of armor.

As soon as I land, I pick myself back up and search for Bram, pulling on my wind elemental. The sky darkens. My storm.

Bram! I call out through the dragon link, but it proves fruitless. He can't hear me. He never will in this form. I'm desperate to find him but he's no longer in the area where he landed.

Thunder claps echo through the air. Rain starts to fall in needling pelts. I welcome it, urging my elements on. I can see clearly through it, can control it. The Occultist won't have the same luxury. I breathe in deep through my nostrils, trying to catch Bram's scent. But I made a critical mistake by calling the storm in too quickly and the water has washed away all smells.

I rip through the trees, charging back to where I left Terek and the Occultist. Somehow, I'm sure that warlock has Bram. Fire burns hot in my veins. Smoke rises from my nostrils, mixing with the mist from the rain. Where are they?

I no longer care about drawing attention to myself, no longer care about this forest or what threats lay within it or beyond. All I can think of is Bram. He risked everything by coming with me on this journey. I can't let him down. I can't be responsible for another Brightcaster's death.

I make it back to the road, the rain pounding harder, turning the dirt into slippery mud. A cry sounds from further down and I charge toward it.

A flash of red magic pulses and I scream. The Occultist is standing next to Bram but Bram can't move. He's been put under a spell. Even though nothing binds him, it's as if invisible ropes tie him up. His eyes bulge with the effort to break free.

I want to call out to him, but I can't in this form, and I don't dare change back into my more vulnerable human body. I growl, readying myself to send a plume of fire at the man, but he beats me to it. He pulls Bram to him, using him as a human shield.

"Come with me willingly," the Occultist says, "or come with me by force."

"Don't trust him!" Bram yells. The Occultist sneers and employs more of his invisible force to squeeze Bram, who cries out in pain. But Bram grits his teeth and continues, "Go! Go, like I told you."

"Come with me, Dragon Princess," the Occultist continues, "Or pay the price."

The elements are demanding to be let free, to destroy this man, but I know that's impossible with Bram in his clutches.

"Go!" Bram cries again. "Save your father. Come for me later."

I'm immobile between the two choices, but the elements continue to build. The rain pelts down harder, the wind blows into a wild hurricane, fire rises around me. The earth shakes.

"Have it your way," the Occultist snaps, howling overtop the noise but it's so loud, I can barely hear a thing. "You'll be coming to me soon enough anyway, whether or not I had your useless prince. Tick, tock, Princess, you're almost eighteen."

Confusion and fear whirl within. A tree cracks and plummets to the road. Lightning flashes through the sky, a clawed reckoning. The Occultist lifts his hand and twists it in an intricate pattern. A glittering symbol hangs in the air for the briefest of moments before vanishing to smoke. Seconds later, both he and Bram disappear.

TWENTY-FIVE

HAZEL

THE WEEKEND COMES FAST AND thank God for that. Each minute is filled with studying for midterms, shoving junk food into my face, and avoiding the gloomy weather. Before I know it, Sunday morning sweeps in and my focus turns to my date with Landon tonight. When he texted to confirm, I replied with a happy "yes" but I couldn't help but notice a little pang of regret. My thoughts have been consumed with Dean. Everything about him is dangerous and wrong, but I can't help myself from wanting more. And being with him, it makes me feel alive in a way I've never experienced. And now Landon doesn't compare. Another thing I can't help. Nor can he.

It's not his fault that he's normal. It's not my fault I'm not.

"Are you sure you want to go on this date?" Cora asks.

"How are you so good at reading me?" I laugh.

We're walking back to the dorm after having a giant breakfast at the dining hall. The bagel and cream cheese I ate at the end of our meal sits like a rock in my stomach and I'm already regretting my life choices. Why don't I love grapefruit and plain Greek yogurt like Macy? It would be so great to crave only healthy food and know when to stop. But in my defense, I secretly think the woman is lying when she says she *loves* all the healthy foods she eats. Who loves kale? Nobody. It's all lies.

"You've been a distracted mess ever since your confession to us," Cora continues, "and I'm sorry, but I don't think your most recent distraction has anything to do with Landon."

"Agreed!" Macy pipes in.

I sigh. They're right. The wind is chillier than normal and it suddenly rushes at us, wrapping us in an icy cold grip. Macy squeals and we take off, running for the dorm. After a couple of hellish minutes, we tumble inside. I'm breathing way too heavy for a seventeen year old. I probably should start working out more often. And eat kale.

"Landon will be good for you." Macy grins. Her hair is piled on top of her head in the kind of messy bun that looks sexy. When I try to do that, I look like a toddler. "Don't stress. Just have fun tonight. I'll help you get ready."

Flashbacks to the white minidress and high heels on that first Friday pop up and I grimace. "Umm, I don't know if I want to go and if I do decide to go, I'm not sure I'll need help getting ready."

"You're really going to cancel on Landon?"

I twist my lips as I think it through. We do have chemistry and he's a fun guy, for my first ever date, Landon's a good choice. "I guess not," I sigh. "He's harmless. I just don't know if I'm interested in him anymore."

"Because of Dean?"

I nod, equally hating and loving how the man has gotten under my skin.

"Well, if anything, the date will just make Dean jealous," Macy says happily. "I'll make sure Deany finds out about it tomorrow." She winks. "No worries, Girl, I got your back."

Cora laughs. "That's actually not a bad idea. Guys like what they can't have."

"So come on, then." Macy cocks her head to the side and studies me. "You have the prettiest coloring. Your hair is amazing but you always wear it up in a ponytail. If you let me curl it, you'll look like Goldilocks."

I gape at her, horrified. "And this is a good thing?"

She laughs again. "*And* I'll do your makeup so it enhances your natural beauty but isn't too much."

We make it to our doors and I continue to think on her offer. My door is the first. Macy's is across from mine, and Cora's is at the end of the hall next to the bathroom. Macy is so earnest and her big blue eyes are so hopeful that I finally relent. "Okay, you can do my hair. But don't get here before five. I need to study between nap sessions."

"You mean nap between study sessions," Cora interjects.

"Yup!" I laugh and unlock my door, slipping inside.

Macy giggles and Cora yells, "If she gets to do your hair and makeup, I get to pick out your clothes!"

I don't answer. I close the door and lean against it with an amused groan. What have I gotten myself into? I should have learned the first time I agreed to be their human puppet.

Once I'm in my room, I crash on my bed. I haven't been sleeping well at night lately and the naps are starting to catch up with me. But at this point, there's nothing I can do about it. If I'm going to be Goldilocks, I need my beauty rest. Wait, that's Sleeping Beauty. Well, same difference.

My phone rings, and I pull it from my pocket to see my mom's smiling face light up the screen. I answer, lying back on my downy pillows.

"Hey, Mom. What's up?"

"Hi, Sweetie." Her voice is clear through the line. "I just wanted to check on you since the incident. How are you doing? Are you safe? Are you sure you don't want to come home?"

I sigh. I knew this would happen. I told the police that I didn't want to call her, but they insisted because I'm still a minor. Mom lost her mind when she found out and has been worrying nonstop since, calling and texting day and night. She's even offered to bring me home and work out an independent study with the school so I can leave before the semester ends. It's only a matter of time before she asks me to transfer to a different school.

"I'm fine," I assure her. "Seriously. It was a wrong place, wrong time, sorta thing and I promise I'm being more careful now."

My mind races back to breaking into Dean's place and guilt prickles hot. I'm such a liar. But I am not lying when I say I am going to be more careful now.

"You know how I feel about it, Hazel. I'm your mom. Of course, I'm worried."

"I know, but can we talk about something else. Please? I'm doing the best I can."

"Okay--"

"What's new with you?"

The line goes quiet for a moment and then her tone changes to its normal cadence. "Nothing new here. What about you? How is your weekend going? Are you feeling ready for your midterms next week?"

I sigh and roll over. "Not ready yet, but I will be. My first one isn't until Wednesday. We get two days of a reading period so there's no classes tomorrow or Tuesday. Good thing, because I need it."

"Well, that's nice. You'll be able to get a lot of work done."

"Yup."

"And you're sure you're liking this college?"

My smile is real and *that* feels *so freaking amazing.* "I actually really like it here. My job pays well and is actually pretty fun. My boss is helpful, as you already know. My classes are super interesting. I absolutely love my new friends." And Dean is here…

Really, Hazel? Stop thinking about Dean! Landon. Think about Landon. Dean isn't right for you. He's a dragon shifter for crying out loud. Besides, he's obviously in love with that Khali girl. And Landon actually asked you out on a date. Did Dean ask you out? No. No, he did not.

Mom's been saying something but I'm so caught in my own thoughts. Oops. "Sorry, Mom. Could you repeat that?"

Her voice is patient. She's used to me getting distracted. Until recently, it was the spirits that caused it. "I was just wondering if there are any boys you're interested in. Have you met anyone?"

I burst out laughing. What is it with everyone reading my mind lately! "I dunno. Maybe. I do have a date tonight, so I'll call you in the morning and let you know if it was a bust."

"Well, that's great. Have a good time and don't put up with anything less than you deserve, Hazel. You're such a special girl." Her voice is back to being all concerned and motherly, and for a second, I wonder what it would be like to have a dad. How would he react to me going on a date? My heart squeezes because I'll never know and it's best not to think about it. That's how I've always coped with being fatherless in the past. But ever since Dean mentioned me not knowing my lineage, it's been on my mind.

I have to ask.

"Mom, I know we haven't talked about this very much, but was my father disrespectful to you? Is that why you never let him come around?"

The line goes silent and, for a moment, I wonder if the call dropped. But then she lets out a slow breath. "You haven't asked about your father in years." Her voice is even. "Are you sure you want to start now?"

"I'm ready to hear the truth. What happened? It's okay, Mom," I say, "I can take it."

Because I'm pretty sure the reason we haven't talked about

it much is because whoever he was, he wanted my mom, but he *didn't* want me. I think she's been protecting me by staying quiet about him. And I love her for it. But what if my father is the reason I'm the way I am? What if learning my history could help me now that I've embraced this mediumship stuff?

She lets out another long breath. "The truth is I didn't know much about your father. He was a one-night stand. I didn't even know his real name."

"What!" I sit up so fast blood rushes from my brain and starts blossoming along the sides of my vision. Shock gives way to laughter. "Oh my gosh, Mom! I never knew you had it in you."

"It was a one-time thing and it never happened again!" Her defensive tone is playful.

"I have to admit, this wasn't what I was expecting." And I am a little disappointed. Not in her, because everyone makes mistakes and I love my mom. Besides, if it weren't for that encounter, I wouldn't be here. So who am I to judge?

No, I'm disappointed because if she doesn't know his name, then it's official. I'll never meet my father. Part of me always wondered if maybe I would. I even assumed it would happen eventually. That one day he would show up and I would have the chance to get to know him, or at the very least, to tell him off for being a deadbeat.

"Can you tell me about him?" I ask gently. "What do you remember?"

Her voice softens, and I can hear the smile on her lips, "He was gorgeous. Tall and broad and really something to look at. You get your stunning blonde hair from him, though your hazel eyes are all mine. He was this mystery I wanted to solve. He had this tortured soul and once I saw him, I couldn't look away."

Well, damn. "Where did you meet?"

She clicks her tongue. "I met him at a bar, actually." She sounds embarrassed but not ashamed, which is good. It means I can laugh at her without feeling like a total brat. And I do! "You know me, Hazel. I'm always trying to heal every broken person I meet. It's who I am."

"No kidding." I'm still laughing, but silently this time.

"And this guy had something about him that was just so sad, but also magnetic. I struck up a conversation with him because I had to, it was like I was being pulled to him by some unseen force."

Okay, that's weird. My mind races and I want to ask Dean if magic could have been a factor that night.

"It wasn't like me at all, and I don't know how to explain it," she continues. "But I had to meet him and see what was behind his sad eyes. We had a few drinks. He came back to my apartment. We were both a little drunk. I was a brand new nurse back then, you know. I didn't have much but he didn't care. He was kind to me. One thing led to another…"

"Okay, yeah, I get it. You don't need to go into details."

"Well, the next morning, I woke up and he was gone. No note. Nothing. I never saw him again."

I lie back down on the bed and stare at the white ceiling. "That's kind of depressing, Mom."

"It was," she agrees. The smile in her voice is gone, and my heart hurts for her. "I barely knew him but I wanted to know more. I really did. He said his name was Jack but I could tell he wasn't being honest about that so I introduced myself as Jill." She laughs. "I was sad to see him go, but you know what? It brought me you. So I could never regret it."

"Aww, Mommy!"

She laughs. "I'm being serious! Hazel, you're the best thing that's ever happened to me. I love you so much. And I miss you. You're so far away. I worry…"

"I miss you, too."

An hour later, after talking about everything and nothing, we finally end the call. I'm no longer tired so I get back to studying. But I'm distracted again. Lost in the revelation of Mom's one-night stand and if there was more going on there than she realized, by the looming date tonight, and still, by the thoughts of Dean and what he is and what it could mean for me.

I skip lunch, opting to snack on the junk food I have in my room and end up crashing into a sugar coma by mid afternoon. I'm pulled from my nap when Cora and Macy come knocking.

"It's time to get ready for your date, Goldilocks!"

I'm basically their Barbie doll over the next two hours. Cora styles me in a white knit sweater that's *the* softest thing ever. It's like butter on my skin and I never want to take it off. When I tell her I'll fight her for it, she rolls her eyes and rummages through my chest of drawers. She pairs the light gray top with my black skinny jeans. Finally, she makes me wear her suede ankle boots. The heels are only a couple inches high and the zippers on the side stabilize my ankles.

"These are the type of heels I can do." I grin and strut around the small dorm room, feeling like a million bucks. Something about the comfortable heels give me an extra boost of confidence.

Macy comes at me with a lipstick wand. "This stuff will stay in place all night." She winks. "Which is perfect for when he kisses you."

I stop, my stomach tight. "You think he's going to kiss me?"

Cora waggles her eyebrows. "Oh girl, you two have been flirting for weeks. I know he's going to kiss you."

Okay. I'll just deal with it when it comes. Maybe I'll want him to kiss me and it will be magical. Maybe I'll turn and run away screaming into the night. Guess we'll find out! What nobody here knows is that I've never kissed anyone before. It's a secret I keep to myself. But in my defense, nobody has wanted to kiss me! It's not like I had a choice. I've had many crushes over the years and would have happily kissed them all.

Macy slides the sticky burgundy wand across my lips. I press them together to smooth it out and then let the lipstick dry. She messes with a few of the already perfect curls she's slaved over, stopping for a second to touch my obsidian necklace. They know all about it now, so even if it doesn't look good with this outfit, neither would dare to remove it or make a negative comment.

Cora rifles through my closet and pulls out my red peacoat. "Wear this one," she says. "Dresses the look up a bit. Makes you stand out. Not that you don't already stand out, because you totally do. You're a babe."

I blush and slide into the coat, hug and thank them both, then tuck my keys and phone into my pocket. Ready or not, it's time for my first ever date. It only took until I was a freshman in college to get asked out, dang it! If only it were a date with a certain someone…

As I walk down the dorm hallway toward the stairs to the parking lot, I decide to give Landon a chance. I *really* liked him earlier in the week when I agreed to go, and I can get back to that feeling if it's the right thing. He's a great guy. He's cute and he makes me laugh. With everything going on lately, I need someone who can make me laugh.

It's settled. If he tries to kiss me, I'll kiss him back. I'm positive that one kiss from him will have me forgetting I ever even met Dean Ashton.

Ha! Yeah, like that's possible.

TWENTY-SIX

KHALI

I DON'T FLY SOUTH. I need answers, and if anyone has answers, it's that damned Fae elf.

Back in my human form, I stalk down the road like a confident predator, no longer caring who, *or what*, has seen me. I'm certain my magicked storm was witnessed from miles away. Drawing on my elements as I did would have certainly scared off anyone, or anything, that wanted a piece of me. At least, that's the silly lie I tell myself. I know it's foolish to stay, but I'm desperate to get my friend back. I need *him* to get us into the human realm so we can find Dean and ask him about my father's hex.

It doesn't take long to find the nearby village Terek spoke of. If he was lurking around this area when he found Bram and I, and was so adamant we went around it, then chances are he knows somebody living here. Maybe whoever that is, can help me find him, and from there, maybe I can help Bram, because I can't leave him with that horrid Occultist. Who knows what that creature would do to him. Maybe I can rescue Bram before going for Dean, or more likely, relay some kind of message back to Drakenon. Either way, I have to do something.

I don't know what I expected of the Fae village, but I thank the Gods it appears to be elfin and relatively normal. Elves, I can handle. It's the other forest creatures, the nymphs and huldras and such that I don't want to deal with right now. I don't know a lot about them, but if they're anything like the terrible merfolk that populate the lake near Stoneshearth's Castle, I don't want the opportunity to find out.

The village is designed much like a typical village back in Drakenon. Most of the homes are meager but liveable, comprised of heavy stone and thatched roofs. Others are built of solid brick and mortar, and a few of the largest aren't ordinary homes but lovely, sprawling estates, laid out with whitewashed walls, dark wooden roofs, and massive lawns with abundant greenery.

I walk right through the center of town, my senses open to anything that might assist me. This place smells of summer evening sunshine and newly budding florals, of yeasty bread rising and sweet tea melting. I search for anyone who might have answers, but the second anyone here spots me, they scatter away. Much like Terek with his feline tendencies, all the elves are animalistic in their features and movements. A pinkish woman, who resembles a tall bird, loops into a doorway and slams the door shut. A child with a crop of yellow hair and ram's horns scampers around a corner. He's on all fours, tufts of fur peeking out from under worn clothes. I frown, wondering again what kind of spell the Occultists used on these people?

Movement from a nearby window catches my eye and I stop. A woman blinks from behind a thin pane of glass. Her eyes are the largest I've ever seen, open saucers of soft brown. I head in her direction, hoping she'll talk to me. Her home is one of the larger ones and well kept, with a bounteous flower garden out front. Before I can knock on her front door, she opens it.

"Come in," she whispers. "Quickly, please."

I hold my breath as I step over the threshold. She appears to be quite young, perhaps no older than myself, but I know better than to assume her age. Elves are immortal. They can be killed, of course, but otherwise, they don't age once they reach maturity. This one is tall and willow thin with skin of beautiful smooth caramel. Little white furred patches perfectly frame her angular face and accent her large, doey eyes. Trademark elven ears poke through long white-blonde curls. She's gorgeous, the fusion of a deer and an elf woman, and from the way she keeps her distance from me, just as skittish. But it seems she's willing to talk, so I smile brightly.

"Thank you," I say.

"Come." Her voice is hasty. "We don't have much time."

I follow her into the parlor with walls of polished river rock. The worn ornate rugs and threadbare furniture are perfectly arranged to feel as welcoming as the woman's startling eyes. This is the kind of place that used to have a staff, but now, its halls feel void of what was once bustling with life. It's as if she's the only one left and she's trying to keep up with appearances in case everyone comes back one day.

"I'm Khali," I say, reaching out a hand. She eyes it wearily and doesn't shake it, but motions for me to have a seat on an emerald green lounger instead. "I'm looking for an elf named Terek. Do you know him?"

She pauses, and then slowly sits down, still not offering a word.

"Please," I continue, urgency rising up in my voice, "my friend is in trouble and I think Terek might know how to help me find him."

"Terek needs to take care of himself right now," the woman snaps.

Worry floods my system. Worry, and anger. That Occultist

was tracking Terek. He led the warlock right to us. I have a right to seek him out!

"What's your name?" I ask sweetly, trying to keep the anger inside.

"Does that matter?" Her expression is grim. "I could die just for talking to you, let alone bringing you into my home, when I should be turning you into the Occultists as they'd wish. Many of my kind have died for much less than opening their door to an outsider. Like I said, let's make this quick, then please, leave here and never come back."

An overwhelming hurt consumes me. I never asked for any of this. If she'd just give me a chance to explain, she'd know that. "I'm not dangerous. I won't hurt you. I'm looking for allies."

"But you are dangerous! You don't understand," she continues in a rush. "It's not safe for us if you're here. You'll lead unwanted visitors into our village who will stir up trouble. We have barely survived as it is, and only from obedience to the Sovereign Occultists." As she says the name of their cult, her face falls into anger, but her voice holds steady.

"So do you know where they could have taken my friend?" I lean forward.

She nibbles at her lip, considering. "There's nothing you can do for your friend," she says. "I'm sorry. They take any creatures they find back to the capital city so they can properly spell them, just as they have with all of us. The more powerful of us or the ones with royal blood, they usually just kill them."

My breath catches and I choke on my words, not wanting to ask about the spells, not wanting to *know* about the murders. Maybe this is what happened to my father. Perhaps he was captured and spelled, but he got away somehow.

"I have to ask," I say. "Are the Occultist's spells why you're all so…" My voice trails off, not sure how to proceed without causing harm.

"Yes," she says, understanding. "The spell they've used on my people has stifled our magic and is turning us into the animals that we once resembled."

It makes sense considering what I've seen today, but it's still hard to imagine what that must be like for this once proud race of magical beings.

"It takes some time," she continues on sourly, "and if we behave, they will release the spell from some of us, or lessen it so it's not as fast. Not many have had that good fortune. The ones who do, well, they're usually the worst of the traitors to our kind."

"I'm so sorry," I say. An entire kingdom, an entire species, will be lost if this doesn't stop. Not only did they kill off all the royal lines, but the Occultists conquered the people and are slowly destroying their minds and bodies. If they can do this to the elves, a formidable, strong, and magical people that have been in this land for centuries, what could they do to the dragon shifters? Are we strong enough to fight them? Are we prepared for this?

"Thank you for answering my questions," I say. "Where is the capital? What's it called?"

She shakes her head violently. "No, you cannot go there. You won't stand a chance."

"I'm the most powerful dragon in Drakenon," I say simply. "I have to try."

She reaches out and takes my hands in hers. The edge of her right hand is rough, having already begun its transformation into a hoof. I swallow hard.

"Don't go there," she continues. "You must go back to Drakenon and convince your armies to help us. We have no other hope. The Occultists have taken over the rest of Eridas. They've killed off so many. If they continue this way, you will have no allies to help you when they come for your kingdom, too."

I don't have the heart to tell her that the Brightcasters would never agree to help. They care about protecting their own hides and nobody else. That's how it's always been.

But with that thought, I wonder how they've reacted to my leaving. To Bram, a prince, being gone as well. They might not need him, but they need me. It won't be until I die that another with my power will be born, and by the time she's eighteen and of age for marriage and childbearing, it could be too late for the dragons, especially the ruling family.

My mind flits back to what that Occultist said about my birthday. He claimed to have met me before, to have spelled me. He said that I would be coming to find him once I turned eighteen. Could it be true? A hurried sense of unease washes over me.

A deep rumbling growl sounds from outside the walls, followed by a hoarse roar that can only mean one thing. I jump up and rush to the window. Outside the house, a black dragon lands, the wind whipping around him. I scurry back from the window.

"Hide," I whisper and stalk toward the door.

The dragon must have shifted back into human form, because a voice shouts my name. A voice I know well. A voice I wish I could never hear again.

"Khali," Silas yells. "I know you're here! Come out before I storm this village to the ground."

When he says storm, he literally means it. Silas could use the weather to take down entire buildings. And as an air elemental, had he been in the area, he would have recognized my magic the moment I used air earlier to try to save Bram. There's no point in hiding. I know what Silas is capable of. He doesn't care about this village. He only cares for himself.

I gather my courage, square my shoulders, and stride through the front door.

"Didn't you get my note?" I say, raising a confident eyebrow. "I didn't want to be followed. But of course, you've never been one to care about my wishes, now have you, Silas?"

Silas turns to me with a haughty glare. He's not alone but that doesn't surprise me one bit. He has a party of at least ten other Dragon Blessed shifters with him and maybe even more hiding somewhere. They're all armed with long swords for their human forms. They have spent all of their lives training for and engaging in battle and the cockiness is hard on their faces as they look at me. I glare right back, my magic raging in a cyclone of elements beneath my skin.

"Fiancé." Silas stalks forward. "You did not have permission to leave, not then, not now, not ever."

"I have to help my father," I spit. "There was no other way. Now go back to Drakenon before you get yourselves killed. I'll be back as soon as I find the cure for my father's curse."

"Your father is a lost cause!"

Anger ripples through me. I hold my stance. "*You* are a lost cause."

"Where's Bram?" Silas asks, his lip curling. "My brother will have to answer for his sins."

I laugh at that. "Don't you dare speak of answering for sins, Silas. Or did you already forget what happened to your twin?"

The men surrounding Silas bristle, a few questioning eyes turning in his direction, but he plays his part well, a confused expression masking his true self.

"Bram was taken by the Occultists," I snap, getting right to the point. "So if you don't mind, I'm going to go get him and be on my way."

"No," he presses, "you're coming home with me."

"I'll return when I'm good and ready!"

I don't hesitate. I shift into my dragon, letting her roll over me like a blanket of power, and lift my wings into the sky. Silas and the men also shift with the cracking of bones and the cries of battle, readying themselves to chase me. But there was only one dragon faster than me and Silas killed him. As my wings pump and I zip over the landscape, I deflect the headwind Silas tries to thrust at me. I push the wind back at them, and summon a torrent of prickling rain. Again, just underneath my hide, I can feel something chasing at my magic, something trying to drain it away. I push it down but it exhausts me. I fear I'm running out of time.

My heart pumps and my thoughts zero in on my next step toward saving my father. I don't know where Terek is and I don't know where the capital is and I can't find the Occultist and Bram without those two things. Now that Silas is on my tail, I can't stay in this kingdom for much longer. The only person left who might be able to help me save not only my father, but now Bram, is Dean Brightcaster. The first prince. My first kiss. My first love.

And so, I fly south alone.

TWENTY-SEVEN

HAZEL

"DO YOU HAVE ROOM FOR dessert tonight? Our tiramisu is delicious." The waiter offers a little black menu, and Landon shoots me a questioning smile.

I shake my head. "I'm way too full to eat more." Plus, I'd feel bad to add to the bill. This place isn't cheap. I was a bit surprised Landon picked it, given that he's a college student and I know where the guy works.

"Just the check, thanks," Landon says and the waiter leaves us to our conversation.

The Italian restaurant is tucked around the corner from Main Street, between a dry cleaners and a karate studio. Inside the owners have kept everything high end, with black tablecloths and crystal glassware, low lighting and authentic Italian decor. There are only a few other parties dining here tonight, giving the place an even more romantic ambiance. It's the perfect date restaurant. The food was amazing. The company was even better.

So why do I feel so guilty? Oh, probably because I know I shouldn't have come on this date in the first place.

A candle's long flame flickers in the center of the table. The fire reminds me of all the unanswered questions I want to ask Dean, questions about where he comes from, questions about what he meant when he asked me about my father. My mind is so full of these questions that it's difficult to focus on anything else. Landon doesn't seem to notice, or if he does, he never indicates anything is off. The guy is as happy-go-lucky as they come.

A few minutes later, Landon helps me back into my coat. On our way out he holds my hand, threading our fingers together, and leads me to his gigantic white truck. He smells like coffee mixed with spicy citrus cologne. It's quite nice. But it doesn't stir me in the same way a certain someone's woodsy fire and rain scent does.

I have to use the foot rail to climb into his truck. He gives me a little boost and as I slide into the seat, I catch his blue eyes staring. They are bright and clear and stunning. But they aren't mysterious. They don't draw me in and hold me suspended. They don't shift from fire to coal.

He smiles that big goofy smile of his. "What are you thinking?"

"Nothing," I say, because I don't have a fair answer to give him.

I study his dimples for a second. I've always loved dimples. Who doesn't? Landon's smile comes easy. I don't have to work for it, and even though I tell myself that's a great quality in a man, I picture the smile I've only witnessed a couple of times. A smile so rare, it's like catching a shooting star on a moonless night.

But no matter how hard I try, I can't stop comparing Landon to Dean. Poor guy.

"Should we head out?" Landon asks. "I want to show you something."

I nod, and he closes the door, running around to his side of the truck. He jumps into the driver's seat, still smiling, and another wave of guilt pummels through me. He doesn't deserve this. I'm leading him on and I should ask to go home. I should tell him I just want to be friends and be honest about my feelings.

But he's so happy and I can't bring myself to wreck that. I'll talk to him about this tomorrow. No need to ruin tonight for him. And besides, I'm totally curious about what he wants to show me. He's lived here his entire life and probably knows all the best spots.

"So why veterinary school?" he asks, sounding genuinely curious. He's not just making small talk to pass the time while we drive.

"I love animals."

"So do I, but you can always have pets. Why not go become a doctor instead? You'll make a lot more money."

I shove down the rising annoyance. "Why does everyone always assume money is the end-all-be-all to happiness?"

"You got me there," he laughs.

"What about you?" I challenge. "What's your plan after graduating? Are *you* going to try for medical school?"

"Umm, yup." His tone is so self-deprecating that I can't help but laugh.

"What can I say?" he relents. "I want to make money. I could lie and act all noble about it but the truth is, I want to pick whatever medical specialty will pay me the most amount of money for the least amount of work. I'm not going to be one of those doctors who's on call all the time."

"So what kind of doctor are you going to be? Because my mom's an ER nurse, and last I checked, everyone who works at her hospital is always busy."

"True." He nods. "But I'll figure it out. I'll get good grades and then find some fancy practice where they'll let me work four days a week and golf on the weekends and all that shit."

He's serious about this plan. Hey, at least the man is being honest. I don't know whether to find it annoying or to keep laughing. "Too bad you aren't getting a huge inheritance, Landon, because you'd be really good at that lifestyle. You could have your own TV show!"

He nods, playing into the joke. "I'm still praying some long lost uncle will turn up dead somewhere. If med school doesn't work out, I'll marry rich and become a kept man." He turns and waggles his eyebrows at me. "But you'd have to be the mistress," he jokes. "You can take care of the stables."

We laugh about it for a few minutes as we drive along the two-lane highway. The last time I was here, Dean drove down one lane like a maniac and then left me to drive back the other way all by myself. I rub the bad memory from my mind and focus on Landon again. He slows and turns off onto a tiny dirt road. The path is so hidden, I'd have never guessed it was there in the first place. The truck bounces up and down on the road, the headlights revealing a thick pine forest on either side. I hold my breath and try not to squeeze my hands into fists. My heart picks up the further we get from the main road.

"Where are you taking me?" I finally ask, but my voice is drained of courage and it comes out a little too high.

"Don't you worry, little lady," he assures me with a smile. "You're going to love it." His hands are tight vices on the steering wheel as we continue down the dirt road. "Everyone loves it," he adds.

"Everyone?" I twist my lips, wondering what he means by that, and okay, now I really *am* getting annoyed with the guy.

He grins but doesn't say anything more. So is this where he takes all his dates or something like that? Is it some designated make-out spot outside of town? I'm a bit confused and trying to let that confusion overpower the fear under the surface, because anything is better than giving into that. I've learned that fear can be all consuming, and I don't want to go there. I want to be calm. Want to trust. I know Landon. He's my friend. He wouldn't do anything to me. So I shouldn't jump to any conclusions.

But what if I'm wrong?

My mind races all the way until we turn off the dirt road onto another one. The second road is even more remote than the first. It's so dark at this time of night, the headlights are bright white against the trees. They press against both sides of the truck, and I'm beginning to wonder if we're going to make it when the road opens up into a huge clearing ahead.

No, not a clearing. A lake.

My stomach drops and Katherine comes to mind. The

headlights glitter on the water as Landon stops the truck and backs it around until the rear of the pickup is facing the lake. He jumps out and I do the same, my boots crunching into the long grass. He opens the tailgate, hopping up to sit on the metal frame. He pats the space next to him and reaches out a steady hand.

I swallow hard and take it, trying to force images of Katherine and dead girls from my mind. He pulls me up and slides in close, putting his arm around me. It's cold tonight but not frigid, and between my coat and his arm, I'm plenty warm. I don't feel warm, though. I'm chilled to the bone. I try to breathe slowly, to relax, to tell myself I'm perfectly safe. Now that the truck's lights are extinguished, the wide open sky fills with far-away stars. My eyes adjust more and more with each passing second, until I can see those same stars above reflecting off the lake's surface. That sight does calm me a little.

"It's beautiful."

"It really is." He leans in closer. "I've been coming here since I was a kid. In the summertime, it's the best swimming spot. But it's also one of my favorite places to come when I want to be alone."

My thoughts cloud over and I'm right back to where I was. "It's not the lake they pulled that girl's body from, is it?" Katherine's memories hover closer than ever now that we're here. It could be the exact same place, it looks like it to me. But in the dark, I can't tell for sure.

"God, I hope not," he says. "But I don't think so. There are hundreds of lakes in the surrounding areas, so odds are, it wasn't. They're lucky they found her at all."

I can't shake my thoughts of her, and I automatically run my finger along my obsidian necklace where it's tucked under the edge of my coat. I'm so glad I have it, so grateful that I met Harmony and got the help I needed to manage my curse. I can't imagine still having Katherine's ghost following me everywhere, and now the cheerleader girl, too? It's terrifying.

The memories Katherine thrust upon me will never leave. Because while I'm used to spirits sending me awful images, I've never had a spirit get so close and show me so much. I've never had one be able to put the images in my mind so clearly, as if I were living them right along with her. No, not with her, but *as* her. And I can't help but think that she wants more than just my help. Maybe… maybe she wanted to warn me.

"What's wrong?" Landon asks.

"Nothing," I squeak. What's wrong? The alarm bells are blazing! I shouldn't be here. I'm pretty sure this *is* the same lake, I recognize the shoreline.

Landon rubs my arm. He's closer now, his body pressed up

next to mine. My face prickles. If I don't say something now, he's going to kiss me. Wasn't it just hours ago that I planned to let him?

Well, I've changed my mind.

When I wasn't in this moment, it was so easy to imagine our kiss. But now I'm here, I don't want it to happen. There are too many things that make it wrong. My feelings for Dean are too strong. My worries about Katherine won't let me go. And this lake… it should be romantic, but it's freaking me out. Because all I can see when I look at it is what it was like for Katherine to see her body pulled from the water.

"Landon, I appreciate—"

His lips take mine. Hard. It's so fast, it throws my defenses off guard and I don't know how to react. I've never done this before. My mind is a racing mess and I'm frozen, numb to his touch. He must take that as a good sign because he wraps his other arm around me and pulls me closer, opening my mouth with his. His tongue is warm and wet and I'm suddenly distracted by how gross this whole thing is. *This* is kissing? This is what all the fuss is about? Are you kidding me? It's so… slobbery!

My thoughts are rolling around like marbles in my head. He lets out a low moan and shifts his weight, overpowering me. He presses me back onto the bed of the truck. The metal is sharp against my hips, painful against the back of my head.

Okay, I'm done!

"Ouch," I cry out, my hands pushing back against his chest. "Wait. Landon, hold on."

He doesn't wait.

He spreads his body over mine, driving me even harder into the cold metal. His hands are frantic now, traveling over me without reservation or care. He reaches for the buttons of my coat, moving his mouth to my neck.

"Landon," I try again, louder, screaming. "You're hurting me. Stop!"

But he doesn't stop. It's as if he doesn't even hear me. Each one of my senses blast into overdrive. I balk against the cold air when he rips open my coat, his scratchy fingers going for my sweater next. He presses his fingers into my stomach and I kick out.

"Stop!" I yell as loud as I can this time, and it echoes over the lake. "Landon, what are you doing? Get off!"

His hands are everywhere. His breath is garlic and hot and so, so wrong. His heat contradicts the cold, jarring and unapologetic. Half my mind is focusing on fighting him but he easily overpowers me with each move. The other half of my mind is observing everything from above, shocked that this is happening. Disbelieving. Floating away.

Landon doesn't stop. He doesn't utter a single word as I beg and scratch and scream and cry. He grips both my wrists and forces them above my head. He locks them in one large hand and squeezes tight. With his free hand, he rips Cora's white sweater right down the middle, exposing my nude bra and heaving stomach. Tears burn my vision. I can't see the stars anymore.

How is this real?

Landon's eyes glisten black as soot to match the darkness as they assess me for a long second, the black has spread to cover the whites of his eyes. *Just like the man who killed Katherine.* How is it even possible? Then he's back on me, his hot mouth nips at my neck before crashing to my mouth again, splitting my lip. I cry out with the pain. His hand travels over my skin, greedy and unrelenting. He is so heavy. He is a million pounds. He is stone and I am dust. I taste the coppery blood in my mouth and try not to gag. He probably tastes it, too. It does nothing to stop him. In fact, it encourages him.

His free hand travels to my neck and he grabs onto the obsidian necklace, pulling. It's too tight against my neck, so tight, that I cough, lost for breath. Terror flows through me, stinging and hot. But then the necklace breaks free and I gasp for air. The circular beads spill out over the bed of the truck, clattering like pebbles and rolling away.

His hand releases my neck and heads south, and I scream even louder. His mouth kisses along my jaw, oblivious to my fear. What is going on? I don't understand how he could do this. I don't understand how I could have missed this in him. I blink up into the darkness.

We're not alone.

A spirit hovers over our bodies. Dressed in a wispy black cape, I can't see the spirit's face except for two glowing red eyes. Evil reverberates from its floating form. It's an evil so dark, it sucks any light from its surroundings. Something about it is familiar. I've seen it once before. Its outstretched arm is reaching right *into* Landon, holding on tight, *controlling him.*

My screams pierce the night.

Landon's head snaps up. His eyes aren't those of the predator anymore, they're not black. They are those of the prey and they're his normal blue. There's something frightened behind them, something trapped and animalistic. But his body doesn't seem to connect when his widened eyes return to black and he bears back down on me.

I finally understand. Whatever this *thing* is, it's possessing Landon. It's forcing him to do this. He doesn't want to hurt me. But we're both powerless to stop it. This isn't right. This shouldn't be happening. The spirits don't have power over us. In all my years, I've never known of a spirit who could. But this isn't a normal human spirit. This is otherworldly and I remember where I've seen it before. I caught just a glimpse of this thing hanging over the man in the alleyway who tried to attack me.

Is this the thing responsible for all the dead girls over the last two years?

The creature and I lock gazes and it feels as if its red glowing eyes are peering into my soul, judging, assessing, deciding my fate.

Judge, jury, and executioner.

Landon's hands wrap around my neck and squeeze.

TWENTY-EIGHT

KHALI

WHEN I WAS SEVEN YEARS old, I almost died. I was playing by the lake with the princes when I saw something pretty, glittering in the water. Innocent as I was, I stomped through the bank to investigate. That's when a slimy hand wrapped around my ankle and pulled me under, sharp claws digging into my flesh. My screams echoed over the surface for barely a second before cold water rushed my lungs.

I had no power then, no way to fight back or defend myself. The fear was so suffocating, that even to this day, I hate the water. I didn't know it then, but the merfolk had kidnapped me with no intention of actually killing me. At least, that's what I've been told in the years since. I'm not so sure about that. I think had they not gotten what they'd set out for, I'd be dead. They used me as a bargaining tool to manipulate the Brightcaster family into a truce, allowing them more dominion over Drakenon water. I'm still unsure of the details surrounding my release, but I do know they magicked me to breathe underwater and held me down there in the freezing darkness for two days while they negotiated with the royals.

I've never been the same since. After that experience, my childhood innocence was lost to that murky darkness. No matter how anyone tried to explain it, I knew from then on that my life wasn't like others, that for as long as I lived, there would be people willing to use my suffering for their gain.

As I fly, gaining distance from Silas, I'm grateful for what I've been through. Because of it, I was afraid, and I trained in secret whenever I could as a way to try to make that fear go away. And as I got older, I began on my weekly excursions with Owen, stealing away into the darkness to see what was possible. I did what I could, used what I had, and now I'm a faster, stronger dragon because of it.

Now it's my turn to use what I am to my advantage.

The cloudless sunset has turned the sky to a swash of coral. I can't let the coming darkness stop me, I have to keep going. I have to fly faster. With worries for Bram centered in my mind, I peer down at the lakes below and muster the courage to fly lower. The sun is gone but my vision in this form allows me to see in the dark. I search the area, trying to match what I'm seeing with Bram's description of where the ley lines meet. I don't know for sure, but I think I've found it.

If this is the area Bram spoke of, then somewhere down there is the very spot where I can draw on my earthly magic to cross from this realm into the next. If only I knew where that spot was! I hate that I'm alone in this. I'm amazed that it only took a few days alone with Bram for my heart to care so much about him, about his well being and his safety. I'd give anything to have him with me now, to be doing this together. I hope Silas cares enough about his brother to try to help him, but I know that thought is nothing more than hope. Dean's all I have left. If he doesn't know how to help my father and how to save Bram, all of this will be for nothing.

I land next to the largest of the lakes and shift back into my human form. My dragon is my comfort zone, but she's also terrifying to anyone who might be lurking around here with answers. Hunger and thirst roll through my belly but I ignore the ache, looking around for signs of life instead. My vision isn't nearly as strong now, and the darkness of night is expanding by the second. There's nothing here but silent trees and still water and an undercurrent of Fae magic. I release a panicked breath. I don't know what to do.

What did Bram say? Ley lines are energetic lines that

connect places of significance, and when lines from our realm cross over with lines from the human realm, then it creates a passageway for those with elemental magic to cross through. But it can't just be elemental magic, because my father isn't an elemental and he's been visiting Dean. Unless Dean helped him through? Or maybe another creature with elemental magic did it?

I have so many questions, a few theories, but no real way to test any of it. I chastise myself for not questioning Bram more on these things while I had the chance! I was foolish to let that opportunity pass me by.

My eyes strain against the darkness, looking for some kind of indication as to where these ancient Fae rituals took place, but there's nothing out of the ordinary. It looks like the same Fae forest from before, with its thick trees and magicked air. The panic swells up again. I take a long, slow breath to settle my nerves and close my eyes.

The ley lines are all about energy staying with the land. Perhaps if I focus, I'll be able to feel it myself. Each of my elementals has a unique imprint, a different sort of current to the magic. Earth is a grounding power. Water is fluidity, and air is light. Fire is the hardest to explain, but it's like a wild calm. And I feel each of those within me now. But they're not what I'm looking for, so I shift past them in search of something unfamiliar.

At first, there's nothing.

But I keep myself fixed in place, exhaling softly, my eyes shut, and imagine I'm like the trees that grow here. Tall and strong, deeply rooted, interconnected, and observant. Patient.

A pulse of ethereal energy flashes through me, soft as a whisper. I welcome it, letting it come again and again, until I'm sure it's real and not my imagination. My eyes open and my feet lead me toward the source of the energy. I walk along the edge of the large lake. It's almost as big as the one in front of Stoneshearth, but I won't let that stop me. The darkness spreads over the water like a black mirror, hiding whatever lurks in its depths. With each step, the energy rises more and more. Hope surges, and I run, careful to stay light on my feet, to keep quiet. But I've got to move. Too much is riding on my success.

Suddenly, the energy stops.

I skid to a halt and look around, searching for what, I don't know. There's no indication that this is where I cross through. I'm still in the Fae forest. I groan and clench my hands into fists, stalking through the area. A glimmer of something, that's what I need. But there's no glimmer, no signs. There's nothing.

I force myself to relax and allow the unfamiliar energy to wash over me once again. It's stronger here than it ever was, but again, it pulls me in a direction. Not around the lake, but toward it.

I hesitate. Fear rushes me, the memories of my time trapped underwater heady and suffocating. But I don't have time to hesitate. I don't have the luxury of fear. I walk forward until I'm right at the lake's edge. The energy continues to draw me in, and I step into the water. It's cool but not icy. It feels like summer rain, and it welcomes me forward. I take another step. And then another. All the while, my breath pumps to and from my lungs, faster and faster.

Are there merfolk in this water, too? Something worse? What hidden darkness lies beneath the surface of the water? I remember what it felt like to have that clammy hand wrap around my ankle as a child. It's a thought that flashes through my mind every time I'm near the water. If it happened again, would I survive this time?

Tears prick my eyes. I'm shaking so bad, the water ripples around me.

"Another one," a voice hisses from the water.

I scramble from the lake, landing with a thud on the shoreline.

"Who's there?"

A head pokes out of the surface. She doesn't look like the merfolk from my childhood nightmares; she's much more beautiful than that. Her skin is moon white and sparkling, her eyes are onyx glitter.

"The real question," she says, rising further from the water, "is who are you?"

I swallow. There is no point in trying to deceive her. "I'm Khali, future Queen of Drakenon."

She tilts her head. "I thought so," she says, coolly. "Have you come to see your prince who lives on the other side?"

"The other side of what?" I ask. Hope swells in my chest.

"The other side of my lake." She lifts a hand and motions a finger toward me. "Come, I'll show you. But I must warn you, if I help you, you'll owe me a debt."

Terror rakes through me because debt is exactly what Bram warned about. *Bram… he needs me.* I stand and step into the water. She's the only lead I've got.

"Fine," I say. "A debt equal to this one."

"How well can you swim?" she asks, her lips curving into a cool smile.

I call on my water elemental and ready myself for the task ahead. She dives under. Against my better judgment, I trust her, and dive under as well. The fear of this being a trap, of becoming subjected to the things that lurk down here, is more real than ever. But I have to be brave, and so, I swim.

The creature is fast, her fins giving her the advantage. But I'm fast, too. And my water elemental allows me to not only breathe under here, but to use the water as a tool for speed. It pushes me forward, past kelp, through the darkness, deeper and deeper and deeper still.

She leads me straight to the bottom of the lake. The energy down here is so strong, it crushes me on all sides, heavier than ever. I try to scream, to struggle, to break free, but it's like fate is pulling me under without my consent. My vision blurs from black to the brightest white. Someone calls my name and my heart leaps with recognition, but it all happens so fast that I lose all thought. I'm spinning. I'm lost. The deep dark returns.

The energy pushes me to my breaking point. And then, it washes away.

The woman leading me is gone too.

The water is no longer that of summer, that of Fae. It's icy cold.

I swim back to the surface, desperate to be free, my legs kicking with unchecked ferocity. The moment my head breaks the surface, I breathe in the cold air, letting it fill my lungs with its freeing salvation. My eyes blink open, my vision settling, and I know. I know what has happened. I know where I am. I can feel it in the change of temperature, can see it in the landscape. But most of all, I can sense it in the way my magic has lost some of its breath. The elementals dancing within are but a wisp of what they normally are. I've passed through the ley lines. I've crossed over from one realm to the next. I blink the water from my eyes, my vision fixed on the dark shoreline.

TWENTY-NINE

HAZEL

MY THROAT BURNS AS LANDON pushes the last ounce of oxygen from my lungs. My vision is nothing but a black tunnel. Stars wink along the edges. And Landon. He is centered in the darkness. It sweeps over me. Fast. Too fast. I claw at his hands and wrists, drawing blood. I snag a long strand of his hair and rip it from his scalp. I kick out and knee him with all the energy I have left. He's unmovable. He's made of stone. Unfeeling. Unshaken. Above him, the robed spirit has taken control, those two red eyes glowing luminous.

I'm going to die.

My limbs grow weak. The panic settles beneath a haze of acceptance, like a single feather floating on the wind. There is nothing more I can do. I have no fight left. My eyelids flutter and just before they close, something darts through the black, something I've seen before. I try to hold onto the image, to place it, to understand what it is, but my memories are drowning in death.

My life doesn't flash behind my eyes. Nothing does.

Landon's hands loosen … then release. I cough and roll onto my side, gasping for air. The oxygen burns hot as salvation, filling my lungs with fire. My head swims for the surface. Blood races through each vein as my pulse quickens. It feels like a millennia until I'm brought back to awareness. I scramble against the truck bed, scooting away from Landon.

It's dark and hard to make out everything that's going on, but even from here I see his expression transform from dazed to horrified. He stares at his hands like they aren't his own. His mouth opens and closes in stunned silence. His chest rises and falls, faster and faster. Then he looks up and catches my gaze. I cower farther away from him.

"I'm so sorry, Hazel," he whispers, his voice raw with emotion. "I don't understand what came over me. I didn't mean—"

But I can't. I can't do this right now. I race over the edge of the truck, landing on my hands and knees in the long, scratchy grass. It's half dead from the approaching winter and stinks of mildew and mud. I scramble to my feet, ready to run, but movement over the lake catches my attention.

Above the still lake's surface, two spirits hover.

The cloaked demon, who moments before was using Landon to choke me, circles the large spirit dragon. It's the very same creature I saw twice before, the black dragon with the cobalt eyes. I stare in shock for the space of a heartbeat. And then, they attack. Their forms fly at each other over the water, but nothing reflects below them. Nothing but the stars. Nothing but the darkness.

I glance at Landon. "Do you see them?" I choke the words out as I point.

He turns and frowns, shaking his head. He doesn't see anything. My heart sinks but I'm not surprised. This sight isn't meant for regular human eyes.

"Hazel, I'm so sorry," he continues, rubbing bloodied palms into his hair. Most of it has fallen out of its bun, the blonde streaked with liquid red. "Please, forgive me. I would never—"

I hold up my hand and cut him off. "Not right now."

The spirits battle. The dragon roars and charges, flying through the air, long claws outstretched and teeth bared, but the black cloaked spirit is otherworldly in its movements. It disappears into wispy smoke before the dragon can touch it. Then it materializes again at the right moment. This time, it's right behind the dragon, its claw-like hand reaching out. As far as I can tell, it doesn't carry any weapons. But it doesn't need to. Its skeletal hands are the weapon. Whatever the cloaked demon touches is brought into the darkness. The dragon is no exception. It arches and cries out, flying away and then twisting back to continue the fight.

I've never seen anything like it, or anything like *them*. Human spirits are in their own kind of void. They don't touch each other. They don't touch us. But these two things have so much more freedom. I'm reminded of that first encounter with the spirit dragon, when it had knocked me down but I'd talked myself out of that being a real possibility. I had told myself I fell out of surprise. Now I know the truth. These spirits, whatever they are, and wherever they're from, I don't know, but I do know this: they can touch each other—they can touch us.

And apparently, some can make humans do horrible things.

I swallow hard, realizing the implications of this new development. Maybe the supposed serial killer isn't one human man. Maybe it's actually this *thing* using whoever it can get its deadly hands on, using multiple men to murder young girls.

The two spirits continue to fight until the dragon is bested a second time, weakening further and skidding against the water. It cries out, a sound that sends a shiver of fear down my spine. It's losing. It won't be long until the dragon flees or is killed. How does a spirit dragon die? I don't know. And I don't want to know. Because once it's gone, Landon and I will be helpless once again.

"Get out of here," I yell at Landon.

"What are you talking about?" He jumps out of the truck bed and approaches me carefully. "I think you're in shock."

"Landon, listen to me. You need to get in your truck and go. Go, before it comes back for you!"

His face is ashen under the starlight, dazed and disbelieving. The dragon cries out in pain again, a sound Landon can't hear. If only I could explain! But I can't do anything about it. There isn't time. I don't wait to see if he follows my instructions. I take off for the trees. I have to hide from Landon and this creature. I have to get to safety before I become like Katherine and those other girls, before I end up as another lifeless corpse at the bottom of the lake.

I'm caged in by the heady scent of pine and blood, of night air and cold fear. I breathe hard even though I don't want to make a sound. Tree branches scratch at my bare arms and torso. I'm only in my bra, skinny jeans, and Cora's suede boots. The heels sink into the mud and catch on the rocks, slowing me down. The cold licks at my skin, but does little to penetrate past the terror that has become a heat all of its own. I push further into the forest, climbing over fallen trunks and through thick weeds.

After a few minutes, I stop to catch my breath and listen. The silence is eerie. It doesn't belong out here. There should be something to fill the quiet. Birds. Squirrels. Larger animals—I'd even take one of the normal ghosts. But there's nothing. No wind. No cries from the spirit dragon. And no truck engine, either.

My insides squirm. Sweat drips down the back of my neck. It's so silent, I can hear my heart beating. And all I can think is that Landon didn't take my advice. There's no truck pulling away. He didn't leave. Oh God, why didn't he leave?

"Hazel!" His voice breaks through the silence. "Where are you?"

I can't trust him. Not with that thing around. And I don't dare move. He could be possessed again. In fact, I'd bet my life on it.

"I know you're out there!" he yells again, his voice closer this time. "I just want to help you."

His tone rings false, but I'm frozen to the spot. It's too quiet out here and if I move, he'll hear me. If that thing is using him again, he will be immune to pain. He'll be so much faster than me. I'll never get away. Hiding is my only option. Inch by inch, I sink to the forest floor and crouch low. Something hard presses against my hip bone and hope swells. My phone!

I fish it from the front pocket of my jeans and make sure to switch the button on the side to silent. Then I cover the screen with one hand and press the "wake up" button with the other. A picture of Macy and Cora's smiling faces light up the backdrop. I'm quick to turn the brightness down, tears burning my eyes as I look at my friends. If I don't get out of here, I'll never see them again.

What if they come looking for me? They could be next.

I hurry to find the contacts and scroll for Detective Sanders' information. When his name comes across the screen, I let out a small sigh. I push the contact and pray.

Nothing happens.

I only have one bar of service out here. I grit my teeth and look around helplessly. How am I going to get service without being seen?

"Come out, come out, wherever you are." Landon's sing-song voice cackles through the night. He's getting closer and closer. He might find me. Maybe I should run. But if I can get this call to connect, I might be okay. And then I realize that even if I make the call, it's not like I can *talk* to the detective without alerting Landon and the creature to my location.

A tear drops loose, splashing against my cheek. I have to try a different tactic. I type in a quick text to the detective, giving my name, what I know about my location, and that I'm in trouble and need the police right away. I press send and watch helplessly as my phone struggles to connect to service. The text doesn't send. I shake the phone in my hand, more tears falling.

"Where are you?" Landon's tone has turned dark and guttural, nothing like his true self. "When I find you, I'm going to teach you about respect."

The hot tears trail down my cheeks and neck unchecked. My breath catches in my chest as it rises and falls in little gasps. My arms are covered in cuts and goosebumps. And I can't move. I know it's true, that the dragon is gone and whatever that thing was is back in Landon. Because there is no way the Landon I know would ever say anything like that to me. Those have got to be the demon's words.

But why me? Is it just bad timing? Bad luck? Were we in the wrong place at the wrong time? Or am I being hunted by the creature for a specific reason? I think back to the black spirit finding me in the alleyway and can't help but wonder if that wasn't a coincidence.

I release a small breath and grab onto what little courage I have left. I press send on my text again and slowly stand, reaching my hand into the air and praying to whatever is up there, to please save me. Please, let the service connect. Please, let the detective see it right away.

"There you are!" Landon snarls. His force knocks me to the forest floor, and the phone skids loose from my hand. He stalks over to where it's lit up in the darkness and scowls. "You won't be needing this anymore."

He stomps on the screen. It cracks and goes dark.

He comes for me, yanks my shivering body up to his and twists my arms behind my back. I yelp, the pain white-hot.

"Landon don't," I plead. "I know you're in there. I know this isn't you. You don't have to do this."

He brings his mouth right up against my ear. The voice that comes out is not his. Not his at all. It's scratchy and putrid, thick with death and heavy with decay. "For two long years, I've been searching for someone like you. Oh, Hazel, you are exactly what they need."

He's been searching for someone like me? What does that mean? Who are *they*?

I slam my head back into Landon's face, feeling his nose crunch under my skull. It doesn't seem to hurt him. He cackles again and squeezes tighter. The sound omitting from his mouth is still not Landon's. It's nothing like his sweet, carefree, happy laugh. The demon is in total control now.

"Don't fight back," he snarls. "Or I will do much worse. You will not have known true pain until you receive it from me."

He lifts me up and squeezes those strong arms around me like a vice, carrying me from the forest and back to the lake. I scream for help the entire time, twist and kick out, try anything I can, but it's useless. Landon's strength is that of ten men with this demon in charge. I'll never break free.

"You are a disgusting girl," the creature spits angrily. "But soon you will be nothing at all."

Oh, God. I don't like the sound of that. I keep trying to claw my way out of Landon's arms, but it's impossible. We approach the edge of the lake.

"It's time to start the ritual." This time, the voice smiles.

THIRTY

KHALI

A DEAFENING SCREAM SLICES THROUGH the night, and I whip around in the water, searching for the source of the noise. A woman's voice cries out again, sobbing, and then goes silent. I should stay away from trouble, should be looking out for myself and my mission in coming here, but I can't stop myself. That merwoman brought me here for a reason. This can't be a coincidence.

I swim in the direction of the sound as quietly as possible. The icy water seeps deep down inside, all the way to the marrow, but I push through the pain with each stroke of my arms and legs. Something base and instinctual has risen within me, screaming that I must get to that woman. I must help her.

My magic isn't the same in this place. It's still there, but it's like it's been softened, muted down. The water elemental barely makes a difference in my speed through the water, and the fire elemental is nowhere to be found in this terrible coldness. Perhaps it's the shock. Perhaps it's the need to get to the woman outweighing the need to figure out what's wrong with my magic. But more likely, it's this human realm. Things aren't the same here.

It's been called the non-magical realm for a reason, and while I can access some of my magic here, it's not nearly the same. I can't imagine what it would be like to stay here long term. It's terrible. Is this what Dean has to live with on a daily basis? Is this what it's like to be Bram, only worse? I hate to think about it, and try to focus on the present moment over the questions.

The Fae kingdom had the sticky warmth of summer to it, even in the late autumn. But here, even though it's technically the same area, it's less autumn and much more biting winter. It's drier and colder. There is no mistaking that this place isn't meant for magic.

So with that in mind, I suck in a breath and quietly approach the shore. The woman is still crying, her voice growing more muffled and strained by the second. There's something about her that pulls me to her, like a string, like I must help her, no matter what.

I emerge from the water, going for the closest cropping of

trees for cover. Even the trees are different here. Heartier pine trees made for all seasons like what we have in Drakenon. They are special, but still lacking in the enchanting hum of the Fae forest. I don't know if that's a good thing or a bad thing.

I crouch low, my clothing, velvet cape, and bag all soaked through and weighing me down. I carefully dispose of the bag and cape and sneak through the trees, moving closer to the crying until I find the source, until I find them. The hem of my dress drags in the dirt. My boots are squishy with water.

The woman is not alone.

I can hardly make her out in the darkness, but she's there, lying on the shore, a large man kneeling beside her. I inch closer, my vision straining to take it all in. She's young, hardly any older than myself. Her blonde hair is matted around her face, wet with water and blood. Her face is wild and afraid, eyes staring into night. Covered in blood, she's nearly dead.

The man next to her is also young. Dressed only from the waist down, his muscled back glints in the darkness and is covered in a layer of sweat. His long blonde hair glistens with blood in the moonlight. He leans over her, muttering some kind of incantation. It's not a language I understand, but something in me tingles with recognition. This isn't a human language; it sounds like something that could be from Eridas.

How many creatures can use this ley line portal to travel between realms?

The idea of great and terrible beasts roaming this human forest sends me to my knees. Can I really do this? Can I really help? But I don't have time to think about the what-ifs, not with this horror scene playing out only a few yards in front of me.

I move in even closer, unable to look away. The man has something in his hand. A stick? Bile rises in my throat as I realize what he's doing with it. Crouched over her, holding her down with his weight, he's got the girl's shirt up and is carving something into her abdomen with the end of the stick, like it's a knife, and not wood. She writhes and screams, begging him to stop, but he's not the least bit deterred. And no matter how much she fights him, no matter when she pulls his hair, when she lashes out at him, drawing blood, he is utterly unmoved.

Anger grabs on tight. I can't sit here and watch this mutilation.

Bringing whatever of my powers I can to the surface, I shift into my dragon, the trees around me cracking with the force, and I charge.

I slam into the man, throwing him off the girl with all the strength my dragon holds. He flies across the grassy meadow, arcing high, and then lands in a heap of limbs on the shoreline. It doesn't stop him. His body shakes and rumbles, and changes. I growl, because that doesn't make sense. Slowly, he stands, blood pouring, bones broken and cracked. But still, he stands. And a dark form steps away from his body. The broken man collapses in a pile of death, his eyes wide and vacant, shining in the reflection of the lake.

"He's dead." I shift back to human and give my assurances to the bloodied girl. But I don't look at her, not when my gaze is stuck on the dark form that has emerged from the human man. Because it wasn't my imagination. It was real.

I've seen it before. Not in person, of course, only the spirit elemental would allow that, but in many textbooks growing up. Everyone knows of the reapers. They are the spirits tasked to take magical souls from one realm to the next life. What is it doing *here*? And how am I able to see it?

It glides toward me, and I blink, still hoping this isn't real. It can't be. But it is.

The girl groans at my feet, her sobs weakening by the second. She's losing too much blood. I kneel and scoop her up. I don't know how to explain it, but something primal is drawing me to her. I can't leave her here, not with that thing. I have to save her.

"We need to get out of here," I say, hoping she'll be able

to help me do that. But her face is snow-white and the life within her eyes is fading fast. I shift her weight so I can carry her. She cries out, then whispers a name. I go still.

"Dean," she says his name again. "I thought you were Dean." Her head lulls to one side. She passed out.

The reaper knocks into us, sending us crashing to the ground.

Not only is the reaper real, it's materialized from the spirit realm and into a physical being. Horror prickles through my entire body. How can this be? It leans over me, the hood covering its unknown face. Only two red eyes glow from within the inky darkness. It reminds me of the Sovereign Occultists, but it's so much worse. Where an Occultist looks like a normal human, this thing is skeletal and putrid and *death*.

"There are two of you," it hisses gleefully. "My master will be so pleased with me."

Then it pounces. Claws dig into my leg, and it yanks me across the mud and rocks, back toward the girl I dropped.

The reaper grabs her too, dragging us toward the water. I kick out but its strength is incredible, built up by something much darker and stronger than magic alone. I scream and call my dragon to me, transforming to my truest form, catching the reaper off guard. I release my full power, snapping at it with my teeth and claws, drawing on the flicker of fire elemental burning within me now that I'm out of the cold. I let that fly loose, too.

The creature screeches, howling in pain, but it goes for the girl, still dragging her into the water. She's passed out, and if he pulls her under completely, she'll drown.

I block him, pushing him out of the way again. He flies across the meadow as the boy did, and stands just the same. From behind him, something massive and black appears. I recognize the dragon the second he comes into focus. It's Dean.

We don't hesitate. We charge. The reaper meets me halfway, wrapping its cold hands into my hide and pushing some kind of unknown magic into me. It's cold as ice, and carries the scent of death with it. It sinks me to my knees, the pain racking through me, all the way to the tips of my wings. I cry out, death fast approaching, but I can't give up yet. I refuse to go out like this.

Dean pushes him off and the reaper lets out a guttural moan.

I call on my magic once again and this time, find more fire there. It burns within me like a newly stoked furnace, and I release it into the reaper's empty hole of a face. Dean stands at my side, joining me. We don't let up. The fire flows from our roaring mouths as the creature falls to its knees. It screeches and burns and burns and burns to ash.

After a few minutes, after I'm sure there's nothing left, I stifle the flames with the water elemental, bringing everything to a muddy, ashen mess. I manipulate the lake, rolling a wave over the pile of ash, washing it all away.

Dean is with the girl, kneeling at her side once again. I shift and join him and run my hands over her, checking her injuries. His face is drained of color, taking in the blood and the symbol carved into her stomach.

"Are you still here?" I ask, gently slapping her cheek. She doesn't wake up.

Her chest is no longer moving.

"She has a pulse," Dean says.

I let out a panicked breath. "Thank the Gods she's still alive. How can we save her?"

"We have to get her to the hospital."

I peer at him. I don't know what this word means.

"We have a lot to talk about," he says. "Firstly, why you're here. I felt your dragon come through the portal and I came straight away, but there's no time. Hazel needs us."

I'm exhausted, drained from using magic, and I can't imagine shifting again to take her to the hospital place. This kind of exhaustion never happens back home. I don't know how Dean manages it. We stumble toward a road. That's good. It's a start.

A high-pitched screech sounds through the still night. Red and blue lights flash against the trees. I freeze and dig my feet into the earth, expecting to battle with another terrible creature. What will it be this time? I don't know if I can survive any more of this, my magic is so diminished.

"We can't be here," Dean says. He lays Hazel on the side of the road, guilt lighting every plane of his face.

"Come on," he says, and sprints toward the tree line.

My legs don't seem to want to work, I'm too mesmerized by what I'm seeing. Something shiny and fast bounds down the road toward me, coming to a halt as blinding bright lights of red and blue shine in my face. Is it an animal? A beast of some kind?

The *thing* opens and a man jumps out and runs toward me, arms stretched out and holding some kind of black contraption in his hands.

"Is she alive?" he calls out gruffly.

I nod, deciding it best to answer honestly. "But she won't be for much longer. She needs the hospital."

Another one of the flashing light beasts bursts from around the corner. It blares so loudly through the night that I have to cover my ears.

"Who did this to her?" the man asks, staring horrified at the girl's mutilated stomach. He drops to his knees next to her. "Did you do this?"

Do I answer? Do I tell him about the reaper? "No," I reply, beginning to shake. I should run, go find Dean, get away from here.

"Did you see who did it?"

I swallow, my knees growing weak. "Something evil did this," I say and point back to the shore. "But it's dead, now. I killed it."

THIRTY-ONE

HAZEL

I AM FILLED WITH LEAD. My arms and legs are sinking into quicksand and I couldn't move even if I wanted to. I try to pry my eyelids open but they're a million pounds. I groan, awareness seeping into the fogginess of my mind.

"Hazel?" The voice is far away. "Honey, are you awake?"

"Mom!" My eyes finally flutter open, bright lights glaring down. I groan again, but relief floods my system. "What happened?" My voice is hoarse and my throat is raw. "Where am I?" I try to sit up but a searing pain shoots across my abdomen and I'm forced back. And then I remember, I remember what he did to my stomach and I burst into tears.

"Oh, honey, it's going to be okay." Mom is right there, but she might as well be a million miles away, the emotions are a wild storm. I squeeze my eyes shut against the overwhelming onslaught.

"Let me get the light," a second voice says, moments before the lights adjust to a dimmer setting.

The pain and tears and fear and emotions keep coming, one after another, until finally, it washes away enough for me to open my eyes once again. I look around, taking in the tiny hospital room. I'm hooked to all kinds of machines, little sticky tabs stuck all over my body, and a needle taped down and pressing into a vein in my left hand. Everything hurts.

"Where's Landon?" I gasp, his name clings to my worst memory in a way that makes it hard to say it. But I can't blame him entirely, can I? I saw what happened. He was possessed. He was hurting me but not of his own will. There was so much blood, but he couldn't stop. *It* wouldn't let him.

"It's okay." Mom leans over and grasps my right hand between hers, squeezing it tight. "Landon is dead. He can't harm you anymore."

"How?" Tears spring to my eyes. Landon didn't deserve to die.

"Your friend saved you." Mom nods toward someone standing by the door, shadowed by the drawn curtain around my bed. The mystery girl steps into the light with a little wave.

"Hi," she says.

My eyes go wide. I know her, but I can hardly call her my friend. I've never met her before.

"Khali." I swallow hard, putting the gorgeous face to the unique name. "*You* saved me?"

She bites her lip and smiles sheepishly. She's as beautiful as she was in the images the dragon spirit sent me. Her long, wavy, dark brown hair shines perfectly, even under the fluorescents. Her eyes are large, wide set, and absolutely stunning, one of ocean blue, the other of rich soil.

She saved my life?

I try to remember her there that night, but after that thing possessed Landon and he started to carve into my stomach with nothing but a sharpened stick, the pain and blood and shock of it all became too much and I blacked out. My breathing speeds up just thinking about it and the little beeping on the machine races to match.

"It's okay," Mom says, running a hand gently down my hair and cupping my cheek. Tears rim her reddened eyes as she holds my gaze steady. "He can't ever touch you again."

I shake my head. "But it wasn't Landon. He wouldn't do that."

A line deepens between Mom's eyes. "Oh, honey, you don't have to protect him. He's gone."

"I'm not worried about *him*." Tears spring to my eyes and

fear pummels my bruised body. "It's that *thing*. It's still out there."

Khali steps forward gracefully, her posture perfect and her voice soft as cotton. She's dressed in normal human clothing that's nothing like the medieval stuff I saw in the visions. It fits her perfectly but she seems about as comfortable in the jeans and t-shirt as I am in high-heels. "May Hazel and I speak alone for a few minutes? I think I can help her feel better about what happened if I tell her what I did."

"I don't know if that's a good idea," Mom says, but I nod vigorously, and so she stands to leave. "All right. I'll go tell the nurse you're awake."

As soon as she's out the door, Khali perches on the edge of the bed and tells me the truth of what happened without hesitating. "Your friend was possessed by a reaper."

I swallow hard. "Like a grim reaper?" It almost seems laughable had I not been there to witness it for myself. "But I never saw a scythe." The word seems silly saying it aloud but then again, I'm past the point of the supernatural being anything remotely silly or fake.

She shrugs. "He was using Landon to perform some kind of ritual on you, I think because you have magic, and he needed someone in this realm with magic to get it to work."

"I don't have magic," I challenge. Even as I say it, the words ring false.

She raises an eyebrow, but doesn't press the issue. "Anyway," she continues, "I believe it completed the ritual because it took total possession of your friend." She pauses for a second, as if weighing how this is affecting me.

"Please," I say, "I need to know everything. I can handle it."

"It was using a language I've only heard used by the Occultists. I don't know what it means. But in the end, it killed Landon, hurt you, and took on a physical form."

My eyes go wide. "Physical? Like you and me?"

She nods. "Reapers aren't supposed to be able to do that. They're creatures meant for the spirit realm only."

Horror crashes over me and I struggle to sit up again. I have to get out of here. I have to do something to warn people about this. "It's alive? It's just walking around out there?"

"No," she says flatly. "I killed it."

I fall back against the pillow and let out a shuddering breath. "You can kill a reaper?" I question. "How does that work? Doesn't it just go back to the spirit realm?"

She sighs, rubbing a hand along her shoulder. "It must be possible to kill it because I certainly did," she says, "but as far as I know, a reaper has never done anything like this before. So truthfully, I don't know if it simply returned to the spirit realm, but I don't think it's in the human realm anymore. This kind of reaper isn't meant for humans. They're for the supernaturals, like me. It shouldn't have ever been here in the first place."

So why was it here?

All this talk of realms and spirits is making my head hurt. I reach for the necklace around my neck, and then remember it's gone. But no, that can't be right, because it's strung around my neck the same as it always is. But Landon broke it.

"Your friend brought that over a few hours ago," she says. "A lady with white hair? She insisted you needed it and your mom agreed. They had to fight the doctors about it but they won. What's it for, anyway?"

I sigh in relief, running a finger over the little balls of cool stone. I don't think I'm ready to trust this Khali girl with my secrets just yet, but as I look at her, I can't help but sense we're connected somehow. We're cut from the same cloth, even if she is a magical dragon shifter and I'm… well, I don't know what I am. I thought I would hate her, considering the man I'm falling for is clearly already in love with her, but I don't hate her. Not even a little bit. She feels too familiar, too much like family.

"Hazel," Dean's gruff voice calls into the room as the door opens a crack. "Can I come in, please?" My heart explodes, the monitor picking it up. Khali raises an eyebrow and I could die. "I've been worried sick about you," he continues from behind the slightly ajar door. "I'm so glad you're okay. If Khali hadn't gotten there in time, you wouldn't have made it."

Geez, I didn't know he cared so much.

"Sure, come in," I say, squeezing my eyes tight. I can't see the look on his face when he finds Khali here. I don't think my heart can bear it.

The door opens and shuts, and the room fades to silence.

"Khali," he whispers. "You're here too. I've been looking for you. What happened to you? Why didn't you come with me?"

I can't stand it anymore and open my eyes. Khali smiles and goes to him, wrapping him in a tight hug. "I've missed you," she murmurs. "We have a lot to talk about. I really need your help."

I wish I knew what they were talking about.

As if sensing my feelings, Khali pulls away from Dean and speaks, "Dean came and helped me finish the reaper off. When those people came to help you, he left but I stayed."

"People?"

"The police," Dean offers. "You shouldn't have stayed, Khali. You don't understand how human police think."

I swallow hard, still stuck on the fact that Dean was there

last night, too.

He's still staring at his friend and I'm sinking into my bed like I don't even belong in my own hospital room. "Khali, what happened to you? Why would you risk coming here?" He takes her hands in his.

"Drakenon needs your help." Pain wells up in her eyes. "Bram needs you. The Occultists have him. And your brother, Owen…" Her voice catches.

"I already know," he whispers in a dark tone, gaze flicking to me. "Owen is dead, isn't he?"

Realization hits me then. *Owen* is the spirit dragon with the blue eyes. He was here to find Dean, to relay a message about helping Khali. My mind goes back to that place, to that moment Landon was choking me, and I remember how Owen's dragon appeared again and fought the reaper long enough for me to get away the first time. But something must have happened to him after that because he disappeared. I swallow hard. I can't bear to say a word about it now. They've already lost him once, they don't need to know the rest.

"Knock knock," the doctor says as he comes through the door. "How are you feeling, Hazel? Doing all right?"

Dean and Khali press themselves into the corner of the room, whispering quietly among themselves, their eyes still trained on me. Two residents, a nurse, and Mom all shuffle into the room. It's filled to the brim now and everyone's looking at me like I'm a broken piece of china they're trying to meticulously reassemble with tweezers and super glue.

The doctor launches into a myriad of questions, all of which I do my best to answer. He tells me my wounds will take a few months to heal but the plastic surgery department did a great job fixing me right up and not to worry. He then goes into a psychiatric referral and says I'll need PTSD therapy soon.

It's all too much to handle. I'm pretty sure he knows what he's doing if he thinks I'm going to need a phyciatrist. Dang, my life is crazy!

"When can I get out of here?" I ask, my voice pleading. "I want to forget this ever happened and get back to my classes and my *life.*"

He answers to Mom. "I think she's going to need at least another few days of observation but it's up to you if you want to start the discharge process sooner."

"Why is it up to her?" I challenge, angry that I'm not being listened to. "It's my body. I should get a say here, too."

He frowns. "I'm sorry," he says, "but since you're a minor for two more months, it's up to your mother."

"December sixteenth isn't that far away," I snap. "I'm not a child. I'm in college, living on my own. I think I'm smart enough to make my own decisions."

"It's okay," Mom steps in, her face soft and her hands up. "Why don't Dr. Saunders and I step outside to discuss the details of discharging you as soon as is safely possible, okay, Hazel?"

I let out a frustrated breath but nod because I know I'm overreacting a little here. She and the rest of the medical staff leave the room. I shut my eyes tight, embarrassed at my outburst, and then I turn to my friends in the corner.

"What are you looking at?" I question. They're staring at me like I've grown a second head or something. Okay, maybe the painkillers are wearing off because I'm starting to get annoyed with them, too. I'm grumpy to the max but who can blame me? The skin on my stomach feels like it's been set on fire, and I'm ready to be alone to sulk in peace and quiet.

"When did you say your birthday was?" Dean asks.

"December sixteenth," I reply. Great, I didn't want anyone to know.

"And you're seventeen right now?" Khali's eyes are round saucers and her mouth is shaped in a cute little "O".

I frown. Okay, this is getting weird. "Yes. Why the sudden interest?"

Khali steps forward, wringing her hands. "I'm seventeen and my birthday is the sixteenth of December," she says. "We were born on the same day."

I shrug. "So, we're birthday buddies. That's cool but it's a coincidence that happens all the time."

She turns to Dean. "An Occultist said he put a spell on me when I was a baby. He mentioned my eighteenth birthday. And I feel this strange magical connection to Hazel, it's hard to explain, but it's undeniable. When she was hurt, I knew I had to save her. And when you ran away from the police, I couldn't leave her. Physically couldn't move. That can't be a coincidence, can it?"

They stare at each other for a long beat before turning back to me. The dancing fire has returned to Dean's coal eyes, and Khali's are just as magical, sparkling with her thoughts. But no, she's reading way too much into this. Our birthdays matching has to be a coincidence. I'm obviously *not* a dragon shifter. I'm human. And I'm not like them, I'm not special except for this annoying "seeing spirits" business, but that's nothing to do with them and tons of humans claim to have that ability.

"Hazel is a psychic medium," Dean says slowly. "Could it be something more than that? Could she be part of the spell, too?"

"It's possible," Khali replies, her voice growing soft and her eyes watering with something I can't quite place. Fear? Love?

She approaches me again and sits on the edge of the bed, this time taking my free hand into hers. When she does, I yelp. The connection between us grew from a spark to an electrical current. It's a charge that I've never felt before. Is this magic? And maybe it is the result of a spell, but it's undeniable. I don't know what to do with this news.

She swallows hard. "You can see the spirit realm?"

I nod.

She considers this, her ethereal eyes pinning me down with her turning mind. "Hazel, I think you might be more than just a medium. I think you might have elemental magic."

Dean is frozen behind her, looking down at me like he's never seen me before. Elemental magic? I'm not sure what that is but it doesn't sound real. It sounds like it's made from a storybook. Then again, my whole life these last few months has been like that. Like I said before, it's like I'm turning into the heroine of some cheesy teen novel!

"Dean's elemental is fire," she says. "I'm all four—fire, water, earth, and air." She lets out a breath and smiles gently. "And you, my friend, are spirit. You possess the rarest element of all. One so rare, it hasn't been seen for over a century."

I burst out laughing. "No, sorry," I say, "that's ridiculous. It can't be true."

"You saw the spirit dragon," she says, "and the reaper, both creatures from the supernatural realm. I don't think you'd have been able to do that if you were a regular human medium."

That shuts me up. I look to Dean. "You think this is real? You think I have some kind of spirit elemental? Something from *your* realm?"

He stands tall, all brooding eyes and hands shoved into his jeans pockets, but he nods.

Khali continues, "I think you and I are linked somehow. There's something else the Occultist said." She talks of this "Occultist" person like I should have a clue about him, but I do know one thing, whatever he is or it is, it can't be good. "He told me that when I turned eighteen, I'd be coming to him, begging for his help." Our eyes are locked and dread settles in deep. "I think we're connected, as part of a spell." Her voice catches. "And I'm not sure what it means, but I think we're both in deep trouble because of it. Have you noticed anything strange happening to you in the last few months?"

I burst out laughing, a reaction to the shock and the morphine and the fear.

"I'll take that as a yes?"

I swallow hard and stifle the laughs, nodding. I don't want to believe her, but believing her feels inevitable just the same. The reaper might be gone for now, unable to terrorize innocent women while he looked for someone with ties to magic, but he *was* here. And what happened to me is confirmation enough. Khali speaks the truth. There *is* something wrong with me. I think I've always known it, have always *hated* it. There's something magical going on with my ability, something reaching far beyond what is normal for a medium, and even if I didn't choose it, it's mine to own.

"My abilities have been stronger than ever, but they've also felt out of control, like I'm attracting unwanted spirits," I say, building as much courage into my voice as possible. I feel like a fraud. "So I guess you and I have two months to break the spell."

Her hand squeezes tighter around mine. "Two months to break the spell, save my friends and family, and stop Silas from enslaving me as his wife."

I blink, surprised and trying to take it all in. All of this *and* I have to get through my first semester. What have I gotten myself into this time?

END OF BOOK ONE

WHAT'S NEXT?

THE DRAGON BLESSED TRILOGY CONTINUES:

KINGDOM OF SPIRITS - COMING FALL 2019

THRONE OF EMBERS - COMING SPRING 2020

ACKNOWLEDGMENTS

KHALI AND HAZEL'S STORY DIDN'T come to me like my others have. It wasn't a dream that sparked an idea or a wayward thought that I grabbed onto and ran with until I had a book. Fact was, I decided I wanted to write about dragons because I had so many readers asking me to write about dragons. The genre has been popular for a *long* time and I wanted to make the readers happy, so I found a way to write about dragons that felt fun and authentic to me.

I love dragons but this trilogy certainly wasn't in the plans when I finished *The Color Alchemist* series. Actually, I was working on a vampire book when I put that aside to write *Crown of Dragons*. So when I start by saying that I have to thank my readers, I really, really, mean that. The readers inspired just about everything in the Bleeding Realms world and I'm so glad they did. Bleeding Realms is rapidly growing into something that I'm not only in love with, but something that has the potential for *many* more books and trilogies featuring different supernatural societies intermixing with humans from our world. I can already tell you that a certain

High Fae elf is demanding a trilogy.

(But, ummm, I still have to finish that vampire book and *I can't wait!*)

There are so many people I need to thank for assisting me with Crown of Dragons. Thank you to my cover designer, Daqri Bernardo, owner of Covers by Combs. The covers are gorgeous works of art and I love them! Kate Foster, you've once again taken one of my manuscripts and helped it to shine. I'm so incredibly lucky to have you and your talent on my team and I can't thank you enough. Thank you to Molly Phipps for some seriously gorgeous interior formatting. As always, you've outdone yourself! And to my proofreader team, Kate Anderson, Sarah Mostaghel, Ailene Kubricky, and Travis Walker, you guys are the best for putting up with my mess and I'm so grateful for your hard work! Thanks to my family of author friends, for the wonderful community that you've brought me into and for all the incredibly support, inspiration, and love. There are too many of you to name individually but you know who you are. Thank you to my awesome extended family, and to my absolutely *amazing* husband and children, my biggest fans and my biggest support system, I couldn't do any of this without you. I love you so much. And finally, thank you to Heavenly Father for taking care of me and my family. Always.

ABOUT THE AUTHOR

NINA WALKER is a *USA Today* and Amazon Top 100 Bestselling author. She lives in beautiful Utah with her husband, two children, and three furbabies. Nina writes YA romantic fantasy with metaphysical magic systems, forbidden love interests, and heart-stopping plot twists. You can learn more at WWW.NINAWALKERBOOKS.COM or find her on social media at facebook.com/ninawalkerbooks or on Instagram @ninabelievesinmagic to join in on the fun.

www.ingramcontent.com/pod-product-compliance
Lightning Source LLC
Chambersburg PA
CBHW032201180726
48284CB00001B/134